Harry, me and boiled bacon

A farmers boy in the 1960s

ANDY COLLINGS

For Florence

January 1965

A two-furrow plough, a tractor with no cab and a big forty-acre field. And it was cold, bitterly cold. So much so, that at the end of each bout, I stopped and clambered up on to the bonnet and cupped my hands over the exhaust pipe to warm them. And when I couldn't bear the agony of frozen feet any longer I'd take my boots off, one at a time and hold them over the exhaust pipe until they became so hot I would grimace with the exquisite pain as I slipped them back on again. Returning to my seat I spread a heavy hessian railway sack over my knees and tried to trap the heat given off from the gearbox below.

An icy wind sliced into me as I turned on the headland to begin the steady trawl back to the other end of the field. I had taken to sitting on one hand to try and keep it warm and sometimes I would sit on both hands, holding the steering wheel between my knees but then the sack would start to slip off onto the floor.

Behind, a flock of seagulls fought and squabbled over the worms the plough was bringing to the surface. Some of them flew so close it would have been possible to reach out and touch them and every so often, a gull would fly too close to the plough and become partially buried in the turning soil, but it always managed to struggle free, a brown smear on its crystal white plumage to record the moment.

It was my fifth day in this field and there was still more than half of it left to plough. Each morning at breakfast time, Alice, Harry's wife, packed me up a boiled bacon sandwich and a bottle of tea which was little more than stone cold by the time I'd driven out of the yard, and had ice in it by lunch time.

By the third day I had started to rebel against the boiled bacon sandwiches. Today I had reached the point where I couldn't face them anymore and threw them, untouched, into the hedge.

Four o'clock and the seagulls had flown away to wherever it is seagulls go on freezing winter afternoons when they're stuffed full of worms, and with the light starting to fade, I called it a day too and headed back to the farm. There were still the cows to milk and it would be another two hours before my work was finished.

Tomorrow would be another day's ploughing and by the end of next week, the field might just be finished. It could be then, that whatever was dining out on my boiled bacon sandwiches would have to start catching its own food again.

***

I parked the tractor under the barn and ran down the yard to the farmhouse, looking forward to feeling the heat of the kitchen. 'I bet you're ready for a hot cup of tea,' Alice said as I burst through the door.

'That would be great.' I sidled round the kitchen table to where the Rayburn was throwing out a pile of heat, grabbed a seat and pressed my stockinged feet against the oven door so they could soak up the warmth.

'I think Harry's bringing the cows in to the yard for you so you've no need to rush.'

With my socks starting to steam, I sipped my tea and began to feel better. Harry came in a few minutes later, pulled his wellingtons off and headed for the sink to wash his hands.

'How did you get on today, boy?'

'It all went well apart from having to ask a crowd of half-dressed people to move their sun beds off the headland, that and the ice cream man running out of double-scoop cones.

'Well, that's alright then. Cows are in the collecting yard and I've loaded up the Land Rover with their feed for you to take out when you've finished milking.'

So, this is farming I thought, as I walked up the yard to where the cows were waiting to be milked; cold, physically demanding, long hours, long weeks and low pay, but I couldn't remember a time when I had ever been happier.

Chapter one

Early days

My parents always thought it strange I should have such a keen interest in farming and, to be fair to them, I couldn't think of a reason either. We lived on an over-crowded council estate on the west side of town which was not only void of all things agricultural, but also of anything else that couldn't be bolted down.

Schools were stacked out with portable classrooms to accommodate the post war baby-boom, of which I was one, and any curriculum relating to rural activities had long been abandoned. And as for me having any family relatives, distant or otherwise with agricultural connections, I can report there was none.

My aspirations only became a concern for my parents when at the age of fourteen I announced it was my intention to pursue a farming career. It marked the end of their hopes that my wanting to work on the land would be no more than a passing phase, something I would no doubt grow out of given sufficient time and suitable guidance.

And while I did eventually convince them that farming was what I wanted to do, I believe they remained forever hopeful it was just a momentary diversion and it could only be a matter of time before I came to my senses and would be hankering after employment in a more appropriate and prosperous profession.

My parents were not alone in their thoughts; their opinions were shared by the school careers' adviser who, when I told him what I planned to do, groaned, looked up to the ceiling and asked me to leave the room and have a think about it. And while I was out there, to send the next boy in.

But I was not going to be swayed. I had become good friends with a fellow pupil who happened to be a farmer's son and spent many happy Saturday afternoons standing in his father's tractor shed, admiring a big blue tractor and discussing with him what it would be like to drive such a machine.

When it was milking time, we would run down to the field where the cows were grazing and gather them into a group by the gate before letting them out onto the narrow lane leading back to the farm. Cars and vans were forced to pull over while the cows ambled by and as the drivers waited for the road to clear, they had to put up with dislodged mirrors and paintwork smeared with slurry, while the cows spent a few leisurely minutes swiping mouthfuls of grass from the roadside verges.

In the summer when the hay was being made, we took sandwiches and caddies of tea out to the men working in the fields and revelled in the chance of seeing mowers and rakes working and, if we were lucky, the engine-powered 'nodding donkey' balers. Everywhere there was always the sweet smell of burnt paraffin; the exhaust from the tractors wafting across the field.

At other times of the year, when it was snowing we clambered on to a sledge and, aided by a manic sheep dog, hurtled down steep slopes time and time again and then, with the farm's water supply frozen solid, helped to take the cows across snowy, moonlit fields to a stream where they could drink their fill before being taken back home again.

I also joined a Young Farmers Club which met every Friday night in a nearby village hall and it was there I rubbed shoulders and mingled with farmers' sons and daughters and tried desperately to become part of their community.

But it was an impossible task. While I could contribute to public speaking contests, help man the carnival float and take part in the farm walks organised for summer evenings, I was always going to be the town boy. I was the one who cadged a lift home to a council house on a crowded estate while others had their farms and houses at the end of tree-lined drives.

There was always a particularly poignant moment in the year when the time came to decide who would be representing the club at the annual Spring Rally. This was an important occasion for Young Farmers, an event when members competed against those from other clubs in a range of classes, including stock judging, sheep shearing and tractor handling contests.

Sadly, it was one for which I had little to offer. While other 'real' young farmers could enter such competitions knowing what was expected of them, the best I could manage was to represent the club in the 'bicycle fault finding' competition and then, having failed miserably in that one, the following year I was entered for the 'wiring up a three-pin plug safely' contest with only slightly better results.

But annoying as it was, deep down I really didn't mind. I was with people I wanted to be with and in my third year at Young Farmers and while I was still at school, I was enrolled on a machine milking course at the county's agricultural institute where there was a herd of pedigree Jersey cows.

Bearing in mind the closest I had ever been to a cow being milked was when I peeped through the doors of my school friend's parlour during their afternoon milking, I didn't think I was an ideal candidate.

Even so, a couple of weeks later, on an autumnal Thursday evening in October, I was feeling very uncomfortable wearing a white hat and coat, holding a milking bucket with strange pipes hanging off it, and staring blankly at the back end of a cow I had been allocated to milk.

'Right then, John. If you want to make a start washing the udder, we'll see how it all goes,' said the examiner, holding a clip board loaded with paper to make his notes on.

I felt nervous and my efforts to clean the cow's teats were tentative and as it turned out, largely ineffective. When I thought I had finished, the examiner took a clean cloth, washed them again and held it up to show it covered in grime.

'Just so you know for next time, there are two more on the other side,' he said, helpfully.

Any further doubts he may have had about my capabilities were soon confirmed when he had to show me where to connect the vacuum pipe from the bucket to the main pipeline and then remind me to turn it on.

'Now then, John,' he said, after making more notes. 'Let me see you attach the cluster to her teats.' He stood back.

This was the part I had been dreading, not because in my innocence I had any qualms about being in that vicinity of a cow but more because I wasn't sure of the correct way to do it.

There was nothing for it though, so I squatted down to floor level and set about attaching a cup to each of the teats, a task which took for ever to complete and when I eventually struggled out from beneath her, I was dripping with nervous perspiration. The examiner then pointed out I had put them on the wrong way round with the pipes coming out from the side rather than forwards under the cow's belly, where she couldn't kick them off or stand on the pipes so easily.

And while he made even more notes, life deteriorated in to a psychological battle between me and the cow. Truth was she didn't like me. She turned her head and stared, her big brown eyes glaring angrily, and I was convinced she was telling me as much. But I was wrong; what she was actually doing was taking aim. Lifting her tail, she gave a loud, deep cough and fired a huge plume of slurry in my direction which landed on my white coat and then, after hanging there for a few seconds, slid slowly to the floor.

'Best not to stand directly behind a cow,' said the examiner who, having filled two pages with notes, was now continuing his report on a third. 'Not a good idea when she's in a mood like that.'

Despite having demonstrated a mega degree of incompetence I somehow managed to scrape through the course and from then on, for the very first time, I felt I really belonged to the Young Farmers Club. I was now one of them, a bona fide member; I had cow shit under my finger nails, stains on my white coat and best of all, I had the certificate to prove it.

Not long after that, I left school still determined to start a career in agriculture and for once in my life destiny was on my side.

In the last hour of the last Friday, when end of school bedlam had already broken out and someone had lobbed the mandatory packet of soap powder into the school fountain, the careers officer scurried bravely into the classroom and made a bee-line for me.

'Ah, Johnson,' he gasped, pushing a note into my hand. 'I've had an enquiry from a farmer looking for a young person to help out on his farm. So, if you really must do it, his contact details are in the note.' And with that he hightailed back out of the room.

Yes, I thought after I had read it, this will do me fine. After all, I'm now an experienced cowman and I know how to wire a three-pin plug. I also wondered if there was a chance my prospective employer would have any bicycles he needed checking over.

I didn't have long to wait.

***

'Well, I'll tell you one thing, if you work for me you'll not have trouble sleeping at night,' Harry Wilcox said, after I had made a miserable attempt to explain why it was I wanted a career in farming.

That Saturday morning I had cycled the ten miles from my parent's house in Northampton to Storeton Green, a village a few miles due east of the town. Church Farm had been easy to find in that I just headed for the church, but it had rained all the way and my drenching had been all the more thorough by riding a bike that didn't have any mudguards.

Convinced such a poorly maintained machine would not create the right impression, I had left it in the street and walked up the steep path to the farm. We were now standing a few yards from the backdoor of the farmhouse and I could feel water running out of my jeans.

Harry, a well-built, robust looking character with rugged, weathered features who I guessed was in his forties, had taken the high ground and was looking down on me, his arms folded in a dominating way.

Clad in beige overalls, wellingtons, flat cap and a waxed jacket with bale string and straw sticking out of its pockets, he seemed oblivious to the wind and the rain that continued to swirl and fall about us.

'What did you say your name was?' he asked.

'It's John Johnson and since last week, I'm seventeen years old.'

'Well John, what sort of things are you good at?'

I tried to concentrate on finding an answer but nothing would come to mind that had even the slightest chance of convincing him I was any good at anything.

'It's something I've always been interested in and now I

want to do it,' I said at last, conscious it was probably the lamest answer anyone had ever given to such a question.

'How about milking cows, driving tractors, mucking pigs out, baling, ploughing, lambing... What do you know about them?'

I stared up at him, open mouthed. Apart from a very brief and not particularly successful encounter with a cow during my machine milking course, I knew absolutely nothing about any of them and I considered this was not the best time to mention how I thought my friend's big blue tractor worked or that I had a good idea of how to wire a three-pin plug.

'Just as I thought, bugger all. So what use will you be to me?' Rain water was beginning to run off his hat and onto his shoulders. 'And anyway, you look as if you could do with a bit of building up before you start on this sort work; a slice or two of boiled bacon to get some beef in to you.' He looked closer at me. 'There's not a lot on you, is there?'

'We all have to start somewhere,' I said. 'Anyway, thanks for your time. It was very good of you to see me.' I turned to go.

'Hang on a minute, there's no rush,' he said. 'What I'm trying to tell you is that it can be tough working on a farm, so you don't come whimpering to me after a few days complaining about it being too hard. Do you want the job, or don't you?'

'Well, yes I do,' I replied.

'Alright, I'll give you a try but I'm not promising anything long term. Let's see how you go for a few weeks. I'll pay you three pounds a week and full board; alright? When can you start?'

I nodded and tried to smile. 'I'll be here next weekend.'

'It'll do. You'd better go in the house and introduce yourself to Alice, my wife, and she'll show you about and if you're lucky, she'll make you a boiled bacon sandwich. And try not to drip water on the floor, she doesn't like it. I'll see you next week.'

Harry walked over to his Land Rover, climbed in and drove off up the yard, a big black collie dog on the front seat beside him and another dancing about in the back on a pile of sacks, buckets and goodness knows what else.

***

And it *was* hard work, painfully so. For the first few days I ached everywhere and my hands, which had held nothing more abrasive than a tooth brush in the last seventeen years and were as soft and as useful as a moorland bog, were now blistered and sore. My head hurt from the sheer physical exertion so that, not long after tea I would be away to my bed.

Try as I did to conceal my sores, such ailments did not go unnoticed and Harry took enormous satisfaction in telling me to use plenty of carbolic soap and to use the nail brush to scrub with when I was washing my hands in the kitchen sink.

'They need a good splash of iodine, boy,' he said. 'That would toughen them up. Or you could try a large scoop of udder cream, as long as you're careful where you put your hands afterwards.'

When I declined this advice, he warmed to his theme and told me there were also some pretty pink oven gloves I could use if I wanted and at this point Alice, nice lady as she was, stepped in to tell Harry to be quiet.

'Oh, Harry,' she said, sipping her tea. 'Leave the boy alone.' And then to me: 'Take no notice of him, John. You'll be alright.'

That evening I took a stroll up to the milking parlour and grabbed a handful of udder cream from the large tub which sat on the shelf between the cubicles. Smooth and cool, the relief was almost instantaneous and, better still, long lasting.

For the first couple of weeks the weather produced nothing but heavy showers and I had been cleaning out pigs, most of which were housed in pens built in what had been a cow shed in earlier years. And it wasn't long before

I decided I didn't like pigs and that they didn't like me. They didn't interact, they showed no interest in what I was doing for them and it seemed as if I was either shoving food into them at one end or clearing up the mess that resulted from the other.

So I could drive down the field to the muck heap and empty the trailer, Harry had given me a short course on how to drive a tractor he had purchased only a couple of months earlier. Resplendent in its red and yellow livery and yet, largely unmarked, I had read that this model was the flagship tractor of the David Brown range and, with its fifty-two-horsepower engine, a powerful workhorse. I looked forward to driving it.

Using the steering wheel to pull myself up onto the footplate, I swung my leg over the gearbox, a large metal block which dominated the centre of the floor space.

'There are eight gears, six forward and two reverse,' Harry started. 'So, you have three forward and a reverse on the right-hand gear stick and a high and low ratio in each of them using the left-hand stick. You should be alright in high first or high second for most things, but low third can be handy on occasions. Top gear gets you about fourteen miles an hour.'

I sat there gazing down at the two gear sticks and wondered what on earth it was he had been trying to tell me.

'Let's fire her up and give it a go,' he said. 'And make sure it's out of gear.'

I fiddled about trying to find the black starter button on the left-hand side of the cowling, and after several futile attempts at locating it, I had to bend down to see where it was. Pressing it in, the engine began to turn over.

'Give her some throttle,' Harry shouted.

I reached up with my other hand and pulled the red lever on the steering column towards me and the engine roared into life.

'That's it,' he said, after he had reached over and closed

the throttle, so we could hear each other. 'You've got it worked out now. Take her out into the paddock and have a drive round for an hour and get used to her. We'll do the trailer reversing later. Mind how you go and don't bend it.'

He stood back a couple of paces and I pressed the clutch pedal and took a stab at finding a gear which would send me in the right direction. I did and the tractor stalled.

'The hand brake is down by your feet on the left,' Harry said.

I groaned and restarted the engine, engaged a different gear, released the brakes and took my foot off the clutch and prayed we would not be going backwards. But it was alright; the tractor lurched forwards and we were moving out of the yard heading for the paddock. And it felt good despite there being no cab for protection from the weather and no springs to stop the bumps jarring my spine - if the couple of inches of foam rubber cushion on the seat was to be discounted.

Out in the paddock I tried out all the gears, including reverse and pulled and pushed every other lever I could find and after half an hour I thought I had become reasonably competent, until it occurred to me that a tractor on its own achieves very little, if anything. It needed an implement to operate or a trailer to pull and that is where the skill of tractor driving comes into its own.

I knew I hadn't even started to learn what it was about, and an impossibly difficult lesson on trying to reverse a two-wheel trailer didn't help at all. I had a long way to go before I could even be considered a useful addition to the farm.

***

Breakfast at Church Farm was the highlight of the day and marked the completion of a host of routine pre-breakfast livestock duties and the start of the day's 'proper' work. It was held in the kitchen where the centre piece was a huge oak table with seven chairs around it.

A large alcove running down one side of the kitchen

was home for the stove and a coal fired Rayburn which, kept alight the year round, ensured the kitchen was always a warm place to be.

On colder days the kitchen was a magnet for the farm's cats and dogs. They would stretch out in a tangled heap in front of the Rayburn and Alice spent a good deal of her day pushing them outside only to have them line up by back door until someone opened it and they could all creep back in again.

Two, highly polished, wide bore copper pipes wound their way out of the alcove and up into the ceiling to take heated water to other parts of the house and while most of the furniture was in keeping with the age of the house, which was several centuries old, the exception was a state-of-the-art, top of the range automatic washing machine.

This appliance was so out of place and it cried out to be in a utility room surrounded by fridge-freezers, tumble driers and any number of other 'white' electrical gadgets and I wondered who had talked Alice into having one. I would have expected her to still be using the copper boiler and a mangle in the wash house.

In the months to come I would realise that the modern world and Alice were not a comfortable mix. Stemming from a farming family herself, an upbringing on an isolated farm had hardly prepared her for the fast-moving technological developments of the 1960s. And while she was kind and caring, there was always an element of 'them and us' about her; 'them', which lived out there and 'us' which were her family and closest friends. It was a view which meant she invariably avoided any route that could cause her to become involved in society at large and this led to an insular way of life and frequent criticism of the way other people chose to run their lives.

Anyway, for some reason the ultra-modern automatic washing machine had slipped through the technology net and I was impressed. And so must have been the tabby cat which now spent a large part of its day curled up in a plastic bowl on the top of it and appeared to be able to sleep through the violent shaking when the spin cycle kicked in. On the few occasions I saw it awake, its eyes definitely weren't right.

Breakfast followed a routine which was never knowingly changed from one end of the year to the next. It started at nine o'clock with Alice laying the table and distributing bowls of cereal. Harry sat at the head of the table and Alice, who needed to be near the kettle which steamed away all day on the Rayburn's hotplate, seated opposite me. It was a large table for the three of us with plenty of room to spread the newspaper whenever I had a chance to read it, but there were also times when friends and relations dropped in and the numbers swelled.

As ever, there was the presence of dogs and these crept under the table and spent their time sleeping and gently passing wind and I seemed to be the only one to notice.

For the breakfast itself, the bowl of cereals was always followed by two slices of boiled bacon carved off a joint by Harry and this was consumed together with slices of bread and butter prepared by Alice.

And when it came to bread and butter, Alice employed a skill that could only have been acquired through years of practice. With a fresh uncut loaf held firmly in her hand, she would begin by cutting off the crust and then spreading the face with a layer of soft butter. A quick change of knives then saw her cut off the slice of buttered bread as she rotated the loaf, a slice which, if she set her mind to it, could be as thin as an eighth of an inch. It was a joy to watch even if it did only amount to less than a mouthful of bread.

Alice was also in charge of the tea which she made in a warmed pot with spooned-in tea leaves and, once filled with boiling water, was kept warm with a colourful quilted cosy. After several minutes' brewing time, the tea was poured through a tea strainer into white bone-china cups and saucers. The first cup was not a straightforward operation though and involved a gentle, pre-tilting of the pot to ensure water isolated in the spout was properly mixed with the main body of brewing tea before it could be poured.

The first cup was Harry's, a splash of milk being added from a jug before it was passed up the table. Mine was the last to arrive and I was always tempted to reach across and take it, but that would have created a pecking order issue and, I felt sure, have resulted in some ramifications. After all, I was at that stage at least, still an example of 'them'.

Shortly after the boiled bacon and bread had been consumed it was the moment for Alice to ask whether more tea was required, and Harry always replied he would have just half a cup. Which I thought was strange; half a cup was hardly a swallow in those cups and he always had a second half a cup anyway.

One Sunday breakfast time, while cutting ever more slices off yet another large joint of boiled bacon, Harry announced his tomatoes were not doing as well as they might. There was, he said, a need to cut back the branches of two trees which were preventing light reaching his greenhouse.

'Ronny's about somewhere so we'll ask him to help us,' he said. And in response to my questioning look regarding who Ronny was, he answered: 'You'll see.'

Chapter two

A light pruning

The orchard was across the yard from the house, just below the dairy and alongside a few small outbuildings. About an acre in size, it was home for Pedro the donkey and no one was quite sure how long he had been there or could even remember him not being there, but he was testament at least, to the first part of Harry's belief that you never see dead donkeys or happy farmers.

Pedro's stable was regularly bedded with fresh straw and he retired to it most evenings as the sun was setting to a supper of fresh hay and, if there wasn't much grass, a handful or two of ground barley.

As donkeys do, he was capable of creating incredibly loud braying noises at the most unusual times of the day, braying that could be heard all around the village and beyond and had, on occasions, given rise to complaints which Harry had ignored.

'He's only doing what donkey's do,' he said. 'And you can't complain about that can you? If I complained about everything humans do, I would be a busy man.'

There were times, in his earlier years, when Pedro had been in big demand to take part in the nativity play held in the church as part of its Christmas celebration. At first, he was a big success and all the children flocked to stroke him and he even had his picture featured in the parish magazine with the caption, 'Popular Pedro'. This success was followed by a request for him to make an appearance at the Harvest Festival, again with a large following.

But then one year his flatulence problem kicked in and, while it was tolerated for a couple of years, it became progressively worse so much so that some members of the congregation were moved to make copies of his photograph and write an amended caption. On his final appearance, maybe five years ago now, he managed to empty the church and caused midnight mass to be cancelled, mainly because no one wanted to risk striking a match to light the candles.

'I think it's down to his nerves,' Harry said when we were discussing Pedro's problem. 'He worries he might embarrass himself. And if truth be known, I think that's why the vicar also stopped asking for him to be at the harvest festival, that and the fact he knocked over the whole vegetable display when he went for the carrots.'

The orchard was, on occasions, also used to keep orphaned lambs in so their demands for bottles of warm milk to be given to them at all hours of the day could be met without having to walk too far from the house. Later in the year, it was a useful, secure area to keep lambs that had been selected to go to market – the trailer could be backed up to the gate and the lambs loaded without a lot of fuss.

But for today's task, the focus of attention was on the two oak trees which grew along the top edge of the orchard and had long, overhanging branches preventing the sun from shining on a couple of greenhouses that, with their moss-stained glass and woodwork, looked to be older than the oak trees but were probably not.

'No good trying to grow big tomatoes in the shade, is it boy?' Harry said, as we made our way across the orchard carrying a long ladder between us. 'That's why sheep only have small feet.'

Harry was also carrying a bow saw and I had an awful

sense of foreboding. In my book, branches when they're cut off tend to fall downwards and that was where the greenhouses were although to be fair, they weren't immediately beneath them but pretty close, all the same.

The first problem we discovered was that the ladder wasn't long enough to reach all the branches needing to be pruned.

'Got any ideas?' Harry asked when we had set the ladder leaning against the main trunk of the tree.

'Well, we could find a way of hoisting someone up there. He'd be safe enough if he was tied on to the tree,' I said.

I was still thinking along these lines when I heard the orchard gate latch being lifted and when I turned there was a youth walking towards us with a sort of aboriginal loping stride so that his rolled down wellingtons scraped through the top of the grass.

'Ah, here's Ronny,' Harry murmured. 'His name's Ronny Brown and he's the youngest of seven children, none of which went in for attending school very often. I had a school inspector round once to see why he was with me rather than at school and when I told him schooling would be a waste of time, he said you never know, sometimes they turn into geniuses when they're like that. Anyway, not long after he was born they had his mother in and took her tubes out.'

'Hello, Harry. Alice told me you needed some help doing something.' Ronny's eyes shifted to the long ladder, the bow saw and then to me.

I looked back at him and noticed the shock of dark hair, the unwashed face, the wisp of adolescent hair on his top lip and the collarless shirt with what were probably the remains of a string vest somewhere beneath it. I would have said he was in his late teens, but it was hard to tell with any certainty.

Ronny nodded at me and reached into his coat pocket and retrieved a packet of cigarettes but there didn't seem to be any in it, at least not whole ones.

Instead, he proceeded to pull the white paper backing off the metal foil that lined the packet and then, having split open a few of the unsmoked tips, re-rolled the tobacco up in the paper to make a cigarette which somehow held together. And then he lit it and drew heavily on the resulting smoke.

'What's up, Ron?' Harry asked. 'Getting to the end of the financial year again or have your ICI shares slumped?'

'Nah,' he replied, smoke billowing from his mouth and his left nostril. 'You can get another five fags out of a packet of twenty and then you can get nearly another two out of those five if you roll them thin.'

Harry, who says he has never tried a cigarette in his life, screwed his face up, not over impressed with Ronny's frugality and turned to me. 'If you fetch a couple of cart ropes from the tractor shed, I'll try and explain what we want him to do.'

I walked round to the yard and spotted the coils of ropes hanging from bolts driven into the ironstone walls. Some were in better condition than others, so I chose two which looked long enough and could hold Ronny's weight.

When I arrived back, they were standing beneath one of the oak trees, staring up into the branches.

'We've had a better idea,' Harry said. 'What we're going to do is tie a rope around Ronny and, with the rope looped over the highest branch, we'll pull him up and then he can saw off the branches as we lower him down.'

'So, we need to get a rope looped over the highest branch. And how are we going to do that?'

'Simple. He climbs up the ladder as far as he can and then lobs it over. It's only another ten feet and we can tie a weight on the end to help him get it over.'

I shrugged. This was not a good time to be a greenhouse. If Ronny doesn't land on them, the brick he's tying to the end of the rope surely will – and that's not counting where the branches he plans to cut off will land.

Ronny took hold of the ladder and began to climb; the rope, with the brick attached, secured to his belt and Harry feeding rope out to him as he went. The top of the ladder was only a few inches higher than the branch it was leaning on and it occurred to me that any bouncing could see the ladder with nothing but fresh air to lean on. And that, I estimated, would just about flatten both the green houses.

'I'm nearly there, Harry' he said.

I looked up and watched him grab the branch with one hand and the brick with the other.

'You'd better get ready to catch it and give me plenty of slack.'

'Don't you worry about that, boy. I'm holding the other end of the rope.'

Ronny leaned back as far as he dared and, moving his arm in a great arc, lobbed the brick in an upward direction, releasing it at the moment that would ensure it sailed over the top branch with feet to spare. I was impressed.

But that was when the trouble started.

Harry let the rope slip through his fingers and the brick descended but it was still swinging wildly as it drew level with Ronny and, as luck would have it, the brick caught him on the side of his jaw.

'Bugger that,' he yelled. 'That bleedin' hurt.'

'Never mind all that,' Harry said. 'Just remove the brick and tie the end around you and we'll make a start.'

And ignoring his discomfort, Ronny did just that.

'Right then, let's give this a go.' Harry said, taking up the strain.

'I think we should tie the other rope onto the end you're holding before we start,' I said. 'He needs to come down sometime and there isn't enough rope to lower him, and he's not going to do an awful lot up there if he hasn't got the bow saw with him.'

'Yes, alright then. Let's do that. We can take the ladder out of the way and pull him up from the ground.'

With the ladder removed Ronny stood at the base of

the oak tree like a condemned man; the rope around his waist and one hand reaching up, clutching the rope which led up into the tree.

And it wasn't the best of places to be standing. Over the years, Pedro had spent a large part of the summer in the shade of the oak trees and there was a thick, greasy layer of donkey droppings on the ground.

'I'm not very happy about this, Harry,' he said.

'That's right, boy. Just remember to keep a firm hold of the bow saw.'

He stood there expectantly as Harry and I took up the strain on the rope which tightened on Ronny's waist and did little more.

'Pull!' Harry yelled. 'Pull like you're pulling the postman off your mother!' And in unison we gave it all our combined weight but while Ronny managed at one point to stand on tip-toe, he remained for the most part on the ground.

'It must be the friction of the rope around the branch,' Harry said. 'We need to pull it at an angle; there's too much rope touching it.'

We moved further out into the orchard and tried again but with little noticeable improvement in that Ronny was still standing under the tree, possibly now wincing a little. It was then that Harry suggested using Pedro to give us some extra pulling strength.

'I'll get him a bucket of ground barley and he'll do anything for us,' he said. 'Make a loop in the rope for his shoulders while I fetch it.'

Pedro was clearly very fond of ground barley, but he much preferred it to be taken to him rather having someone hold a bucketful a few inches away and being restrained by a length of rope around his shoulders from getting any closer.

'You stand in front of him with the bucket and I'll give him some encouragement from behind,' Harry said. 'Let him have a good sniff of it first.'

Pedro plodded forward a few paces until the rope was taught and I moved the bucket ahead of him and then, without any warning, Harry suddenly started clapping his hands and shouting like a mad man which not only startled me but also Pedro who flattened his ears, took flight and, despite the restriction of the rope, passed me at something nearing a canter.

I looked over to where Ronny should have been, but he wasn't there. All I could see was a rapidly ascending pair of legs accompanied by a strange high-pitched whimpering noise that changed into a strangled cry as he disappeared up into the branches.

The problem was Pedro wouldn't stop pulling. Both of us were now behind him and he was going like the clappers, that is, until Ronny reached the branch the rope went over. And while that brought Pedro to an abrupt, rib cracking halt, he was still doing his best to keep going, pawing the ground like an enraged bull.

'Stop him, Harry!' There was a desperate cry from somewhere up in the foliage. 'For pity's sake, stop him.'

I picked up the bucket, rattled it and called his name. 'Pedro. Come on boy. Good boy. Come and have some barley.'

He stopped, turned around and trotted over towards me and, as he did, the rope slipped off his shoulders with the result that, released from his bonds, Ronny began a rapid descent which ended in a dreadful splat as he landed in the donkey poo below.

I gave Pedro a handful of ground barley; I felt he'd done his best and deserved something for his efforts and then ran across and joined Harry who had stopped a yard short of Ronny who, like a demented prehistoric snake, was slithering about trying to get to his feet. And when he managed it, he looked awful. His trousers and shirt were well covered in donkey mess and try as he did to wipe it off, he only succeeded in spreading it even further.

'I think I'll be on my way, Harry,' he said, slurring

slightly due to brick damage. 'I've a few jobs I ought to be doing in the village.'

And then he loped off across the orchard, hands in pockets and his rolled down wellingtons scraping their way through the grass.

'Well, boy,' Harry said, turning to me. 'I suppose we should be getting along too. I mean, the shade from the trees isn't that bad. Pedro enjoys it and, if push comes to shove, I could try growing tomatoes in the cloches, or even outside, come to that.'

***

That evening Harry and Alice took me with them when they went to visit her brother who runs the family farm where she was born and raised. About three miles out of the village, the entrance to Rose Hill Farm was a ten-foot gate tied shut with bale string which drew some derogatory comments from Harry.

'It's a bit poor when the first thing you see on a farm is held together with bale string,' he said. 'Why don't they get a proper gate latch and, while they're at it, put in a twelve-foot gate and fill some of these pot holes in.'

'You say that every time we come here,' Alice said.

'Well it doesn't seem to make any difference.'

'Exactly.'

The track meandered its way across the fields until, after about half a mile, arrived at the farm buildings and Harry brought the Land Rover to a halt beside a large three-story house. It was like one of those 'House on the Prairie' type places where generations of a family all live under the same roof.

And that was how it was at Rose Hill with Alice's parents living alongside her brother and his wife and their four children; three generations. Making things more complicated was that the principal male in each generation had been christened William and whoever had the job of opening the post must have had an interesting time.

'You must come on in and have some tea,' said Alice's sister-in-law when she saw me standing on the back doorstep wondering where I should be, since Harry and Alice had wandered off somewhere. 'It'll be a good opportunity for you to meet everyone – we always like to get together on Sunday evenings.'

I thanked her and stepped into the kitchen where there was a large table along with, numerous seats and countless cats and dogs. Over in the corner, next to the range sat an old man in an easy chair with a blanket over his knees.

'That's William senior, my William's father,' she said. 'Oh, and I'm Kate, if no one has told you.' And while I smiled politely at William senior, she turned to the other end of the kitchen and waved her hand in the direction of an old lady reclining in a similar chair. 'And that's Ethel, William's wife; she doesn't have a lot to say these days either. Anyway, come through to the front room and meet everyone else.

I followed her down a windowless corridor which must have been all of fifteen yards long and had dog-height stains along the yellowing walls. Light was provided by two naked, low-watt light bulbs hanging at each end of the ceiling.

The door which marked the end of the corridor was already half open and I could hear voices, young sweet voices. Kate pushed the door open wide and clapped her hands for some attention.

'Quiet everyone,' she shouted. 'I want you all to meet John who is now working for Uncle Harry.'

Everyone was seated at a large round table which had several plates of sandwiches and cakes on it and I noticed the room's occupants included three girls.

'Well, where shall we start?' said Kate looking round the table. 'Over there is William junior our son and he's sitting next to his father, William.'

William junior was about my age and he smiled back at me in what I interpreted as being a sorrowful way.

Although being heir to the farm he had probably already realised there was not a lot to look forward to.

His father looked as if he still had a good few years left in him, there would be few opportunities to sample off-farm life and, unless something changed, he was staring at a lifetime standing about in ankle-deep cow shit, an occasional trip to the village fete, and if he could work it, a surreptitious subscription to Playboy.

His father looked a dour sort of character with gaunt features which included a sharp pointed nose with a perpetual 'ten-gallon' dew drop on the end of it. He managed to make a slight nod as he looked at me and we both tried to ignore the resulting splash. I wondered how it was he had managed to meet up and marry someone as pleasant and outgoing as Kate. Perhaps her car had broken down by the gate.

'And over there are the girls,' said Kate, interrupting my thoughts, 'In ascending ages they are Elsie, Emily and the oldest, Elizabeth who has just turned seventeen.'

I found myself worrying for the postman again but only briefly. I knew I shouldn't stare but I couldn't stop myself. Elizabeth was enchanting; her long dark hair, her fresh, youthful complexion, she was beautiful. She looked away from me, a slight blush rising in her cheeks. And then I heard the giggling of her two sisters followed by some inane whispering.

'Very pleased to meet you,' I said, because it was the only thing I could think of saying and sat down on the chair Kate had pulled out for me.

'Now where have Harry and Alice got to?' she asked.

'They'll be looking at the cows,' replied dour William. 'He wants to buy the Friesian which calved last week but he's not having her, is he boy?'

I assumed he was speaking to his son but before I could be absolutely sure I heard footsteps in the corridor and Harry and Alice appeared. They were greeted by yells of welcome from their nieces and nephew.

'Sit down and make a start,' Kate said. I'll fetch the tea.'

'I'll give you seventy for her, you can keep the calf and I'll pick her up tomorrow,' Harry said.

'Make it seventy-five and we have a deal,' dour William said, starting to spit on the palm of his hand to seal the deal but stopping when he realised where he was.

'There you go, John, another cow for you to milk.'

'That's good,' I replied and looked across the table at Elizabeth who smiled back at me.

Kate returned with a large pot of tea and fussed about with the tea cups. 'Just so you know, these here are boiled bacon,' she said, pointing to the largest plate on the table.

Chapter three

My girls

By July I felt I was getting into the routine of it all and I liked to think I was starting to contribute to the running of the farm. But there was still a lot to learn.

Each day began with a six-thirty morning call from Harry which as far as milking cows goes, was not a particularly early start. But since I had begun to frequent the local pub for the odd underage pint of bitter and a game of skittles, it was a time which was becoming increasingly tougher to meet.

'Morning, boy,' Harry said as I strolled into the kitchen several minutes after he had called me. 'I see we're heading for the trussing needle treatment.'

'The what?'

'The trussing needle treatment.' He reached for the shelf which ran along the top of the alcove and scooped up a needle that must have been a foot long.

'What's that used for?' I asked.

'Well, normally, it's used to truss chickens and turkeys up after they've been plucked and had their innards removed.' He pointed to the eye where the string would be threaded through and the sharp point. 'But, in your case, it's for waking up those who can't wake up on time.'

'Oh, great; that is something to look forward to. I think I'll buy an alarm clock.'

Harry laughed and disappeared upstairs with a cup of tea for Alice. I sipped mine and took a closer look at the trussing needle before putting it back on the shelf.

'Right then,' Harry said when he returned. 'I'll bring the cows in and you bring the bucket of hot udder washing water.'

I swallowed the last of my tea and walked into the hallway to get my wellingtons and coat on and went across the yard to retrieve the bucket. There was no hot water in the dairy so I had to use the house supply.

Ever since the cow shed had been converted to pig pens, the cows had been milked in a milking bail designed originally as a self-contained mobile unit that could be taken out to the field where the cows were grazing during the spring and summer.

The idea was that the herdsman went to the cows and brought the milk back to the farm, rather than the cows walking back and forwards to the parlour when they could be grazing and making milk. It also meant fields in other parts of the farm could be grazed, fields too far from the farm to walk back to twice a day.

Somewhere along the way, Harry had acquired a milking bail and had set it up as a permanent fixture at one end of a concreted area, sharing a wall with the church graveyard. The cows were outside all the year round and consisted mainly of Red Polls which were classed as a 'dual purpose' breed capable of producing an acceptable yield of milk and, when crossed with a Hereford bull, some fine beef cattle.

Over the years though, the herd size had slowly expanded to about forty cows with the introduction of different breeds – Friesian, Angus, Ayrshire and, as Harry put it: 'Anything else which looks as if it could put a few gallons in a churn.

With a relatively small number of cows I soon became well acquainted with each of them and, in time, I grew to love them all. Not at first though. There were those which could be deliberately difficult and set out to make my life miserable – kicking off clusters, kicking out when I came near them, making piles of cow slurry in the milking area and refusing to leave the bail when they'd been milked. They could be challenging.

But I worked on gaining their trust, holding a handful of feed out while they waited to come in to be milked and feeling their tongues reaching out to take a trial lick and, when nothing nasty happened, taking a longer lick. I would stroke them on top of their heads and behind their ears, talk to them softly and be as patient as they wanted me to be while they were being milked.

It took some time but gradually they settled down and they became 'my girls' who I could approach in the field and have a few words with whenever I was passing through. On warm Sunday afternoons when we weren't too busy, I would go down to their field early and sit down with them, leaning against one of them and discuss the weather and the current political situation in south-east Asia or whatever.

If I was lucky I would be rewarded with a long rasping lick and then I would say it was time to go and they would just look at me in a 'do we have to' sort of way until I strode off and then they would decide to follow.

There was one of them though, and I never discovered what breed she was, who was a particular tyrant; her delicate features and subtle colouring suggested she may have had a bit of Jersey or Guernsey in her but I couldn't be sure. The only one in the herd to have horns, she didn't seem to fit in with the rest of the girls and she was an absolute loner who would always be some distance away from the rest of the herd.

At milking time, she invariably came in last and kicked out as soon as I put the cluster on her and then started getting upset about everything.

But I persevered. When she kicked off the cluster I would put them on again and if it happened again, as it usually did, I would simply put them on her again. No shouting, no tantrums, just soft talk and an encouraging stroke. We had all the time in the world and when she eventually discovered that kicking off the cluster produced no response other than for them to be replaced, she stopped doing it.

One day I managed to milk her from start to finish without any trouble and I told her how clever she was. For me, it was a landmark event and although during the next few days she tried her hardest to be good, there were one or two relapses. Soon though, she was as good as gold and even started coming in early to be milked and I also began to make a fuss of her with a few handfuls of feed and the odd ear tickle.

Horns, as I called her, turned into a wonderful cow – a real special girl - and when I walked in front, as I brought them up for milking, she always walked directly behind me. Every time I looked back she would shake her head and snort, a silly sort of endearing smile on her face.

One of the most satisfying parts of it all was that when the girls were in the collecting yard waiting to be milked they would be relaxed and calm and this was reflected in the small amount of mess they made. As any cowman will tell you, nervous cows produce mountains of slurry and I have often thought that those who feel the need to shout and use sticks to dominate their cows cause themselves a lot of work.

***

The first few cows were arriving in the collecting yard when I arrived at the bail carrying the bucket of warm water. I placed it out of the way in the corner and wished them all a good morning as I walked round to the compartment which housed the single cylinder Lister engine to power the vacuum pump.

Turning on the petrol and adding a dash of choke, I cranked the engine over and as it settled down to a kind of even running, I closed and bolted the door before pulling the gate to the collecting yard shut.

The bail could take four cows at a time – two would be milked while the other two were having their udders washed or, if they had just been milked, let out and two more allowed in from the collecting yard. Cows were milked directly into churns – the churn lids were replaced with a unit which used a rubber seal to create a vacuum in the churn and from this came the milk and pulsator pipes.

By the time I had returned from the engine bay, the lids on the two churns had sealed and the pulsators were clicking and hissing as they should. All I had to do was place a scoopful of ground barley into each of the troughs, open the gate to let four cows in, and milking could begin.

I made a note not to over-fill the churns before changing over to empty ones because that just sent milk up the vacuum line. The problem was that, short of lifting them up to see how heavy they were, there was no way of knowing how much milk was in the churn. Over time I developed a sort of gut feeling to when the churns should be changed over.

The bail may have been a convenient and low-cost way of milking, but it could also be a very cold place in the winter. When the cows came in with frost on their whiskers I would reach deep into the warm water bucket for the cloth and give their udders a slow wash, not that they had a lot of milk to give in such icy temperatures.

And after they had finished being milked I'd push my hands up between their udder and flank and spend a few seconds warming my hands before I put some udder cream on their teats to stop them becoming chaffed and sore.

Being entirely open at the front meant snow and rain could also be a problem but that was how it was and that was how they were milked. They were some tough old girls who seemed to cope with some extreme weather conditions and I wished I could be as tough and resilient as they were.

There were occasions though, when it was too bad even for them to go out and then they were given a barn to shelter in and some hay to chew on.

When the last cow had been milked it was time to swill down the bail and spend a few minutes clearing up any mess there was in the collecting yard. I'd give it a more thorough swilling down when I had dealt with the milk.

Taking the churns of milk down to the dairy was always a challenge and to avoid having to carry them – the combined weight of ten gallons of milk and a steel churn was too much to carry far - I had to learn how to roll them on their edge across the collecting yard. Harry was an expert in churn rolling and could roll, turn corners and bring them to a halt with extraordinary precision.

'Be careful you don't over lean them,' he said. 'You have to find the balance point and keep it steady.'

I also discovered that churn lids didn't always sit that tightly and it was possible for one to come off and then there could be real problems; like a churn on its side spewing ten gallons of milk all over the yard, and me still holding the lid.

The churns were rolled from the bail across the collecting yard to a hand gate in the corner and it was here they were loaded onto a hand cart – three at a time – for the journey down the yard to the dairy. It was a distance of about thirty yards and the trolley was brought to a halt by leaning down on the handles so the rear skid dug into the gravel.

Before the milk could continue its journey down to the stand in the street where the churns would be collected by a lorry, they had to be cooled by passing cold water through pipes which were immersed in the milk. It worked but it was slow and there was always the risk the milk lorry would arrive before the milk was properly cooled.

Not that this was a problem for the previous evening's milk which had been cooled and stored overnight in a large, walk-in fridge.

Having stood in there for a dozen hours, the cream would come to the top and, right on the very top was the thickest layer of cream which, being ice cold, was delicious to have on cornflakes with just a sprinkle of sugar. It was sweet, creamy and crunchy and incredibly addictive.

Milk lorry drivers were not renowned for their patience and if the milk churns were not ready to be collected they would, if their mood took them, just leave a few empty churns and drive on. So I would take down the evening milk first while the morning milk was still being cooled and then make a couple more trips with the morning milk.

The full churns were loaded on to the trolley and with just a gentle push, set off down a slope which started gently but became increasingly steeper as it continued, and the speed of the trolley increased rapidly as a result.

With thirty gallons of milk on board, all I could do was hang onto the handles and keep the weight on the skid but on the smooth concrete slabs, the braking effect was negligible. A small correction in the steering was required to see the trolley safely through a hand gate and then it was a straight, unstoppable run for about another thirty yards down to the street.

When it was dry there was an element of control but should it be icy or snowy it was just a matter of hoping there were no vehicles or pedestrians coming along the street, or the postman making his way up to the farm.

On rare but memorable occasions, I was met by the Milk Marketing Board inspector, usually a lady in a white coat, who was there to check on the temperature of the milk.

'You tell Harry, he'll have to do better than this,' she would bark at me as she looked at the thermometer she had just removed from the milk which was clearly still too warm. 'If it happens again he'll get more than a warning – he'll be getting his milk back. You could make hot chocolate in this.'

There was no arguing and, as I was the person

responsible it didn't seem to make sense to mention it to Harry. I would just have to try and finish milking earlier and allow more time for cooling.

Before the churns left the dairy they each had a label tied to one of their handles to inform those who needed to know how much milk was in the churn, how many churns were being sent, the date and who the supplier was.

And it was one of these labels Harry took the trouble to tie to the collar of the neighbour's in-season collie bitch which had come to visit the farm's dogs. "Served and ready for collection," he wrote on it, adding: "Stud fee to be agreed."

With the milk sent on its way, there was just time to return to the bail and the connecting yard and have a good clean down using plenty of water and then, with the cows out on the grass and everything clean and the milking equipment in soak ready for Alice to strip down and sterilise, it was time for breakfast.

There were some mornings when I used to look forward to a slice of boiled bacon, but not very often.

Chapter four

Haymaking

Harry was in a philosophical mood. 'Farmers always go on about their haymaking experiences,' he said. 'They'll tell you about the time when the sun shone for days on end and how they mowed the grass one day and baled it the next, and also about the disastrous haymaking times when it rained continuously throughout the entire summer and crops were ruined.'

These "I remember when..." moments were, I believed, an indication of an ageing mind and they were also incredibly boring.

'I can remember when old Joe Parker came round to borrow four drums of diesel. He wanted it to help burn the grass they had mowed three weeks before and was still lying on the ground. The grass was now so rotten it wasn't worth the cost of baling, so he thought he would have a go at burning it – and I don't think he even managed to do that. Mind you, it's a fact that more bad hay is made in a good time than in a bad time.'

Harry paused and, because I could tell he had more to say on the subject, I asked him why that should be the case.

'Well, when it's a good dry time and the sun's out, as it is today and doing its job, people are out with the baler too soon. The hay looks and feels alright but it hasn't been properly made and a few weeks after its been in the stack, the bales start to heat up and get so hot they catch fire and the whole lot goes up in flames.'

'Really?' It sounded a bit far-fetched to me.

'It's a fact,' he insisted. 'You would be amazed at the temperatures produced when poorly made hay is stacked in a heap. Barn fires were once a regular occurrence but now people are more careful, but you still hear about the odd one.'

We were standing in the middle of a ten-acre field Harry had mowed two days ago and I had been given the task of tedding it using a machine which had a rotor with tines on. These picked up the cut grass and threw it out the back, leaving it in a light, airy swath so it could dry out and make more quickly.

I reached down and grabbed a handful of grass and gave it a twist and, rather than feeling brittle and crisp, it felt tough and there was still some dampness about it. 'How long will it be before this is ready to bale?'

'The baler usually tells you whether it's fit or not. If the first few bales come out weighing a ton and looking green then it's time to put the baler back under the barn. Anyway, we'll see what this afternoon brings.'

***

Two days earlier, with a bright, dry day forecast, we had set out with the new tractor attached to a single-bladed reciprocating mower and the farm's other tractor, a Fordson Major, hooked up to the tedder. The plan was that Harry would mow the grass and I would shake it up and kick some life into it with the tedder.

'Mowers can be temperamental pieces of kit to operate,' Harry said, as he undid the clip which allowed the cutter bar to be lowered to a horizontal working position. 'One minute they can be cutting with no problem at all and then, for no apparent reason, they start to bung up and make an awful mess of it.

'What happens if you hit a rock?' I asked.

'You swear loudly and hope you haven't broken

anything. If it's a big obstruction, the whole cutter bar will swing back and hopefully lift at the same time but even that can go arse up if it feels like it.'

I had the impression mowing wasn't Harry's favourite job. If so many things could go wrong with the mower why didn't he try another one?

'They're all much of a muchness,' he said when I asked the question. 'It's the concept that's wrong. They were designed for use with horses and employed a land wheel drive to reciprocate the blade, a system which needed next to no power to operate. There should now be mowers which use the power available from modern tractors – a flail system or something that doesn't rely on sharp blades or perfect standing grass and can cut ten acres an hour not the ten acres a day these mowers manage, sometimes. Anyway, this isn't getting this lot mowed, is it?'

He climbed up onto the tractor and put the drive shaft in gear and soon there was the rapid clicking noise of the blade moving back and forward between the fingers on the cutter bar. He lowered it down to ground level and drove of around the field, the tractor's wheels running close to the hedge, leaving an uncut width which would have to be mowed later.

I waited for him go round a couple of times and then started up the tedder which used its tines to lift the grass and leave it in a fluffy swath that could take full advantage of the day's good drying conditions.

Late morning and the work came to a halt for a blade sharpening session. Harry removed the blade and placed it on the front axle of the tractor and then, with me holding one end of it, proceeded to use a long dry stone to sharpen the individual blade sections.

'They don't need a lot of sharpening,' he said. 'Just enough to take out any burrs and put a shine on the edge.'

Even so, it was almost half an hour before we slid the blade back into the mower and reattached the connecting rod which moved it backwards and forwards.

'You'd better have a go now, boy. I'll just give her a bit of a grease-up.'

With everything set, I drove over to where Harry had left off, engaged the drive, set the throttle as instructed and set off. And it cut very well, the cut grass falling back over the knife as it moved forwards and the large wooden swath board on the end of the cutter bar, deflecting the cut grass over in a great wave to create a gap for the tractor wheels to run on next time round.

Slowly but surely the area of uncut grass became smaller and the time to get round it reduced. I was all set for the finish when Harry waved his arms for me to stop when there was only the size of a tennis court left to cut.

'We'll leave this bit,' he said. 'I don't know if you've seen them but there's a couple of nesting partridges in there somewhere and they've some young chicks running about. It would be a shame to cut them up for the sake of a bale or two.'

I looked across the uncut grass and saw nothing but with the engine stopped I could hear them – a series of high pitched chirping noises.

'Can you hear them?' Harry asked. 'Their mother will be fretting for them so we'll leave them to it.'

And as he spoke, I counted six fluffy balls of chicks emerge from the standing grass and flutter their way along the edge.

'There they go,' I said.

'Don't forget to do the outside of the field,' Harry said as he climbed back on to his tractor.

I nodded and drove over to where the mowing had started and, suddenly, the field looked awfully big again and a long way round. This time, I had to travel in the other direction to cut the grass nearest the hedge. And it wasn't easy. The grass had been run on by the tractor and the fingers struggled to push their way through and get under the grass. But bit by bit, I managed it and the job was finished and I looked across a field with swaths of grass, and there was the scent of freshly mowed grass hanging heavily in the evening air.

For me, it had been a perfect day. I had achieved my first piece of mowing; the machinery had worked well and the weather had been warm and drying so you could almost see the colour of the grass changing as it dried out.

***

The sun scorched down as we walked back up the yard after lunch, kicking the dust up from beneath our boots, I could already feel the heat burning down on my shoulders. The dogs were nowhere to be seen and were probably standing nose deep in a water trough if they had any sense. Looking out across the paddock, I could see the cows lying down, cudding away in the shade beneath the trees, their tales flapping idly to keep the flies on the move.

'If you give the hay one more run through with the tedder, I'll get the turner and start putting two rows in to one behind you,' Harry said. 'And then we'll see if we can get some baled.'

By mid-afternoon, the hay had been rowed up and was ready for the baler. Every so often a wisp of a breeze would ghost its way across the field and create small whirlwinds in its wake, whirlwinds that lifted strands of hay high in the air and seemed to float for ever before they descended to the ground.

With the baler in the field I had my first chance to see the sledge – a system used to create stacks of bales and reduce the amount of running about with trailers when the bales were loaded and taken out of the field.

And it didn't look very inviting. At the front end was a wooden platform about a yard and a half wide and behind this and open to the ground, was an area which could hold six bales on their edges and then have three layers of four bales on their sides stacked on top of them. When there were eighteen bales a lever was pulled and the restraining bar at the back swung open to allow the stack to slide out of the sledge.

'The bottom bales are on their edges to prevent the bale strings being damaged or broken as they're dragged across the ground even though there are a number of flat metal strips for them to run on,' explained Harry.

'And I'm the one who stands on the wooden platform and stacks the bales as they leave the baler,' I said.

Harry nodded. 'There are other types of sledges which just hook on the back of balers and collect the bales as they drop out,' he continued. 'You can get about eight bales in them before you have to pull the rope to open the door and then they need to be stacked after that.

'Of course, eight bales weren't enough for Joe Parker; he welded up a monster of a sledge which could hold about thirty of them.'

'Did it work?' I asked. 'It did for about an hour but then, with a full load and Joe trying to get just one more bale in, there was a big ripping sound as the back of the baler was torn off. But worse than that, Joe always used to bale with the rope he pulled to release the bales twisted around his wrist so when the sledge pulled the back off the baler, he went with it, pulling him straight out the back of the tractor. And with no one on the tractor to stop it, it carried on motoring until it hit the hedge.'

'Was he alright?'

'Oh, he was alright apart from a dislocated shoulder and a bit of bruising to his ego. I think they ended up using the framework of the sledge for the side of a barn.'

With the baler's pick-up swung over into its offset position so the tractor didn't have to run on the swaths, the spools of string threaded through to the knotters and the sledge hooked onto the rear of the baler, all was set.

Harry engaged the drive and the shaft started to turn and with it I heard the plunger sliding back and forwards accompanied with the clatter of the pickup tines and the rhythmic scraping of the feeder arm which took the crop into the chamber.

'It sounds alright to me, boy. We'll give it a go. You'll

find the first few bales a bit loose until the chamber gets really full – it's the resistance of the clamps in the exit chute which dictates the weight of the bale.'

I walked to the rear of the baler and stepped aboard the sledge platform and wondered how I was expected to stay on it with nothing to hold on to. The first bale was not long arriving. It landed at my feet and promptly collapsed into a bundle of loose hay, nothing like a bale. I grabbed the strings and pulled them off before kicking it all over the side. The second bale wasn't much better so that followed the same route but the next one was definitely heavier and more bale shaped, so I thought it was worth keeping.

I bent down to roll it over onto its edge and push it to the edge of the platform and did the same with the next bale but when the third arrived there wasn't any space to move it and I was in a mess. I waved at Harry to stop.

'What's up, boy?'

'There's no room for the third bale,' I said. 'At least, not with me standing on the platform.'

'There's been blokes a lot bigger than you on the platform and they managed alright,' Harry said, making his way towards me. 'If you put the first one on the far edge, the second one on the other edge, there's room for the third in the middle and all you have to do is stand behind them and push them off. Drop them into the sledge and they'll slide to the back of it. Do the same again for the next three and then start stacking them in fours on top. Four layers high and you pull the lever to release them and try and drop them off in a line across the field.'

Harry walked back to the tractor but before he left me, he picked up a bale to see how heavy it was and then went and screwed down the clamps to make them heavier. 'No point wasting string,' he said.

It took a little while but eventually I got the hang of it, juggling bales about on a small platform that bobbed up and down as it slid across the field wasn't easy. Nor was walking across the bales to stack more on top of them; it was like trying to stand on the back of a pair of galloping horses with no reigns to hold on to.

With my first full stack completed I leaned down and pulled the lever to release them and it was a satisfying moment watching it slide out. Some of the other stacks were not quite so pleasing, though. For some reason, they would stick in the sledge and wouldn't slide out properly which meant I had to give it a shove to help it on its way, and there was always the danger of a stack starting to move and then stopping when it was only halfway out. This left a gap of open ground in which I had to start hopping up and down to prevent being jammed up against the stationary bales.

It was relentless. The bales never stopped coming and with no opportunity for a rest, my hands were starting to suffer. The strings were cutting into me, re-opening old blisters and there were thistles in the hay which all seemed to end up in the sores. I resorted to a handkerchief in one hand and the end of my T-shirt in the other.

Eventually, we stopped to top up the string using the spare spools stored in a cabinet on the side of the baler.

'How's it going, boy?' Harry asked, as he ripped open the bag containing the twine.

'Oh, not so bad,' I replied. 'Do we have any water?'

'No, we don't but Alice said she would bring some tea down to us about half past three.'

Harry joined up the spools of twine by taking the strand from the middle of the new spool and tying it to the strand on the outer edge of the one being used.

'You always pull the twine from the centre of the spool and it helps if you smooth the joins so they don't snag on the guide loops or the needles which present the string to the knotters,' he explained.

I would have liked to ask him how the baler ties the knots when a bale is made but I thought that could wait.

Back on the platform I reached for my handkerchief

and the edge of my T-shirt and waited for the bales to start coming out again. I found that once I had managed to get the six base bales where they should be, the stack could be built up from the back by creating a series of steps.

I felt rather pleased with myself for achieving this but then I thought, that this is the way it's probably been done for years. Was there any other way?

Looking across the field I could see my stacks, most of them in a reasonably straight line which would help when we brought the trailers in to start carting them back to the farm.

Shortly after half past three Alice arrived and I was pleased to see she had Elizabeth with her. We headed over to where they had parked the pick-up in the shade of a large oak tree.

'Hello, Elizabeth,' I said when I had brushed some of the hay off my T-shirt.

'Hi John. You must be sweltering out there today.'

I grinned. 'You're telling me it is. But it's good haymaking weather.' She smiled back at me and then reached up to take a strand of grass out of my hair.

'Are you two with us, or what?' Alice said.

We sauntered over to where Harry had pulled a few bales together for us to sit on, and Elizabeth and I shared one.

'This is more like it, boy,' Harry said as he sipped on his mug of tea and leant back against the tractor wheel. 'Everything always tastes better in the field.'

Alice opened a large tin of sandwiches. 'I bet you're ready for one of these,' she said, offering them to me.

I reached in with some trepidation and took out a sandwich. Surely, I thought, they couldn't be boiled bacon. Not again. But they were and I munched bravely into it.

'Harry, are you going to have one?'

'No, I'll have jam, please.'

What! Nobody mentioned jam to me and I felt Elizabeth's elbow jab into my side and I could hear her stifling a laugh.

Alice reached into her bag and brought out a second tin and even before she opened it I swear I could smell the strawberry and when Harry brought one out, the bread was cut really thick and the jam sat in a generous layer between heavily buttered slices like a sponge cake with the cream and jam oozing out down the sides.

'Now this really is more like it, boy,' Harry said, mug of tea in one hand and a door-step of a jam sandwich in the other. 'Like I say, it always tastes better in the field. And why have three or four sandwiches when you can have it all in one go, eh?'

I took another small bite from my wafer thin boiled bacon sandwich and smiled my agreement.

'Anyone know what Ronny's doing? We could do with him for a few days to help us with a spot of bale carting.'

Alice thought about it. 'Well, I saw him walking down Doctor's Hill yesterday so he's about - you know, not in prison, or anything. I'll have a drive up the village on the way back and see what he's doing.'

Harry pushed the last of his jam sandwich into his mouth, licked his fingers and got to his feet. And when he had finally swallowed: 'Right then, boy. If you're ready, we'll carry on. Another hour should crack it.'

I climbed back onto the platform and, as Alice and Elizabeth were on their way out of the field I waved, but they probably couldn't see me.

***

By the time I had finished milking, it was almost dark and as the cows ambled across the paddock for their evening grazing they were silhouetted by the last vestiges of a setting sun spreading a golden glow across an azure sky – a sky in which the stars were already putting in an appearance.

Harry had left the Land Rover at the top of the yard with half a dozen bales of hay stacked in the back of it - buffer feed for the girls and, for me, the most enjoyable task of the day. I slipped into the driving seat and was surprised to see Elizabeth sitting in the passenger seat.

'Hello,' I said. 'What brings you here?'

'Well, I'm still waiting for dad to pick me up on his way back from town. I just thought it would be good to help you take the bales out.'

'Oh right.' I started the engine and drove off across the paddock.

The cows knew I was on my way and had assembled by the far wall where they seemed to enjoy spending the night. Not all of them though. I had taken to stopping and giving a wad or two of hay to a rather old girl who was not now the quickest in the herd and always arrived too late for her share of the hay.

'This lady is a bit slow so I give her a few wads of hay on the way over to the rest of them,' I said, drawing to a halt beside her.

'Stay there, I'll break open a bale and give her some,' said Elizabeth, opening the door and jumping out.

My mind was in a whirl. There was this wonderful girl out with me and well, I didn't know what to think.

The passenger door opened and Elizabeth climbed back on board. There were strands of hay sticking to her jeans which she brushed off.

Meanwhile, the other girls were waiting for us near the wall and when we arrived we pulled out the rest of the bales, cut them open and scattered the hay over a clean area for them.

When all had been spread, Elizabeth and I stood together and watched the cows pulling contentedly at their feed, the red sky behind them heralding the soft, gentle onset of night and without thinking, I slipped my arm around her waist and felt her head rest on my shoulder.

'I think we should be heading back,' she said.

'Yes, I suppose we should.'

Chapter five

Bale carting

July was turning out to be a warm, dry month and many farmers' thoughts were now turning to harvest and there were those on lighter land who had already started on their autumn sown barleys. Harvest at Church Farm though, was still a couple of weeks away due to the main cropping being the later ripening spring barley. It had turned a golden yellow but the grains were still 'cheesy' and needed to ripen properly.

Instead, our focus was on bringing in the hay crop and we had baled the first ten acres and there were another ten acres which were very nearly ready.

'I think we'll bale what's fit this afternoon so we'll use the morning to pick up the bales we've already made. If Alice makes you a spot of lunch, you can row up the hay as soon as we've loaded the trailers and we'll let the bales sit and breathe until we need to cart the rest of them.'

'Sounds good to me,' I said and turned to Alice. 'If you just make me a bottle of tea, that will keep me going, thanks. I won't have any sandwiches.'

'Well, if you're sure. I was going to give you the rest of the strawberry jam sandwiches I've had in the fridge, but I dare say they'll keep a little longer. Harry can have them later.'

After breakfast, I walked up the yard with Harry, his two sheep dogs, Ross and Bob, jumping playfully by his side. 'Good boys,' he said, giving them both a pat on the head. 'It's going be too warm for you out here today. Go lie down and keep cool.'

And then, moving out from the tractor shed, cigarette in hand, wellingtons scraping along the ground and doing his best to compete with a cloud of flies, appeared Ronny.

'Ah Ron,' Harry said. 'Just the chap we needed to see.'

'Hello, Harry. You need some help with the bales.'

'That's right. You up for giving us a hand?'

Ronny sucked heavily on his cigarette and then while he exhaled the smoke, he clipped the end off, placed the tip inside the packet for future processing and announced: 'I'm ready, Harry.'

'Good. Right then let's get some trailers organised. If you put the Fordson on one of the two wheelers, we'll hook the David Brown up to the four-wheeler.'

I couldn't help noticing the wild look in Ronny's eyes as he savoured the prospect of driving a tractor and it would not be the last time I would see it. 'I'll give him a hand hooking up,' I said. 'Do we need any ropes?'

'I'll bring those down along with the pitch forks,' he replied and as he said it I felt a sudden wince in my hands. This had all the making of another painful experience.

Ronny and I drove out of the yard in a convoy, if two tractors and trailers qualify for such a description. We were heading out to the field just off Samuels Lane, a ten-acre field of grass which had been under-sown into a crop of spring barley last year. We needed to make our way to the other side of the graveyard and that meant cutting across Farm Close, through the allotments and then across the Naseby Road and down Samuels Lane.

Farm Close was one of a number of fields around Storeton Green that during the early part of the last century had been quarried for iron ore and when they were worked out and the land reclaimed, the company discovered there was a distinct shortage of soil to bring the fields back up to somewhere near their original level – like about twenty feet of it.

Land, such as the roads and bridleways which had escaped the draglines, the steam shovels and an army of pick-wielding navies, were left high and dry so that the majority of fields now had steep slopes leading into them. All of which made entry and departure something of a challenge, particularly with trailer loads of hay or straw.

Harry was waiting for us when we descended into the field and we drew to a halt beside him.

'Ronny, take your trailer over to the stack on the headland over there,' he told him. It was the furthest stack from the field entrance. 'Doesn't make sense to haul bales away from the farm and then haul them back again. We'll leave the four-wheeler here until we've loaded Ronny's.'

And with that, he climbed into the Land Rover started the engine and began to drive off. 'Come on, boy,' he shouted. 'Trailers don't load themselves.'

I sprinted after him and got one foot on the loop of metal tubing protecting the rear lights from being smashed, lunged up to grab the roof bar and felt the vehicle accelerate. Harry in one of his mad moods. I soon discovered it was possible to ride the bumps and hollows by bending my knees and before long, far from being terrified, I was enjoying the ride.

'Yeah, go for it!' I screamed, the wind rushing over my face. And I think he would have done if he hadn't been running out of field. Instead the brakes came on and we skidded to a halt by the far hedge.

Ronny arrived a few minutes later. 'Bloody hell, Ron, where have you been? We could have had half a load on by now,' Harry reached into the back of the Land Rover for the pitch forks. 'Right then, whose pitching and who's stacking?'

'I'll stack if you want,' I offered.

'OK then, jump up on the trailer and we'll make a start.

Having never stacked a trailer before I needed some tuition and by the time I had half a dozen bales on board, I realised I hadn't a clue where to put them.

'You need to stack them so they all bind in with each other,' Harry explained. 'On the bottom course put a row down the middle and then put the other bales out to the edges on each side and make sure you get the front and back square. And then on the next course it's one long-ways on the edge and two across and then on the third it's one long-ways on the other side and two across and make sure you keep the sides straight.'

Well, I tried to stick to the plan but it sort of got away from me and however hard I tried I ended up building overhangs and the front was far from being square. Matters weren't helped by Ronny throwing the bales up like a man possessed.

'How high are we going?' I shouted down. 'And as I spoke, I felt the load lurch and the bales on the front half of the trailer began to tumble onto the ground.'

'Bloody marvellous,' Harry scowled. 'We've not been here ten minutes and there're more bales on the ground than when we started. I've seen a few loads fall off but they usually made it out of the field beforehand. Yours didn't even get to move before half of it was on the ground again. Weren't you ever given some bricks to play with? Get up there Ronny and try and sort it out.'

Ronny climbed onto the trailer and I jumped off. I was in disgrace. But then things became even worse. In an effort to level the load out Ronny pulled some bales out from the remaining stack and then they too fell off the trailer with Ronny ending up underneath them.

'Look what you've done now,' Harry cried.

It would have been good to have reported that that was the end of it. But sadly no. The disaster continued when, with all the weight of the remaining bales now on the rear end, the trailer became detached from the tractor and tipped backwards, the drawbar high in the air. All the remaining bales slid off the back of the trailer and then with the weight removed, the front end came crashing back down to the ground.

'Well, that was impressive', said Harry. 'There's not a bale left on the trailer.'

'I think we should see what's happened to Ronny.'

'Why? If right now I was lying unconscious under a load of bales I think I could be very happy about it and I wouldn't want to be disturbed.'

I walked over to the bales and began to pull them away. Two bales down, I found him. 'Are you alright?'

'Just get the bales off my arse and I'll let you know.'

I did as he asked and he struggled to his feet. 'Where's Harry?'

I pointed towards the gate at the far end of the field and the figure climbing over it. 'That's him just leaving the field.'

'Oh right. I guess we should carry on loading the trailers, then.'

'I think that would be a good idea. This time I'll pass the bales up to you,' I said.

A couple of hours later and we had the two trailers filled, both to six layers and with a few more on top. We had roped them and I just hoped they would stay put when we drove out of the field. I counted up the stacks of bales still to be carted and reckoned another four trailer loads would just about do it.

Before leaving the field I had a look in the Land Rover and found a bottle of water and I made sure I had a drink before Ronny did, especially after he'd wiped the top of the bottle under his armpit before having his swig.

'When we get back to the farm I'll have to go and give the other field a run through with the tedder,' I said. 'We'll just have to hope Harry's about to help you load the other two trailers.'

***

As the day drew to a close, I made my way back to the farm along the dusty track running alongside Church Close and the Paddock, and reflected that, apart from the disaster with my load of hay, it had been a good day. All the bales from the ten acres in Samuels had been cleared – they were standing on trailers in the rick-yard waiting to be unloaded, and the ten acres in one of the lower fields had been baled and stacked in heaps. Tomorrow, or the next day, we would have a session carting and stacking bales and haymaking would be over and harvest could begin.

The cows were waiting for me as I drove down the yard. One or two of them were letting me know they had other things they would rather be doing than standing in a collecting yard, but I pointed out that if it wasn't for them we wouldn't be working hard to make sure they had something to eat this winter.

Later that evening I went out to have a look around the cows. Sally, the big Friesian was close to calving and she was restless and had taken herself off to the other side of the field.

I reported the news back to Harry who assured me she would be alright but even so, before I went to bed I slipped out again to have a look at how she was getting on. She was where I had left her and, as I shone the torch over her, she was totally engrossed in licking her new born calf – a beautiful heifer calf. As I watched, the calf struggled to its feet and stood for a few moments on a set of wobbly legs before taking a tentative step towards her mother's udder and taking her first feed.

Sally made some encouraging noises as the calf latched onto a teat and began to suck and I told her she was a clever girl as I reached into my pocket for a few feed nuts which she took from my hand.

And then I left them to it – Sally and her new born calf.
***

The next morning, as usual, Harry brought the cows into be milked and Sally came in with them but I turned her away and told her to go and look after her calf. Another day would give her a chance to grow stronger but I knew deep down I was just putting off the moment when the calf would have to be removed from her – it would be reared in the calf pens while she would be milked.

This was something I would never get used to and while I knew farming was a commercial business with little room for sentiment, the separation of a mother from its calf was never going to be a pleasant task.

And on this occasion it was even more difficult because during the day, Sally had taken her calf and hidden her in the middle of a large patch of nettles in the corner of the field. When I came to fetch the cows in for the evening milking she was standing with the rest of them and went through the milking bale as if everything was normal.

While the cows were in the yard though, Harry had driven across the field, found the calf and brought her back to the farm.

Sally was distraught as I have ever seen a cow to be. That evening, when I had let the cows out into their overnight field and fed the hay bales, she looked everywhere for her calf, running from one end of the field to the other, her udder swinging wildly beneath her, bellowing and shaking her head, snorting, her nose and eyes running.

I tried to tempt her with a wad of fresh hay but she was having nothing to do with it. Exhausted and breathing heavily, she just pushed her nose into my chest and stared questioningly at me with her big dewy eyes.

There was no consoling her and I shared her sadness. Farming could be a cruel, unfeeling business and while I had never questioned my involvement in it before, I found I was doing so now.

'Don't be upset John,' said a voice behind me. I turned and there was Elizabeth.

'Where did you come from?'

'Alice told me you were out here so I walked down the track to meet you. It's not nice having to take calves away is it? I hate it when dad does it.'

'No, it really isn't,' I replied turning away from her as

the emotion of it all consumed me again.

'Hey, come on. It's not your fault.' She put out her arms and pulled me to her. 'It's just so good you care, that's what really matters.'

I put my arms around her and we held each other close. 'Thanks, Elizabeth,' I murmured. 'You're terrific.' And then, for the briefest of moments her lips found mine.

'Come on, we need to get back,' she said, breaking free. 'Everyone will be wondering where we are and you never know, you could be missing out on some boiled bacon.'

I caught her hand and spun her round to face me.

'Don't say it, John. Please don't even think it,' she cried.

'Think what?' I said.

She suddenly became more serious. 'Don't say it because I think I'm thinking it too and it frightens me.'

We walked home in silence and I held her hand until we reached the top of the yard and then she broke free and ran off down towards the house.

Chapter six

Pedro power

As was usual, the second Saturday in June saw the Storeton Green annual show taking place in a field just off Smith's Lane. A show which in past years had been notoriously unlucky with its weather, this year the organisers had been promised two days of warm sunshine and they had made sure that everyone in the village knew about it.

'What are you entering?' Harry asked me at breakfast time.

'Sorry,' I said. 'Entering what?'

'At the show, boy. The village show; what are you entering?'

'Well I wasn't thinking about doing anything. I thought I'd just go along and see what was there.'

Harry was shaking his head. 'It doesn't work like that. You've got to enter something. Everyone does. No one goes to a village show just to have a look, for pity's sake; we'd all be home by lunch time. Tell him Alice.'

Having poured out the tea, Alice replaced the tea pot on the tray and began to push a cup up the table to Harry. 'What do I say, John? No one can make you enter anything but nearly everyone does, and it would be good for you to join in and have some fun.'

'Well what sort of thing do you think I should be entering?'

Harry reached behind him and caught hold of the latest issue of the village magazine and passed it over. 'Have a read though that and decide what you're going to do. And I shouldn't be long about it, we shall have to be there in half an hour.'

'What's the rush?'

'If you hadn't noticed, Alice has spent most of last week baking cakes and biscuits, so she has to be there to set them out for the judges. You won it last year didn't you, love?'

"Only in the sponge cake class but I didn't get a look in the chocolate biscuits or the fruit cake. Needless to say, that Mrs Brown with all her la-de-da kitchen equipment won those classes, again.'

Oh, you'll be alright this time, just you see,' Harry said. 'Anyway, boy, what have you decided? The welly-wanging competition, tossing the bale, long distance raw-egg catching, dog handling...? Well, if you can't decide I will. We'll put you down for the Donkey Derby.'

Alice put her cup down. 'Oh, that is a good idea Harry, and Pedro will be so pleased to see his friends again. You know, I was only thinking that the other day.'

'The what?' I asked.

'The Donkey Derby. That's always a good one and draws a huge audience – even gets them out of the beer tent for a few minutes.'

'But what do I have to do?'

'Just sit on Pedro for a couple of circuits of the field. He's done it before. Hang on to him and you'll be a hero.'

'And what will you be doing?'

'I'm the anchor man for our tug-of-war team. Never been beaten in five years but come on, boy, we've just about time to give Pedro a grooming and see if we can find you a saddle or something.'

***

We drew up to the entrance of the show and Harry slid the window of the Land Rover open and waited for the man on the gate to come over to him. Already, I could hear music being played over the public-address system.

'Hello Harry,' he said. 'Haven't seen you since last year.'

'Well you wouldn't have, would you?'

'That's right. Anyway, how are you?'

Oh, not so bad. There are three of us this year.'

'And that will be one pound and ten shillings please and the horse goes free.' He nodded to the trailer. 'Are you entering the gymkhana? I hear the competition's pretty strong this year.'

'No, we're going to win the Donkey Derby.'

'Oh no, you haven't brought that donkey again, have you? Not the one that...'

'Come on,' interrupted Harry. 'Just give me my change and you can start letting some other people in.'

'I think it was in the church wasn't it...?'

Harry grabbed his change and drove off down to the bottom end of the field where there were trees and generous amounts of shade.

'You normally go past the marquee so I don't have so far to carry my cakes,' Alice said.

'I just wanted to be sure we could park in the shade to keep Pedro cool. But don't worry, I'll carry them across to the marquee for you.'

He stopped the Land Rover and we climbed out. Already the heat of the day was climbing steadily into the mid-seventies. Today was set to be a scorcher.

'It might be best to put a halter on Pedro and take him out,' Harry said. 'I've put a churn of water in the back so you can pour him some out into the bucket and the halter is also in there along with a net full of hay.'

And with that, he set off towards the group of big tents which were at the other end of the field. I didn't think Alice's biscuits were probably going to make it with their chocolate still intact.

I reached over the tailboard of the Land Rover and grabbed the leather halter and then tried to make some sense of what looked like a random collection of straps and buckles, nothing which even looked like it would follow the contours of Pedro's head.

After some struggling, I identified the nose band and worked back from there and everything then seemed to fall into place. The problem was that I had still to open the small side door to climb into the box to put it on him and when I had done that the halter had taken on a completely different shape.

But I persevered and thankfully Pedro was in a tolerant, forgiving mood and he allowed me several goes at it without complaining. The sticking point was his ears which, compared to a pony for which this halter had been designed, were quite a bit longer and, with the nose band section in place, getting a strap behind his ears was next to impossible.

I didn't want to make a big thing about it because that would upset him, so I undid the strap and re-connected it when I had placed it in the required position. All I needed to do then was to connect the chin strap and the job was complete.

'There,' I said, giving his velvet muzzle a gentle stroke. 'That wasn't too bad was it?'

It was a question he answered with a loud flutter of passing wind that echoed around the box and made the sides shake. I took the hint and, after tying his rope to the ring at the front of the box, retreated into the fresh air and went to the back and lowered the main door.

The stench was over powering; not unlike the inside of a warm truck tyre but probably worse. 'What on earth have you been eating?' I asked him, as I waited for the air to clear. 'I hope it's not the old nerves, kicking in again.'

Untying his rope, I reversed him gently down the ramp and looped it around the nearest tree. With plenty of shade, a bucket of water and a net of hay to pull on I reckon he was about as comfortable as a donkey could be.

But I was wrong. Other donkey owners had chosen to

park nearby and had also tethered them among the trees and Pedro was not long spotting them. I recalled Alice saying how much he would enjoy seeing his friends again and as I watched him, he drew in a great breath and let go a mega bray that, at just a few feet away, was deafening.

And he kept doing it. Between breaths I could hear other donkeys responding and braying their necks off.

What was I meant to do? Harry and Alice had disappeared and it looked as if I was stuck with looking after Pedro; so much for seeing the other events at the show.

About half an hour later, Harry arrived back looking flustered. 'What are you still doing here, boy? Haven't you been listening to the announcements?'

'He's been making so much noise, I haven't heard anything at all,' I said. 'My ears are ringing.'

'Well, it's time for the parade of all the animals taking part in the show and you have about five minutes to get him up to the main ring, get him booked in and be given a number.'

'Which way is the main ring?'

'Just follow the crowd.'

So Pedro and I did just that and it wasn't long before we found ourselves in the main ring heading for the show organiser's office where there was a long queue of people waiting to be registered. We took up a place a few yards behind a large grey horse which, with its ears flattened didn't look as if it was enjoying us being there. The girl holding him was having a job preventing him gadding about and every so often the horse reared up. We moved further away; it didn't make sense to be too close to the rear end of that one.

The queue moved on slowly until eventually it was our turn to step forward. 'Name?' asked someone who was wearing a black bowler hat and a white coat.

'Pedro.'

'Pedro what?'

'Did you mean my name or the donkey's.'

He looked up from his notes and sighed. 'Your name,' he said.

'John Johnson,'

'Class?'

'Donkey Derby,'

There was a quick raising of the eyebrows before he spoke again. 'Right then, you'll be number six.' He reached out behind him and one of his assistants gave him two cards with the number six on them. 'Secure one of these each side of your saddle and be in the collecting ring at half past twelve. And if he runs as well as he farts he should do well. Next.'

We then did a circuit of the main ring which ended with everyone being ushered into the centre for few brief moments of utter chaos as horses, cattle, sheep, donkeys and a pig mingled together, before departing back down to the shade of the trees again.

There was no rush. I had at least a couple of hours before anything happened so we took our time, idling along, listening to the music which fired out of the speakers surrounding the main ring.

'Hello John,'

I heard Elizabeth's voice but couldn't place where it was coming from until I realised she was on the other side of Pedro.

'Elizabeth. I rather hoped you would be here. You're looking wonderful.'

'Just at this moment, I'm rather too warm,' she replied, giving me that smile again. 'But not too bad. How about you?'

'I think I'll be better when the Donkey Derby is over.'

'Oh no. Harry hasn't entered you for that, has he?'

'It would seem so,' I replied. 'Do you know anything about it or what I'm supposed to be doing?'

'Well it's quite a mad affair and there are not a lot of rules,' she said. 'If you're not careful other riders will try and get in the way of you and cause all sort of trouble. Normally, only about two or three manage to finish, the rest, well, pull up, lose their riders or just simply decide to go home.'

'That doesn't sound too good. Perhaps I should just stay at the back.'

'That's not a choice you have. What with all the shouting and yelling, the donkeys tend to charge off the starting line and keep going. Control is not something you will have a lot of.'

'Harry didn't mention any of this to me.'

'I'm not surprised.'

We arrived in the shade and I topped up Pedro's bucket with water from the churn before sitting down alongside Elizabeth, leaning against the side of the Land Rover. She slipped her hand into mine and she turned to face me.

'Kiss me, John.'

And I did. A long lingering kiss that drove out all other thoughts from my mind other than knowing I had fallen in love with Elizabeth.

***

Elizabeth had left to meet up with her family when Harry arrived. Before she went she pleaded with me to be careful and told me she would be watching.

'All set?' Harry asked.

'No, not really.'

Pedro was still tethered to the tree and looked as if he had nodded off and I had to admit that if there had been a choice, I would sooner just stay here in the shade rather than risk life and limb in a donkey race.

'We haven't a bridle for him so you'll have to use the halter; I'll clip some reins on it for you to hold on to. The good news is that we have a saddle.'

Harry produced it from the rear of the Land Rover and at first glance it looked to be little more than a piece of cloth with girth strap. And it didn't look a lot different when I took a second glance at it. He took it over to Pedro and placed it on his back and looped the girth strap under his belly. It was when he felt the strap tightening he began to take exception and jumped about a bit.

'Steady, boy,' said Harry, patting his withers. 'You've had a saddle on before so you know what they're like.'

The stirrups were very short and they hadn't an awful amount of adjustment in them so when, with the help of Harry, I climbed aboard, even at full extension my knees were almost bent at right angles.

'That looks good,' he said. 'Very professional. Now, where are your numbers?'

I passed them to him and he clipped them onto the saddle.

'Shouldn't I have one on my back too?'

'No, there's no need. It's the donkey people want to know about, not the rider.' He stood back. 'Right then, all set?'

'Well not quite. I thought you were going to give me some reins so I can steer him.'

'Well spotted, boy.' He felt in his pockets and pulled out two lengths of baler twine and proceeded to tie one to each side of the nose band and pass the ends up to me. 'Now what I suggest is you jump down and lead him up to the collecting ring and just do what everyone else is doing and you'll be fine.'

It was a lonely walk and when I arrived I discovered there were upwards of twenty other donkeys and riders milling around. Some of the riders were wearing silks and jodhpurs and really looked the part. My jeans and T-shirt, which Elizabeth had taken great delight in telling me bore the message, "Young farmers do it in wellingtons", singled me out as an also ran before I even climbed on Pedro.

Everyone except me seemed to have someone to talk to so I took to plodding around the ring trying not to show the bale-string reigns to too many people.

Harry was right about one thing though, the Donkey

Derby drew a large crowd and, as he had said it had also emptied the beer tent, judging by the tone of the jeers and the colourful comments some of the crowd were yelling.

A loud crackling from the public-address system quietened the crowd and the announcer began his work. 'All competitors of the annual Donkey Derby should now make their way to the middle of the ring. The course is the same as in previous years and it is two clockwise laps of the field running between the yellow marker flags.' There was a pause as the commentator waited for the riders to gather in the middle of the ring.

'Now listen carefully. Anyone who deviates from the course – like trying to take a short cut as some of you did last year - will have me to answer to, as will those who use excessive force or ride dangerously.' He cleared his throat. 'Gentlemen, mount your steeds and make your way to the start.'

Pedro had now worked out why he was here and was livelier, making it difficult to get up in to the saddle. But I received a helping push from one of the people in the ring who also wished me good luck.

The start was at the beginning of a short straight which linked up with the main course and I noticed most of the riders – there about twenty of them - were lining up on the right side – a position which would shorten the distance to the course and the first bend by a few strides. I thought about doing the same but then, having listened to Elizabeth's comments about wild riders and keeping out of trouble, I took a more central position.

The starter, dressed in an ill-fitting demob suit and an oversized bowler hat, held a flag in one hand and a half-consumed pint of beer in the other. He asked everyone if they were ready, didn't bother to wait for a reply, then dropped the flag and raised his glass. We were off.

Pedro, keen to stay with his friends, broke into a trot which in the paddock at home was exceptional for him, but not really fast enough to win this race. I urged him on and he eventually got the message and started to canter which was still a gear or two short of the flat out gallop I would have preferred.

We started on the climb up from the spinney in last place, but some riders had set off too fast and were now slowing. Pedro, old soldier he is, had paced himself and was now slowly gaining ground on the leading group and in the last few yards of completing the first lap we were in sixth position, and still going well.

Rounding the bend at the start of the second lap, the leading donkey appeared to slip and went down taking two other riders with him which left us in third position. But then the dirty tricks began. The rider directly in front of us, one of those dressed in jodhpurs and silks, used his crop to hit Pedro's head, not just once but several times. I switched him to the other side and started to draw up alongside but then the rider pulled his donkey out and blocked my way and we had to veer over to the other side of the course.

Shortly after that we were at the spinney again and the finishing straight was almost in sight. I brought Pedro back across the course and was just ahead of the second-place rider. He made to lash out with his crop again but this time I caught it and wrenched it out of his hand and without it, he began to slow.

Second place and less than a hundred yards to run; the crowd was screaming and there were arms waving everywhere. I used my knees to urge Pedro on and we were making ground. Stride by stride we were moving into overtaking mode but then, too soon, we crossed the finishing line and the race was over. I pulled on the bale strings and we slowed to a trot and then to a steady walk. Another ten yards and we would have won.

There was nothing more to do other than to slip down off the back of Pedro and give him a big pat and a stroke on his neck. He had done well, better than I could have hoped for and I told him as much.

Together, we walked back into the collecting ring where I loosened his girth strap and continued walking around so that he could catch his breath and cool down a little.

'John!' Someone was shouting at me. I looked round and saw Harry, Alice and everyone I could remember from Rose Hill farm heading for me, a pack I was relieved to see, also included Elizabeth.

'You did well, boy,' Harry said, clamping his arm around my shoulders. 'I think all those weeks of intensive training and the careful planning of our race strategy really paid off. Those early morning gallops, the strict diet control, my stop watch recording...'

'Yes, Harry, I think they probably did.' And as I spoke my eyes were on Elizabeth and I moved towards her and put my arms around her and lifted her off the ground. 'Put me down,' she screamed but I could tell she was laughing so I lifted her up again.

'Well, if I could just interrupt here,' Harry said. 'You might like to know that the judges just called it a dead heat – so you came equal first.'

This time I turned to Pedro. 'Did you hear that old fellow, we came equal first. 'Come on we'll take you down to the shade and give you a good rub down along with a cool drink of water.' I gave Pedro's bale string a tug to get him going and set off across the field.

'I'll come with you and give you a hand,' said Elizabeth. 'As long as you promise to lift me up again, but not with everyone watching.'

I laughed. 'That's a deal.'

And aware that all her family's eyes were on us, I took her hand and held it as we walked down towards the spinney – Pedro in one hand, Elizabeth in the other.

Chapter seven

Preparing for harvest

'It's time to sort the combine harvester out,' announced Harry as he carved the boiled bacon. 'The barley is about ready.'

The way he said it made it feel like he was heralding the end of time itself. But then, in many ways, harvest actually was the end of one farming year, and the start of the next.

'How much is there to cut,' I asked.

'Well, there's forty acres down the bottom of Brier Hill, fifteen in Samuels, twenty-seven near the old railway cutting and a few other odd bits.' He paused while he did the sums. 'I reckon we've about ninety acres but in past years we've also ended up doing as much again for Smiths – the big farm at the top of Copse Hill.

They've hundreds of acres to do and it's been said that whenever their manager spots a combine harvester coming along the road, he hijacks it and tells the driver to take the turning up to his farm, find a field and get stuck in. We also bale a field or two of straw for them – they need every bale they can get for their cows.'

The combine harvester, a big red Massey Ferguson, lived under the barn in the rick yard and I had on occasions climbed up the steps to see what it was like to sit in the driver's seat. Just what lever did what was something to find out and a walk around what was an enormous machine gave me little idea as to how it worked.

'It's all about separation,' Harry said. 'If I gave you an ear of wheat, how would you set about getting the grains away from the rest of the ear – the chaff, stem and all the rest of the bits?'

'Tell me,' I said.

'Well you'd put the ear of wheat on the palm of your hand and rub it with the palm of the other hand, right?' He went through the actions.

I nodded.

'And then when you have the grains out what would you do with it?'

'Blow on it?' I suggested.

'That's right. Blow on it to remove the lighter material. And that's just how a combine harvester works. The crop gets cut by the cutter bar at the front and then everything is taken up an elevator and forced through a narrow gap by a rotating wheel with rasp bars. This rubs the corn heads against stationary steel bars and it is there that most of the grain is separated out; the grain falls down on to sieves which, with a draught of air to blow the chaff off, cleans the grains and these are then taken to the grain tank.'

He pointed to the big tank on the side of the combine.

'The straw, which will still have some grains mixed in with it, passes to the straw walkers where it's given a really rough time to shake these grains out as it is 'walked' to the back of the combine and out onto the ground, leaving the grains behind.

And that's basically is it, a design which hasn't changed significantly since the first threshing drums my father used to tow about the county. If I was to have a bet with you, I would say that it's a design which won't change for generations to come. Combines will get bigger, a lot bigger, but the threshing system will stay very much the same. You mark my words.'

Who was I to argue with that? I bent down and looked up under one of the side panels at the innards of the machine and saw a nightmare assembly of belts, pulleys and bearings. Belts which, according to Harry, could slip and over heat before disintegrating; pulleys which could split, and bearings that could and regularly did, collapse and spit out ball bearings.

Harry stood back and looked at the combine harvester, his hands on his hips and a resigned look on his face. 'Do you know, this machine might look as if it's a few years old but this will be its sixth season and in that time I wouldn't think it's done anywhere near a year's work in total. I ask you, if you had bought a car, a tractor or anything else you can think of and it clapped out less than twelve months after you bought it, you would be jumping up and down. But not with a combine harvester which spends ten months of the year stuck under a barn and only a handful of weeks being used. Oh no. These machines can collapse in a heap of bent metal after just a few months' work and no one expects any better; it's monstrous.'

He was having a rant and I was beginning to think it was all part of a pre-harvest ritual which required the combine to receive a good verbal bollocking in the hope it might just behave itself during the coming season and stay in one piece.

'And another thing,' Harry continued, kicking a tyre. 'It always amazes me you can have a machine working perfectly well when you put it away at the end of a season and then, when you come to try it out at the start of the next, there's suddenly a hundred and one things which need to be repaired.'

I chose to say nothing. I wasn't even sure he was still talking to me. Harry's mood had been deteriorating since he had climbed aboard the combine and pulled the starter and, far from hearing a four-cylinder diesel engine turnover and roar into life, there was a dull groan followed by a click and then silence.

'The battery's flat,' he said.

Which, even with my limited experience of all things

mechanical, did not appear to be too much of a surprise considering it had stood idle for ten months. 'Where is it?' I asked as Harry climbed down the steps from the operator's platform.

'Behind the seat. Take some spanners and take the one off the Fordson while I get this one out and put it on charge.'

I located the battery under the Fordson's bonnet between the engine and the radiator and loosened the two terminals trying hard to avoid the sparks as one lead shorted out on the chassis.

The battery exchange was achieved without too much hassle but from that point on the day slowly went downhill. Having started the engine successfully, engaging the threshing system resulted in some horrendous noises and Harry leaped off the seat and ran around the machine in an attempt to locate the source of the problem.

'Bugger,' he said, when he had disengaged the drive and stopped the engine. 'One of the sieve bearings has collapsed.'

Harry dived under the combine for a closer look at the problem area and emerged to announce we needed to strip this lot down. He waved a hand in the general direction of the combine, 'And then remove the old bearing and fit a new one.'

'Right,' I said. 'Do you think it would be a good idea to mark the bearing we're aiming for – just so we know when to stop unbolting bits?'

'No, not really. If we're still pulling pieces apart and you can see daylight on the other side of the combine, it could be a good time to stop.'

Harry had his favourite wrench in his hand when I returned; a 15-inch adjustable, the sort they use on railway lines, and not far away was a huge lump hammer.

And so it was that, by mid-afternoon, there was a sea of bits lying on a large tarpaulin that had been spread on the ground beside the combine. After numerous trips to the workshop, Harry now had all the spanners, hammers and wrenches the farm possessed, adding to the general assemblage of metal, rubber and grease that covered the surrounding area.

***

At five o'clock I left Harry to it and went off to milk the cows. The day had been one of sweating, fuming and swearing as stubborn bolts refused to loosen and belts fought hard to stay on their pulleys, despite the leverage of long bars to lift them clear. But the bearing was getting closer.

By the time I had finished milking and brought the churns down to the dairy and placed them in the walk-in fridge, Harry had rigged some lights up, which I found rather worrying. Did he intend to work through the night?

'I'll just take out the feed and I'll give you a hand,' I said as I walked passed. There was a grunt of agreement followed by a clout with a hammer.

With the Land Rover stacked with bales I drove out across the paddock and in to Farm Close. As ever, there was the old lady hanging back behind the rest of the girls and I stopped to give her a large wad of hay which she tucked into.

I always expected a few more to try the dawdling approach for a personalised waiter service but whether it was out of respect for the older cow or the thought of missing what could be better feed delivered at the other end of the field, no one had tried it yet.

Stopping by the drystone wall I stepped out to pull half of the bales out the back and split them open and then drove on a few yards more before I emptied out the remaining bales so all the cows had room to eat their share.

I dropped the bale strings into the back of the Land Rover and reversed away so I could watch them tucking into their supper – a happier bunch of girls you would struggle to find.

Best of all, was to see Sally, the big Friesian joining in.

***

I had never seen a bearing replaced before but I felt sure Harry's, 'Hammer the bastard until it drops', approach was probably not included in the methods advocated by the majority of repair manuals.

Harry was lying on his side, chisel in one hand and hammer in the other, bashing away at a bearing housing that was reluctant to leave the rest of the combine.

'Sometimes they just drop out and others, like this one, sit tight and the only way is to chisel the sods out,' he said, giving the chisel another bash with the lump hammer.

I dropped down to my knees to have a closer look. I could see what Harry was chiselling but it was lost on me for what purpose. But then he gave it another blow and there was a ringing sound as a circular piece of metal dropped onto the floor.

'That's done it,' Harry cried. 'It's out. You should come and have a look at things more often, boy; I've been bashing at that little bugger for the last couple of hours.'

I still had to get the churns down to the ramp so any further help I could provide was going to have to wait. In the dairy, the milk cooler had just about done its job on the first churn but there were still another three to do before the milk lorry appeared.

Swapping the cooler over onto another churn without turning the water off was guaranteed to result in a soaking but time was pressing. I scribbled some labels out and tied them onto the handles. And then with three full churns on board the trolley, I launched myself off on the slide down to the ramp in the street.

With three down and three more to go, it was going to be a close call. There was also one more churn of milk to cool and, when I had pulled the trolley back up the slope the first thing I did was move the cooler over on to it. I then loaded two churns and left the third one cooling until I heard the milk lorry make the turn into Church Street.

I didn't have to wait long. The milk lorry had made the turn at the top of Station Road and was now coming along the street. There was nothing more to do than remove the cooler, load the trolley and get them down to the ramp.

Not too sure what it was that caused me to ram the side of the lorry, perhaps it was the urgency of the occasion and I pushed off a little too fast at the top of the slope but the lorry driver was now looking at a bent side panel he had lowered down so he could lift the churns from the ramp onto his lorry.

'Well, that's buggered that,' he said. 'Don't suppose it will shut now.'

'Don't know what happened there,' I said. 'Must have hit a greasy spot on the way down; anyway, the churns and the trolley are alright.'

'Bugger the churns and the trolley. What are you going to do about my lorry?'

'Nothing,' I said. 'You'll just have to be more careful where you park next time, but I can let you have some bale string if it would help.'

With that, I left him to it and began the long haul up the slope with my load of empty churns. Breakfast was beckoning and I was hungry.

***

'Does anyone want more tea?' asked Alice as breakfast was being concluded.

'I'll just have half a cup,' Harry said, pushing his cup down the table.

Alice then turned to me and held her hand out for my cup.

'Yes please,' I said.

She swilled the contents of the teapot around, grimaced and reached round for the kettle. 'We need a top up.'

'I shall have to shoot off into town to get the new bearing, boy. I just hope they have one.' Harry said. 'While I'm gone, go up the loft in the barn and find as many sacks as you can, check them for holes and tie all the good ones up into bundles containing twenty sacks.'

'What are they for?'

Well, assuming we ever get the combine working again, the grain tank holds just about a ton, so it needs twenty sacks to empty it. And while you're at it, find some bale string and cut it up into foot-long lengths to tie the top of the sacks up when they're full.'

'I could squeeze out another cup if anyone wants one,' said Alice.

'Just half a cup then,' Harry said, sliding his cup back down the table.

I left them to it and walked up the yard and cut across in front of the old cow shed and up the ramp which led into the stone barn. The temperature dropped by about ten degrees as I entered, and I shivered; thick walls have amazing insulation properties and these walls were at least three feet thick at the base.

Access to the barn was through two large doors which faced each other across the width of the building so that horses and their carts could enter through one and depart via the other without any complicated reversing. Further into the barn there were, at intervals, narrow slit windows set in the walls which were probably used more for ventilation than for light.

Sturdy as the walls were, the same couldn't be said for the wooden steps which led up to the lofts. Years of wear had thinned the steps to the point they flexed as I trod on them and I wondered how they could possibly cope with the extra weight of a sack of grain on someone's shoulders.

Up in the loft was a wide expanse of wooden flooring with a small heap of barley at one end near the hopper which fed the grain down to the grinder on the ground floor. It was one of Harry's jobs to fill the hopper each day and start the grinder going so there was enough fresh feed for the cows, pigs, calves and, if he was lucky, Pedro too.

The pile of sacks was nearer to the top of the stairs and I could see from the start that this was going to be a dusty job in fact, I was fast learning that everything to do with grain – its production, harvesting and processing – had the potential to be a dusty experience.

And it seemed I wasn't the first to have had something to do with these sacks. I had only just started to inspect them when I found a nest of mice and, by the size of some of the holes they had also been frequented by a large number of rats.

I worked my way through them creating a pile of usable sacks and a pile of not so usable and, by the time I had finished they were about even with the best part of three hundred in each.

Having tied the damaged sacks into a couple of rolls and kicked them down the steps, I split the rest into the required twenties, tied them up and sent them on their way in the same direction.

By the time I had taken the sacks across to the combine, Harry had returned and ready for the big reassembly programme to start.

***

Slowly, the combine came together. Pulley by pulley, shaft by shaft, belt by belt the combine's drive system was reassembled and while I wasn't too much help, I could at least fetch and carry pieces for Harry when he needed them.

The result was a completed combine harvester with a brand-new bearing on the sieves. When we had finished, I was half expecting there would be a few pieces left over, it was that sort of job.

'Well,' said Harry standing back and wiping his hands on a piece of cloth which looked about as filthy as his hands. 'What do you reckon - do you think she's a goer?'

'Let's give her a run and see how she sounds and find out,' I said.

'Right, you climb up there and start her up and I'll have a listen before we try the threshing system.'

Keen as I was to start the combine's engine there was

77

just one problem; I hadn't a clue how to do it. There was a key which needed to be turned but after that I was at a loss.

'Harry,' I shouted down to him. 'What do I need to pull to start it ?'

He appeared at the front having walked round the machine. 'You see that handle sticking out of the floor by your right foot, pull it up and the engine should turn over,' he explained. 'The throttle is beside the key.'

I did as he told me and raised the handle upwards and heard the starter gear engage and the engine turn over. After a few seconds of doubt, the engine fired up and, after a few coughs and splutters, was soon running smoothly.

'Sounds like a sowing machine,' Harry said. 'Sweet as a nut. We'll let her warm up and then we'll see if it all works.'

Harry climbed up onto the driver's platform and we swapped places. He sat down on what was probably one of the most uncomfortable seats I've ever seen or sat on; a sack of thistly hay would have been better than the black, plastic covered wedge which offered about as much padding as a couple of house bricks.

Opening the throttle slightly he placed his hand on the big lever which, when pressed down, would engage the combine's threshing system.

'This is it, boy,' he said as he lowered the lever to the floor.

There was a creaking of pulleys and belts as all the different components began to turn, shake or blow but these individual sounds soon faded as everything moved up to speed and the noise, while still being loud, merged into one.

Harry jumped down and walked along the side of the combine listening as he went. And then he bent and looked into the innards to see how the new bearing was settling down. 'Well it looks alright on this side,' he yelled before moving around the back to look up under the hood to observe the straw walkers riding up and down on their cranked axles.

At the front of the combine the sails, which draw the crop into the combine were rotating slowly, and the knife with its many triangular serrated sections slid from side to side as they moved between their finger guides.

I looked questioningly at Harry. 'Everything working?'

'It looks good but we need to run it at full speed.'

He climbed back up onto the platform and pushed the throttle lever over as far as it could go and the engine began to roar as the speed of all the components increased. No longer a sedate machine ticking over gently, the combine had turned into a beast which shook, vibrated and bounced on it wheels. I stepped back and wondered who was responsible for inventing such a fearful monster.

Harry was now pulling levers. The header with its rotating sails, knife and auger was being raised off the floor and the combine was moving slowly forwards out of the barn. He beckoned me over and I climbed onto the platform with him as he pulled the lever up to bring the threshing system to a halt.

'We'll make a start in Badger Close,' he yelled in my ear. 'I'll take the combine down and you hook a tractor on the flat trailer and meet me down there – and don't forget the sacks you sorted out.'

I nodded to him and climbed down onto the ground again and watched Harry squeeze the combine through the yard gate. There was only an inch to spare. And then I set about organising the required tractor and trailer, remembering to take the pile of sacks and the handful of bale twine to tie them up with.

By the time I had made it down to Badger Close, Harry had made a start and the combine was leaving a trail of straw as it moved slowly through the crop of barley. I parked the tractor and trailer on the headland and ran after him, my boots brushing through the stubble and an increasingly uncomfortable feeling around my ankles as barley awns worked their way into my socks.

When I managed to draw level with him I grabbed the hand rail, pulled myself onto the steps and climbed up and stood beside Harry. Watching the crop being cut and then pushed onto the table by the sails was mesmerising, particularly when it seemed to hesitate briefly before being swept to the centre of the header by the large auger and then disappear into the combine.

'How's it going?' I asked.

'It's going well. Everything is shining up and it just starting to sound as if it wants to be working.'

I felt like saying that was down to the firm, no-nonsense lecture he gave the combine when we first started getting it ready, but I thought there would be a better time. Instead, I asked him how the grain was.

Harry looked behind him at the grain tank which was being slowly filled with barley delivered from a conveyor which brought it up from somewhere in the bowels of the machine. 'You can see for yourself. Grab me a handful while you're at it and we'll see how dry it is.'

I climbed onto the tool box behind the seat and reached over the side of the tank and caught a handful of grains and offered them to Harry who took a couple and placed them into his mouth and bit on them.

'I'd say that's dry enough,' he said, taking another grain from my hand and giving it the same test. 'Yes, that's alright, about fifteen percent moisture, I'd say.'

Seemed a bit precise to me, but who was I to argue. About an hour and two circuits of the field later, the tank was nearly full so we headed over to the trailer and Harry brought the combine alongside so the unloading auger and its chute hung over the trailer.

'Right then boy. This is where you earn your keep. The tank holds just about a ton of grain so each batch of twenty sacks should empty it.'

I took hold of the first of the sacks and opened it out

in front of the chute.

'It comes out fast so you'll have to be ready for it.'

I nodded, took a firmer grip on the sides of the sack and planted my feet as firmly as I could on the trailer floor.

'Ready?'

'Yes.'

Harry pushed down on a lever and the unloading auger began to turn. A few seconds later a wall of grain started sliding towards me and when it hit the sack it was all I could do to hold it open. Harry then stopped the auger and the sack was full.

'Tie that one up and then you can lay it down and use it to lean the other full sacks against it,' he said.

And so a tank emptying routine began which would continue throughout harvest. Harry would bring the combine over to the trailer and I would hold the sacks open for them to be filled, and while he carried on combining, I had ample time to tie up their tops and then stack them, so they gradually filled the trailer.

Some of the sacks were larger than others and Harry insisted on filling them up to the top which hardly left enough loose sacking to tie them up with. These extra heavy sacks were also difficult to move and I struggled to move them to where I wanted them to be. I was beginning to dread being asked to carry such a weight up the loft steps.

Mid-afternoon and Alice drove into the field in the Land Rover. 'I don't know whether this is lunch or tea,' she said, spreading some tins and flasks of tea across the tail board. 'It's only a few boiled bacon sandwiches but I thought you had better have something inside you to keep you going.'

I sat in the shade of the trailer, leaning against one of the wheels, and munched into one of them.

'How's it all going?' Alice asked.

'Well,' Harry said. 'The crop's fit and judging by the number of sacks we've filled the yield isn't too bad either.'

'What's a good yield?' I inquired.

'For spring barley, anything over twenty-five hundredweight an acre and I'm happy, and I reckon this field will just about do that. After you've finished tying up the sacks you'd better take them up to the farm and bring a fresh trailer down. You'll need to go steady – and park it undercover somewhere.'

Declining Alice's offer of a second sandwich, I drained my cup of tea and jumped back onto the trailer to finish tying the sacks. Harry meanwhile, strolled over to the combine, restarted the engine and engaged the threshing system with the result a large cloud of dust spewed out and descended on Alice, who was gathering up mugs and tins.

I looked over towards Harry and saw he was laughing.

'Glad that wasn't me,' I said to Alice.

'Yes, well you boys have a strange sense of humour. He does the same thing every year. It's all part of growing up but for some people it's never going to happen.' She sounded cross and was looking at Harry.

Later that day, after I had finished milking and had taken the buffer feed out to the cows, I wandered down the track to Badger Close. The sun was now well low in the sky and the mist had started to move up the valley. Parked in one corner of the field was the combine harvester, its work done for the day and before it, casting long shadows, were rows of straw looking like a giant knitted jersey.

I turned to make my way back to the farm. If the weather held, tomorrow was going to be a busy day and the thought of bath, a pint of beer and an early night seemed to be a good plan.

Chapter eight

Harvest hassles

There are some mornings on a farm when everything feels to be about right. A clear blue sky heralded another hot sunny day, the cows all seemed to be in a good mood and even the miserable old sod who picks up the milk churns managed half a smile, but then it might have been the cigarette he habitually held between his lips getting too short.

Having finished milking, I took the girls down to their field and was pleased to see Harry had moved the fence to allow them some fresh grass to graze on. Not that they were remotely interested in it because as soon as they had all had a good drink out of the water trough, they headed for the trees and settled down for a quiet day's chewing the cud in the shade. I wished I could have joined them.

'Hope you're feeling strong today?' asked Harry as I sat down at the breakfast table, having pushed one of the dogs out of the way so I could get some room for my feet.

I was beginning to think heavy sacks and loft steps. 'No more than usual,' I said. 'Why, do you have something planned?'

'Give the boy another shake with the cornflakes, Alice. He'll need some extra energy.'

Alice looked at Harry. 'You're not thinking of asking him to carry those sacks up to the loft, are you?'

'They won't take themselves.'

'Well just be careful,' she said. 'We don't want any accidents.'

I dug into the boiled bacon slices and thought it through. Harry, I guessed weighed a good hundredweight and a half and with a sack of grain across his shoulders that would be two and a half hundredweight. There was no way those loft steps were going to take that sort of weight.

'Right,' Harry said. 'Let's see how we go. If you bring one of the trailers around to the front of the stone barn, I'll see you there.' He pushed his cup and saucer down the table towards Alice. 'Just half a cup, if there's one in the pot.'

The tractor was still hooked up to the second trailer we had used yesterday so, as Harry had requested, I pulled it along the track to the stone barn. With this load and the sacks on the other trailer I estimated we had the thick end of six tons to off load, more than one hundred and twenty sacks to carry up the loft steps.

'You climb up on the trailer and pull them to the edge,' Harry said, tightening his belt by a couple of notches.

'He stood with his back against the trailer as I did my best to lower the first sack down on to his shoulders but inevitably, the sack dropped the last few inches making Harry swear.

And then he set off towards the loft steps walking solidly as only a person carrying over a hundredweight across his shoulders can. I watched as he put a hand out to grip the bannister and then took the first step and then the third, the fourth and the fifth. It was when he put his weight on the sixth I heard the splintering of wood and a leg shoot through, accompanied by a loud yell.

I jumped off the trailer and went to see what I could do which, after a few seconds I realised was not a lot. The sack of grain was still on Harry's shoulders, one leg was out straight and nearly touching the floor and the other was doubled up under him.

'What do you want me to do?' I asked.

'Well, for starters, you can shift this sack off me.'

There was very little room on the stairs and the sack had not landed in a very mover-friendly position but I tried to pull it clear, but with no success.

'Climb up over me, get behind it and give it a push,' Harry said. 'And don't take too long about it.'

'But how am I to get up there with you in the way?'

'For pity's sake. Just get up there.'

I climbed up over Harry trying not to tread on anything too delicate and eventually I was in a position to use my feet to push the sack off his shoulders and down the steps to the floor. It was big ask and the sack seemed to be reluctant to go where I wanted it to but eventually it started to move and after one big push with both my legs, it finally slipped over Harry's head and tumbled down the steps.

The sack wasn't there anymore but Harry was, and he started to make some efforts to release himself, swinging his vertical leg and reaching out with his arms to pull himself clear. All in all, it was not a particularly dignified exit but at least he was back down on the barn floor in one piece.

'Well that wasn't a good start, was it?' he said, rubbing the top of his leg.

I had to agree with him and wondered where we went from here. It was not a day to be wasted lingering in the barn, when the combine harvester should be on the move.

'Right then. This is what we'll do,' Harry said. 'We'll off load these sacks of barley on to the floor down here for now and we'll work out how we're going to get them into the loft later. I'll make a start doing that while you go and fill four five-gallon drums up with diesel and then, when you've done that come and help me finish here and we'll head for the combine.'

'Sounds like a plan to me, Harry,' said a voice from behind us.

I knew who it was. You could smell Ronny before you

saw him, stale tobacco providing the main clue, but if that wasn't enough evidence the sudden increase in the fly population had to be an absolute clincher.

'Ronny,' Harry said. 'Just the person we wanted to see. Give me a hand with these sacks and then we'll see if we can get some harvesting done. And Ronny... put that cigarette out.'

With Ronny turning up it meant he and Harry could get on with the combining and I could make a start baling the straw. But before all that could happen we had to prepare the combine for its day's work. And, as Ronny and I found out, it wasn't the best moment of the day.

'Fill the diesel tank up while we grease up,' Harry told Ronny. Which was clear enough but with the combine's fuel tank about five feet off the ground, directly above the rear axle, it could prove to be a tricky job to achieve without becoming soaked in diesel.

It may have been easier if I had remembered to bring a funnel but Ronny, five-gallon can in hand, climbed up on to the axle, removed the tank filler cap and upended the can into the tank; which was fine until he came to the fourth can and this one didn't quite make it. Half way though emptying, the fuel tank was full and the excess diesel spilled out and over him.

'Bloody hell Harry,' he cried. 'I'm soaked.'

'Never mind, boy. It'll help keep the flies off you but I shouldn't try lighting a cigarette too soon.'

Ronny's misfortune was not alone though. Harry asked me to empty the stone trap, a small area into which any incoming stones can fall out of the crop before it enters the threshing area. Emptying it requires crawling under the combine to open a door and if care isn't taken the contents, which invariably include a volume of barley awns and black dust, as well as stones, will fall on the person emptying it.

And that is what happened to me. The day had only just begun and I was already as filthy as it's possible to get.

Worse, the barley awns worked their way into my shirt and before long I was itching and scratching all over.

Harry thought it amusing. 'You've made that job your own from now on, boy. Well done.'

Well, I'm not so sure about that, I thought.

'Right,' he continued, while making a big thing about brushing a small piece of straw off his shoulder. 'You go and make a start with the baler in Badger Close and don't make them too light, it wastes string and barn space. Screw the clamps down tight so you get a good firm bale.'

'How about the sledge, who's doing that job?'

'Didn't I tell you? When I brought the baler down this morning I took the new sledge with it – it's one which holds about seven bales and then you pull the rope to release them. Try and drop them in a line across the field. You'll work it out.'

I felt I needed to know a bit more about using the new sledge which I had yet to even see but Harry had turned away and was heading for the combine steps.

Badger Close was two fields closer to the farm and as I walked back along the track I felt a growing excitement at the prospect of using the baler and its new sledge for the first time. Harry had left it on the edge of the field and I walked round it to see what the sledge looked like, not that there was much to see. Basically, it was a tubular steel frame with an open floor having metal strips to provide some support for the bales as they were dragged along the ground.

The bales dropped into it and when there was about seven, a rope was pulled from the cab and this released the gate at the rear to let the bales slide out; when the last bale had departed, the gate swung shut and the filling began all over again.

Having checked there was a plenty of twine available, I climbed onto the tractor, started it up and started baling – the first bale to emerge from the chamber was the last of the hay which looked a bit the worse for wear but then the straw came through and they were bright, yellow bales.

After a few had been made I stopped to check they were good and as firm as Harry had requested. They seemed alright but, just to be sure, I wound the chamber clamps down a bit further to create greater resistance and make the bales heavier.

Which seemed a good idea but when I came across a place where Harry had stopped the combine and the straw had continued to pile out of the back of to create a large heap, the intake tines took a big mouthful and swept it all into the chamber in one go. This gave the bale ram too much to cope with and the result was a very loud bang, a flywheel freewheeling and the rest of the baler's workings at a standstill.

The shear bolt on the drive shaft had broken, as it was meant to when the loading is too high, and this meant I had to start pulling out armfuls of straw to clear the blockage before the baler could be restarted.

As it turned out, clearing the blockage was the easier part. Replacing the shear bolt took a little longer after I dropped the nut into the straw and took about ten minutes to find but, before long, I was on my way again and taking care to slow down when I encountered other places where there were large volumes of straw in the swath

Meanwhile, the new sledge was filling working well. I couldn't see just how many bales in it but I reckoned there must have been at least seven so I gave the rope a pull and the gate opened to allow the bales to slide out, shutting with a loud crunch as soon as the last one had left.

I took care not to wrap the rope around my wrist, having heard what happened to Joe Parker when the sledge pulled the back of the baler off – and him off the tractor.

By lunchtime, there was only the outside swath to do and it was at this point I realised I would have to stop and move the bales I had made when I started the field. They had been dropped just where I needed to run the tractor so, with numerous stops and starts, the outside swath took the best part of half an hour to complete.

When I was on the far side of the field I saw Alice drive down the track and stop to drop me off some sandwiches and a bottle of tea. She waved and then drove on to where Harry and Ronny were working.

So, finding a shady tree, I made myself comfortable and settled down to spend a few minutes having lunch.

'I bet it's boiled bacon,' said a voice I had come to know so well.

'Elizabeth! What are you doing here?'

'Oh, nothing really. School holidays can be pretty boring so I thought I'd visit Auntie Alice for the day. And here I am.' She shrugged her shoulders and smiled at me.

I put out my hand and she took it. 'Come and dine with me. I've heard it said that boiled bacon is at its best this time of the year.'

She leant forward and kissed me. 'Sorry, can't stop. Alice will be on her way back up in a minute or two to pick me up. I think I can hear her coming now.'

She got up to leave, brushing dust off her jeans. 'I'll try and see you after milking,' she whispered, as the Land Rover pulled to a halt beside us.

Later that day, Elizabeth and I took the hay out to the cows and then continued down the track and stopped on the top of Brier Hill. We looked out across at the fields which spread before us and watched the sun descending, the first golden strands reaching out across a cloudless sky, lengthening shadows of hedgerows and trees becoming lost in a harvest haze.

I placed my arm around her, her long auburn hair falling across my shoulder as I held her close. We kissed and at that moment I was the sanest man alive and everything in the world was perfect.

Chapter nine

Danger in the barn

'We need an auger,' Harry said. 'I don't think we have any other choice.'

'What's an auger?' Alice asked.

'It's a long metal tube about thirty feet long and four inches in diameter with a spiral in it which, when turned by an electric motor, lifts the grain being poured in to it at one end and delivers it at the other.'

'It's like an Archimedes Screw,' I added.

'Like a what? Harry asked.

'An Archimedes Screw,' I repeated.

'Well that doesn't sound like very suitable language for the breakfast table, boy.'

I sighed. 'It's nothing like that. Archimedes, you know, the Greek mathematician who was having a bath when...'

'I think I'll stop you there, boy,' Harry interrupted. 'I'm as broad minded as the next man but I don't think now is quite the place for those sort of jokes.'

Archimedes would have to wait. 'Like Harry said, it's a tube with a spiral in it.'

'Sounds a bit technical to me,' Alice said. 'What I don't see is how you get a sack full of grain up a thirty-foot tube that's only four inches in diameter.' She held up her hands and made a circle with her fingers. 'But anyway, if it means you don't have to carry them up the loft steps ...' She left the sentence unfinished.

'There aren't any loft steps,' I said. 'At least not many which will take the weight of Harry and a hundredweight of grain on his back. The auger is a really good idea; we could put the delivery end through one of the loft windows so it empties in the middle of the floor and have the other end in a tub of some sort. All we have to do is empty the sacks into the tub and the job is done. You could probably pile it higher and get more up there.'

Harry nodded. 'I'll get onto the dealer and see when they can deliver one,' he said. 'If Ronny's out there, take a couple of trailers down to Badger Close and load them up with bales. I'll sort the combine out and by the time you get back it should be dry enough to start harvesting and baling.'

And so the day's activities commenced. Ronny and I brought up two enormous loads of straw bales and parked them in the rick yard, we unloaded the sacks off the grain trailer and then, while he went off to meet Harry at the combine, I took a tractor down to the baler, remembering to take a couple of packs of twine with me.

As I pulled out of the yard, I was met by the dealer's lorry delivering a thirty-foot auger.

'That was quick,' I said as he drew to a halt beside me.

'Well in a few weeks when harvest is over you won't need it and you'll cancel the order so that's why it's here now.' he said. 'Where do you want it?'

'If you could lay it down alongside the stone barn and cover the motor with something waterproof that would be great.'

***

Proving that even the best laid plans of mice and men go oft awry, the dark, threatening clouds which had rolled in during the morning decided to deliver their goods, and by mid-day it was raining, not just a shower but the really heavy stuff that arrives after several days of hot humid weather along with thunder and lightning.

And everything came to an abrupt halt. I parked the baler alongside the combine and we tried to put plastic sheets over the grain tank and the operating platform –one to keep the tank dry and the other to keep the seat from becoming soaked. I knew from my own experience that a foam rubber seat can take days to dry out and even longer to stop causing a perpetually wet bum when sitting on it.

Ronny had taken shelter under the rear hood of the combine where the straw comes out and was in the process of rolling a cigarette, but Harry didn't give him a chance to complete it.

'Come on Ronny. Don't bugger about. Get that load of barley up to the farm and undercover and then meet us back down in Badger Close.'

I looked questioningly at Harry. 'We'll stack these bales up and try and keep some of them dry,' he said. And with that, oblivious to the rain which was now sheeting down he strode out into the field and began to make small stacks of bales from the groups of seven I had dropped out of the sledge. 'Put the bottom two on their edges and the rest flat,' he yelled as a sudden clap of thunder rattled and roared overhead.

I joined him and together, we worked like men possessed to build the stacks, moving as fast as we could across the field as lightning streaked earthwards and thunder crashed around us. Like Harry, I was soaked to the skin and I could feel the water squelching in my boots.

With all the bales stacked in one field, we moved on to the next in Badger Close to stack those we didn't have room for on the trailers this morning. Ronny joined us and, from somewhere, he seemed to have found an umbrella – a yellow one with red tassels – which he tried to hold in one hand while he moved bales with the other.

'Oh, very pretty,' Harry said, when the job was done and we stood under a tree and drew breath. 'Don't tell me you found that in the tractor shed.'

And before Ronny could answer, Harry held up his hand. 'I really don't want to know. Come on, we've done all we can down here. Let's head back to the farm. Ronny, you can drive.'

We clambered onto the tractor, Harry standing on the drawbar at the back and me on the footplate leaning on the mudguard, close enough to Ronny to hear the squelch as he sat down on the foam rubber seat.

***

With Alice's words ringing in my ears that I would catch pneumonia if I didn't change into some fresh clothes, I went to my room and did just that, but not before I grabbed a quick bath.

When I brought down the sodden clothes I had been wearing Alice asked me to put them in the washing machine.

'Don't know how I'm going to get them dry but at least they will be clean,' she said.

I looked at Harry and recalled the combine's stone trap experience.

After several days lunching on the side of a field with sandwiches and cold bottled tea, it made a pleasant change to be sitting at a table with a bowl of hot soup in front of me. Harry was sitting at the top of the table and had somehow managed to change his clothes in the time it had taken me to go to my room.

'They delivered the auger then?' he asked.

'Yes, sorry, I should have said. I got him to drop it off by the barn.'

'Prompt service.'

'That is what I told him.'

Alice passed the teas round and I drank it while watching the cat curled up in a bowl on top of the washing machine which was vibrating wildly. Strange cat that.

'I suppose Ronny's gone?' I asked.

'Well, I don't think he's here but just where he's gone, I don't know,' Harry said. 'And when he gets there I shouldn't think he knows why.'

'That's not a very nice thing to say about him,' Alice said. 'Surely he deserves a little more respect than that.'

Harry wasn't going to be drawn into that one. 'Come on, boy. Let's go and see if this auger's any good.'

We walked up the yard and around to the front of the barn to take a look at it. At one end, where the grain went in was a mesh guard and at the other, some thirty feet away, was an electric motor which provided a belt drive to turn the auger.

'Looks pretty straightforward,' Harry said. 'Looks like we need to hoist the delivery end so it hangs over the middle of the loft and try and have the loading end somewhere down here in the dry. How heavy is it?' He pointed to the electric motor.

I grabbed the metal hoop, which was clearly designed to be used as a suspension point and give the exit some height. It was heavy, too heavy just to be carried. It needed some sort of pulley.

'Well, that's simple enough. Nip down to the tractor shed and bring the pulley blocks and a good length of rope. I'll see what we can use as an anchor point.'

Harry's belief that setting up the auger was going to be simple was wide of the mark. In fact, as it turned out, he was miles off it. The anchor point up in the loft ended up having to be a steel bar which needed attaching to the apex of the roof, a section needed to be cut out of the side of the loft so that the auger could be angled down to the floor of the barn, and when after three hours the motor was finally connected to the three-phase electricity supply, the auger rotated the wrong way.

But we persisted and, with half an hour to go before I needed to bring the cows in for milking, we just about had it set up. All we needed was a bowl for the loading end to sit in while the sacks were emptied over it. I thought of the cat and the washing machine but the bowl wouldn't have been big enough, but there again, the old bath tub Harry dragged into the barn was perhaps a tad on the large size. In the end, we settled for a circular sheep trough which looked as if it should fit the bill.

'Right,' Harry said. 'This is it. He pressed the start button and the auger clattered into life, the exposed flights at the loading end bounced about, awaiting their first feed of grain. And that wasn't long coming. I dragged a sack over to the trough and untied the string and, together we lifted it and began pouring the grain out.

It was good to see. The grain disappeared up the tube and, when I raced up the steps, I watched it arrive and pour out onto the loft floor. Brilliant.

Harry pressed the stop button. 'Well that's going to save a bit of grunting carrying them up there,' he said. 'But what we need is a sack barrow to bring the sacks over and a ramp or something to raise them over the side of the trough.'

'I'll think about it but I'd better make a start getting ready for milking,' I said.

'Is it that time already?'

'It certainly is.'

***

The rain that had sheeted down to bring harvesting to an abrupt halt in the morning had moved on to become more of a warm drizzle which, by the time I had walked down to fetch the cows, had all but stopped. But for the cows, rain was rain, whatever type it was.

They had taken shelter under the trees and because there was a delay in the precipitation arriving at the base of the trees as it worked its way down through the leaves, they were all convinced it must still be raining. And there they were determined to remain, despite me standing out a few yards away from the trees and waving my arms about to show them it had stopped raining.

'Oh, come on girls. Look, it's stopped raining out here. The only place it's raining now is under the trees where you're standing. Don't any of you see that?'

They stood there slowly cudding away as they looked at me with wry smile across their faces. I was the idiot standing in the rain. I could put up with it no longer and headed into the group to find Thrifty, a black Red Poll/Angus cross who was as soft and as gentle as cows go when it comes to man/cow interaction. You could do anything with Thrifty, pick her feet up to inspect them if she was limping, stroke her under her chin, sit down and lean against her when she was out in the field, and so on.

'Come on Thrifty,' I said, patting her rump. 'Show all your friends it's not raining anymore.' She looked round at me as if to ask if I was sure, after all, it was still raining where they were standing.

She decided to trust me and started to walk out onto the track away from the trees, and the others then followed, adopting their gentle, unhurried saunter as if they hadn't a care in the world.

I walked in front so I could open the gate into the paddock and as I waited for them to all pass through, there was steam rising off their coats.

'Told you it wasn't raining,' I muttered to Horns who had hung back so she could walk across the paddock with me.

Alice had prepared all the milking equipment and all I had to do was fetch a bucket of warm water from the house, start the Lister engine and milking could start.

As I walked past the barn I could hear the new auger rattling away as Harry emptied sack after sack into the trough. It would be interesting to see how many he had emptied.

With plenty of grass to eat, the cows were milking well and the amount they produced had been increasing for some weeks, helped by a couple of fresh calvings, some generous buffer feeding and a scoop of milk nuts and ground barley when they were being milked. The evening milking would almost fill five churns which meant a couple of trips had to be made with the churn trolley down to the dairy.

By the time I had washed up, cooled the milk and placed the churns in the walk-in fridge, and loaded the Land Rover up with hay bales, Harry had shut down the auger and retreated to the house.

While I could have really done with a cup of tea and something to eat, I couldn't resist spending a few minutes looking in the loft to see how much barley he had managed to send up there. I climbed the steps and had a look. He had done well. There was a mountain of grain which, at its deepest was at least five feet high and even at the sides of the loft it was well over two feet deep, more than there ever could have been if sacks had been emptied out.

As I came back down the steps I noticed the curve in the joists holding up the floor and I could swear they were bending more. The floor was on the verge of collapsing.

'Harry!' I yelled as loud as I could and looked around, desperately trying to spot something I could prop the floor up with. Lying alongside the wall were some railway sleepers and I ran over and grabbed the end of one of them and pulled it across the floor to a point directly under the main beam. Raising it up, it very nearly fitted but it needed another three or four inches to make contact. I hunted around trying to find a stone or a piece of plank that I could use. I could hear the beams creaking.

And there, under a pile of bags I found it, a six-foot length of scaffolding plank. By the time I had lodged it in place on top of the sleeper, the gap had closed so it was now a tight fit. I sped over to the sleeper pile and pulled another one over and placed that under a joist. This time I didn't need any extra packing, and then I did a repeat trip to place a third sleeper under another joist to provide support at the far side of the loft.

At the end of all that I was out of breath. But as I watched the floor, the sleepers seemed to be taking the weight and preventing a disaster which would not only have destroyed or damaged the grinding machinery but put all the barley back down on the floor again. And that would have made Harry's day.

I heard footsteps approaching. 'You alright, boy?' Harry asked. And then he spotted the sleeper supports and guessed what I had been doing. 'Oh no. The floor wasn't...'

'Afraid so,' I replied.

'And you managed to put these up to stop it.' He pointed to the sleepers.

I nodded.

'You could have been killed if the floor had collapsed,' he said.

'Well it didn't and now it should hold. But I don't think it needs any more barley up there.'

Harry went over to inspect the floor and the supports, giving them a tap with his hand. 'They're taking the weight. Lucky you were here.'

There was nothing more to say so I jumped in the Land Rover and took the hay out to the cows.

Chapter ten

Pop-pop to the rescue

Over the last few days, Harry had become increasingly tetchy and irritable. It had rained almost continually for a week or more and, as a result, the combine hadn't moved during that time. Sheeted down on the edge of a half-cut field it made for a depressing sight which did little to raise anyone's spirits.

We were now into the third week of August and there was still over sixty acres of barley to combine and the straw to bale.

I kept my head down at the breakfast table by either reading the paper or the Farmer and Stockbreeder magazine which was also reporting on the wet conditions the agricultural industry was having to cope with.

'It will soon be too wet to drive across the field, let alone harvest the grain,' he said.

I grunted a reply. There was nothing I could think of saying that would make the situation any better.

'We've had some wet harvests in the past but this one beats them all,' he continued. 'I was down at Long Field checking on the sheep this morning and the barley in Forty Acres is starting to go down and the pigeons are moving in.'

I looked up at him and grimaced.

'I blame the Russians,' he said. 'They're messing around with the weather. It's part of their master plan to dominate the world. We should fire off a few missiles in their direction, show them who's in charge and tell them to get the weather back on course.'

I looked up and wondered if Harry was being serious. I assumed not and suggested we should send Ronny over there. But I had misread him.

'Now that's a really stupid thing to say,' he said.

'Does anyone want more tea?' asked Alice, holding the teapot up.

'I'll just have half a cup,' said Harry and, as he pushed his cup down the table he outlined his plans for the day. 'We'll unload your straw trailers and then we'll get the rest of the barley up in the other side of the loft – and we'll put some supports up for the floor before we begin to fill it this time.'

'The auger needs to be moved,' I said.

I wandered up to the rick yard. The two trailers we had loaded were still parked under the Dutch barn and needed to be moved so the bales could be dropped off and stacked in the bay they vacated. When I had fetched a tractor, Harry was waiting by the trailer for me to reverse up to it.

'You're getting better,' he said, when he'd managed to push the pin into the clevis which connected the tractor to the trailer. 'This time you only took six goes at lining the tractor up with the draw bar.'

I took it as a compliment and waited for the trailer's drawbar jack to be raised clear of the ground.

'Where are you going to take it?'

'Out in the paddock and then I'll put the other one in front of the bay and I'll throw the bales off to you.'

Harry nodded and walked over to open the gate leading out to the paddock.

Unloading the first trailer was easy. I just dropped them down to the ground and Harry stacked them in the bay.

The first course of bales he stacked on their edges to stop the strings rotting and breaking out the bales when they came to be moved, but from then on, the bales were placed string-side up with those on the edge of the stack placed first to ensure the side was straight.

It all became rather more difficult when it was the turn of the second trailer to be unloaded. The height of the bales in the barn was now about level with the height of the trailer floor but it was not long before I was having to lift them higher to get them on to the same level as Harry.

I resorted to using a pitch fork and rued the time I had screwed down the baler's chamber clamps to produce heavier bales.

'Come on, boy. Let's be having the bales. We want to be here today and gone tomorrow, not here tomorrow and gone today.'

Well, I didn't understand it either, but I think the message was to work faster, which I tried to do.

By now the sun was burning down and there was a steamy haze across the fields as the damp from the previous night's rain lifted. In the rick yard the atmosphere was almost tropical and the sweat poured off me.

When the last bale made it onto the stack I was feeling distinctly queasy and I went and stood in the shade and drank half a bottle of water.

'What's up, boy?' Harry asked. 'Had a touch of the sun?'

'Just a bit dehydrated,' I said. 'I'll be alright.'

'Well it's starting to dry out so I thought we should see if we can get the rest of the bales picked up. What do you reckon?'

'We might as well. It will need a good day of this weather before we can think about combining again.'

Harry looked at his watch. I could see he was torn between moving the auger over to the other loft and picking bales up.

'Right then let's take a couple of trailers down and

make a start with the bales. No sign of Ronny, I suppose?'

'Not today. He could be having a wash or attending his university graduation ceremony,' I said. 'It's bound to be one or the other.'

Harry laughed. 'You're getting as bad as me, boy. Come on let's get doing something.'

***

Two days later the combine harvester was rolling and the countryside became alive again as all the other farmers fired up their machines and continued with their harvesting. But this time I could sense there was a greater urgency about it. The wet weather had caused valuable time to be lost and now the days were noticeably shorter, the morning dew took longer to lift and the evening dampness arrived earlier.

'If the weather holds up we should be finished by this time next week,' Harry said, when I managed to scrounge some time to stand on the combine as he made the first cut around Forty-Acre.

By saying that, he probably knew he was tempting the wrath of those who hand out the favours in this world and it should have been no surprise when, half an hour later, just as the grain tank was about full, he hit a wet spot and the combine sunk up to its axles and was going nowhere.

I walked over to him and had a look at the problem. The front drive wheels, which probably take about eighty percent of the weight of the combine, were well sunk in the ground while the rear wheels were still on the surface. It set the combine with a serious nose-down attitude.

'Going to need a tow out,' I said.

'Yes, but first we'll see if we can empty the grain tank. That'll take some of the weight of her. Bring the trailer over here and try not to get stuck on the way.'

Well, I tried but the closer I went to the combine, the deeper the wheels sank into the ground until, about ten yards short of my goal, the wheels started spinning and the tractor could go no further.

102

'Looks like we're walking back home,' Harry said as he surveyed the situation. 'And we'll probably have to give the Marshall a run with its winch.'

'The what?'

'The Field Marshall tractor – haven't you seen it yet? It lives in the shed across the orchard.'

We started to walk back to the farm, across a couple of grass fields and then began the climb up Brier Hill.

'Never been there,' I said.

'Then you're in for a treat.'

As luck would have it, we met Alice coming down to see us in the Land Rover.

'Don't tell me. You're stuck and you need the pop-pop?'

'That's just about it,' Harry said, sliding across into the middle passenger seat.

'The length you'll go to just to get that tractor out and running.'

'Well, it's not quite like that,' Harry said.

We arrived in the yard and piled out. You go over and open the shed up and I'll get some blotting paper,' he said.

'Blotting paper?' That one had me beaten.

The shed doors were reluctant to open and I had to lift them clear of the ground to stop them scraping on the ground. But when I looked in, I was amazed. This was a pre-war built Marshall with a huge fly wheel on one side and an exhaust pipe which had a half-way expanded barrel in it - similar to those used by old American steam trains.

I walked round it. There was no seat, although I could see where one would have been and at the back was a large winch drum wound with cable.

'What do you reckon to her?' Harry asked when he appeared clutching a few sheets of pink blotting paper.

'She's amazing,' I said. 'Where did she come from?'

'My father bought her new in 1937 and she's been on the farm ever since. I can tell you more when we get her started. Can you fetch a couple of buckets of clean water;

we need to fill the radiator up.'

I did as he bade and having turned off the drain taps Harry poured the water into a large oval hole in the bonnet. He then unscrewed and removed a brass cap from the front of the tractor and, having set fire to the blotting paper which glowed rather than flamed, pushed it into the hole and replaced the brass cap.

'It helps to heat the fuel and makes starting easier,' he explained.

Harry then reached for the starting handle and inserted one end into the centre of the flywheel and then asked me how strong I felt. I shrugged.

'You see, we'll really struggle to turn the engine over until the flywheel is up to speed – it's a big single cylinder – so what we do is raise this small metal jockey wheel to run in the grooves on the edge of the flywheel. That releases the compression in the engine and makes the flywheel easier to turn until the jockey wheel winds itself off the flywheel; the groove it runs in is a thread.'

I nodded my understanding.

'Now the question is, how many turns with the starting handle do we make before we have enough speed in the flywheel to turn the engine over? And when we've decided that we will know how many grooves we need to set the jockey wheel at before it drops off and we have the full compression of the engine to cope with – at which point the engine will hopefully start.'

'I really don't know. How many do you normally set it to?'

'Well let's try placing it in number four, while we're fresh,' he said. 'If we're still trying to start her in an hour's time we'll increase it to six.'

The starting handle was a real two-man job with the handle bar itself about three feet long. With the cranked end inserted in the centre of the flywheel, we took up our position standing side by side, poised to make a start.

'There's just one thing you should know,' Harry said.

'When the engine starts, the starting handle can sometimes stick in the flywheel and then it's time to run for your life because you don't know where or when it's going to fly off. I've seen it fly in the air and travel for hundreds of yards.'

It was not a comforting thought and I looked round to see which way I would run. The orchard seemed to offer the best line of retreat.

'Right then. Are you ready?'

'Let's do it,' I cried and, in unison, we stood side by side and turned the handle, gradually picking up speed. I counted the revolutions and watched the jokey wheel moving ever closer to the edge of the flywheel until on the top of the fourth revolution it slipped over and the piston met the compression in the cylinder. It was as if someone had suddenly put the brake on.

'Keep going, boy,' yelled Harry.

The engine coughed but that was all and the momentum we had generated to keep the engine turning was quickly lost, and the flywheel came to a halt.

Breathing heavily, Harry went to the front of the engine and unscrewed the cap and placed a fresh piece of glowing blotting paper inside.

'You can get these with a cartridge start system,' he said. 'You put a special twelve-bore cartridge in a small compartment on the side of the bonnet and then wind the engine over until the piston is just on the start of its reverse stroke and then hit the cap to fire the cartridge. The explosion sends the piston down the cylinder and, with a bit of luck, starts the engine running. It usually comes down to the last cartridge in the box before it decides to start. Failing that, you can have a long walk home.'

We took up our positions again and Harry said that this time he had set it for five turns of the fly wheel.

'Ready, steady go!'

I gave it my all and by the fifth revolution I don't think

I could have made the flywheel turn any faster. The jockey wheel slipped off the edge and the engine coughed and coughed again.

'Keep going, boy. She's nearly there.'

I pushed and pulled like I'd never done before and my arms and shoulders ached with the effort but then I discovered I didn't have to - the engine was running and the flywheel was turning on its own. And better still, I was holding the starting handle which meant it wasn't about to spin off into the unknown.

Running at a gentle, relaxed speed – slow enough for it to be counted - the horizontal single piston worked back and forwards and the whole tractor began to bounce on its tyres. I could see now why Alice had called it the pop-pop because that was the sound it made; a sort of hollow pop-pop.

Harry looked happy. This tractor was his pride and joy and held many memories for him and an excuse to get it out and working was not to be missed, even if this occasion was to pull the combine harvester out.

He climbed up onto the back and held the steering wheel as he depressed the clutch and engaged a gear. And then the tractor, its engine turning on the power and billowing clouds of black smoke, moved forwards out of the shed into the orchard.

'Come on, boy, jump on we've a combine harvester and a trailer to pull out.'

By the time we had driven down to Forty-Acres my face was covered in black spots and Harry had the same affliction.

'There's a splash oil feed for the piston, some of which escapes through the exhaust pot,' he said. 'You want to try standing here all day to see the real effect.'

I thought I would pass on that one but I did ask why there wasn't a seat.

'Well there was one but when I had the winch fitted a few years ago it just got in the way so I took it out. You can always lean on the mudguards. A lot of the work this tractor has done involved providing a belt drive for threshing machines.' He pointed down at the wide pulley on the side of the engine which, he added, was also the clutch.

In the field, he reversed down to within about thirty yards of the combine, making sure he stayed on dry, firm ground and then we had the job of pulling the cable off the winch, which wasn't that easy, particularly as we approached the wet ground near the combine. But eventually we made it and Harry used a shackle to secure the end to the rear axle.

Back on the tractor, Harry drove further away from the combine – as far as the cable would allow and then released the large metal anchors which would hopefully prevent the tractor from sliding back towards the combine when the cable was winched in.

The moment had arrived. Harry pulled a lever, engaged the winch drive and then slowly released the lever which set it in motion. The cable began to tighten until it was really taught.

'Don't go near it, boy. If it snaps it could take your head off.'

Nice, I thought. But then, where Harry was standing was probably no safer.

The tractor's anchors started to dig in to the ground and it was clearly a question of whether the tractor could put up sufficient resistance for it to move the combine. It was a tug-of-war and at this point in time it looked as if the combine was winning. The anchors were burying themselves deeper into the ground, heaving up enormous banks of soil.

But then, after a few yards, the tractor gradually stopped moving and the winch was still winding in cable.

'Either the combine's moving towards us or the back axle is being wrenched off it,' said Harry.

I stood back and watched the combine and there was

no doubt, it was moving and for every inch it eased backwards, it seemed to move more easily.

'Yes!' yelled Harry, slapping the tractor's mudguard. 'The old girl's done it again for us. Find me a modern tractor which could have done that.'

When the combine was back on firm ground he stopped the winch and went over and inspected the combine's front end, where it had been buried. There was plenty of mud around but nothing seemed to be bent or broken.

'We'll pull your trailer out and then fire up the combine, empty the tank and check it over,' he said, releasing the cable from the axle.

After all the drama of pulling out the combine, retrieving the tractor and trailer was a breeze and then all we had to do was let the pop-pop rewind the cable and drive forwards so we could lift up the anchors, having kicked all the mud off them.

From then on, the day went reasonably smoothly, at least, compared to the disasters we had endured at the start of the day. Next time round, Harry gave the wet spot a wide berth and managed to keep the combine going without any further mishaps.

'Have you seen how the holes where the combine was stuck have filled up with water,' he asked as we sheeted the combine down at the end of the day? 'You could make a feature of it.'

And then he told me I could drive the pop-pop home while he took the tractor and trailer with its load of grain.

'I suppose you want a hand starting it though,' he said.

Chapter eleven

Harvest home

The last ear of barley disappeared into the combine on the afternoon of the twenty-second of September, more than a week later than normal and marked the end of a harvest which had been a stop-go affair with the weather.

With no way of drying the grains we had to wait for the sun to do its job after every shower of rain and, once into September, the amount of time available for harvesting dry, storable grain was normally limited to just a few hours a day.

But it was finished. Harvest was over and I for one was pleased. The combine was trundled into its parking bay to remain there untouched and unmoved for the next ten months, a few days later the last bales were brought up to the farm and the baler itself reversed into its shed to await the start of next year's haymaking season.

Up in the rick yard, the open sided Dutch barns had been filled to the eaves with straw and hay bales, sufficient to provide feed and bedding for the livestock during the winter months, and the lofts, with their floor supports, were piled high with barley.

Breakfast was starting to return to a more leisurely occasion with Alice having to refill the teapot as more cups of tea were consumed. The boiled bacon supply though, continued as ever and I think I had just resigned myself to consuming a couple of slices along with bread and butter every day of the year.

Anyway, boiled bacon always reminded me of Elizabeth who I hoped, with harvest now over I would be able to see more regularly.

There was a knock on the door and one of the dogs beneath the table stirred and managed a half growl before collapsing onto the floor again. Alice got up and answered it.

'Harry, it's the vicar,' she said. 'He says he would like a word with you.'

'Oh God, it's not that time of the year again,' Harry muttered. 'You'd better ask him in.'

Simon Fanshaw entered the kitchen; a small, balding middle-aged man who wore small wire-framed glasses, a dog collar half buried in his neck and a heavy, full length dark coat.

'Morning vicar,' Harry said. 'How are the sinners of Storeton Green coping with life? I see you've added a telephone number to your new poster – you know, the one about being, 'Tired of sin? - then come on in'.'

'Is there? I don't recall putting a number on there.' He looked aghast.

'Well there is now and there's also a note saying it's for people to ring if they're not.'

'Not what?'

'Tired of sin, I suppose. You have a look at it and see what you think.'

'I will but I wonder whose number it could be.'

'Give it a call and find out,' Harry said.

Alice grimaced. 'Well that's enough of all that. Will you have a cup of tea, vicar?' she asked him, holding up the teapot.

'That would be wonderful, Alice. Thank you.'

'Well sit yourself down then,' Harry said. 'And tell us where we're all going wrong.'

'I'm afraid I think it may be a bit late for that, Harry. But tell me, who's the new lad you have here?' He swivelled in his chair and looked at me.

'That's John, he's been with us for what, four or five months now. He is our champion Donkey Derby rider and wants to be a farmer.'

'Well there are worse professions as you well know; anyway, very nice to meet you, John.' He held out his hand which I took and shook briefly. 'I hope you're enjoying it.'

It seemed to be my cue to speak so I said I was.

'That's good then. Now Harry,' he paused and steepled his fingers. 'I think you probably know what I'm here to ask you about and I'm just hoping you're going to be a little more agreeable than you were the last time we had this conversation.'

'If it's about the Harvest Festival then I don't think Pedro would really enjoy the experience. Not after the last one.'

'Yes, but that was several years ago and he must have got over it by now. And so have we, but he's so much older now and probably a lot calmer too. I really think it's time to give him another chance because the children think he's wonderful. And the other thing is that if everything works out at the Harvest Festival, as I'm sure it will, it's only a few months before we can do the nativity play and, as you know, Pedro would have a key part in that one. What do you think?'

Harry sighed. 'What do you think, Alice?'

'Well, you'd have John to help you this time and as Simon says, Pedro is older and more tolerant these days.'

'Yes, but that's probably because he doesn't have to attend the Harvest Festival or put up with a lot of screaming kids at the Christmas do,' Harry said.

There was a silence and I think Harry knew he was beaten. Simon Fanshaw was not above using the salesman's technique of keeping quiet when the sale's pitch had been concluded.

'Alright, we'll give him one more try, but if he's not happy with it, he's not doing the Christmas gig.'

'Oh, that's fine,' said the vicar. 'Thank you so much for that. I'll put the word out and I'm sure the congregation will double or even treble in size when they hear that Pedro will be there – he's a local celebrity.'

He finished his tea and got up from the table. 'We'll see you all next Sunday then,' he said. 'And John, you must come along to our services more regularly.'

'You could put him in the choir,' Harry said.

'Yes, well, first things first. Anyway, I'll get on. Good-bye and thank you for the tea, Alice.'

Harry waited until the door shut and put his head in his hands. 'Why did you let me agree to that?' he said.

***

I spent the rest of the week cleaning the pigs out and it was quite a task. In the run of things the aim was to clean them out every couple of weeks but with hay making and harvest, nearly two months had passed. And there were tons of it. If they had been left any longer the pigs would have been able to step over the tops of their barriers, the muck was so deep.

Digging it out was hard work and by lunch time I'd only managed to clean two of the pens out and there were eight more to do which meant I'd still be doing this job on Saturday.

But there wasn't any choice. You have to take the rough with the smooth and, to my mind, anything to do with pigs would always be the rough, the seriously rough.

Sunday arrived and I don't think Harry's mood had improved. Memories of previous Pedro disasters seemed to haunt him and he asked me, as he had been asking me all week to be sure to help him out at the service.

Of course, I agreed, just to be there and see what all the fuss was about but with all the tension it created, I thought it wouldn't be a bad time to ask him about me putting in for my driving test. I needed his blessing because the only vehicle I had to drive and practice on was the farm's Land Rover.

'Yes, boy,' he said. 'There's no trouble with that. No trouble at all. You tell me when the test is and I'll arrange to use a tractor or something while you're taking it.'

'I could really do with some practice on the road before the test,' I explained. 'I'll get some L-plates and then I can drive while you sit back and relax, but you will need to change the insurance.'

'Yes, boy. That will be fine. You haven't seen the halter you were using at the village show, have you?'

I wandered if he had been listening to a word I was saying regarding my planned driving test. His convivial replies suggested he hadn't.

'I think I saw it in the garage. Didn't you unload the Land Rover in there when we came back from the village fete?'

'You're right,' he said. 'I did.'

'Listen John, you wouldn't do me a favour, would you?'

'If I can, Harry, of course I will.'

'I've got this dreadful harvest festival thing this evening and they want Pedro to be there for a bit of local colour. You know the sort of thing.'

After a week of hearing Harry going on about the Harvest Festival it would have been difficult for me not to know all about it, but I nodded, fearing the worst.

'Well, it's not really my sort of thing and as you seem to have struck up a rapport with Pedro, I was wondering if you wouldn't mind taking him to the service. You don't have to be there long. Once the first few hymns are out of the way you can lead him home again. Job done. What do you say?'

'And you wouldn't be there at all?'

'No well, not exactly but I won't be far away.'

'You mean in the belfry,' I said. 'Ringing the bells.'

Harry nodded and looked away. He was definitely not a happy man.

'Oh, alright then.'

He brightened up. 'What? You mean you'll do it?'

'That's what I said. But you won't forget my driving lessons will you.'

'No of course I won't. You've as good as passed the test already, just you see.'

'If you get Pedro ready, I'll make a start on the milking.'

'It's a deal,' he said. 'The service starts at seven, so you want to be in there and sorted by about quarter to.'

I think the girls expected me to sit down with them when I walked into their field; they just remained where they were and waited for me to come across. On any other fine Sunday afternoon when we were quiet, I would have been pleased to spend some time with them but today it was not to be.

'Come on girls. No lounging about we need to get on,' I shouted as I walked around them and started to pat a few rumps. Everyone slowly got to their feet and, after a stretch, began the trek back to the farm. Everyone, that is, except for Thrifty, the latest member of the herd to calve. She remained lying down.

I went over to her. She wasn't well, her ears felt cold and her nose, which was usually cool and moist was bone dry. She had turned her head into her flank and her eyes were not focussing.

'What's up old girl?' I asked her, rubbing the sides of her ears to try and warm them up. But she wasn't interested and I started to worry about her. Ignoring the rest of the herd I ran back across the field and up the track just hoping Harry would still be about when I arrived there.

He was in the paddock grooming Pedro. 'Harry,' I panted. 'The angus cross, the one which calved last Wednesday has gone down. She's not well.'

Harry stopped what he was doing. Sounds as if she has milk fever,' he said. He left Pedro where he was and ran into the house and returned with a couple of large brown bottles and a rubber tube.

'Come on, boy. We'll give her a dose of calcium. With a

bit of luck that should sort her out.'

We climbed into the Land Rover and set off down the track steering a way around the cows coming up to be milked.

'Bugger,' Harry said. 'We should have shut the yard gate. They'll be down the yard before we get back and halfway up the village.'

We arrived where Thrifty was still lying down, her head still tucked in alongside her flank and in some distress.

'Bring one of those bottles while I sort the needle out,' he said.

Having attached one end of the rubber tube to the bottle cap and the other to a hypodermic needle at the other, he asked me to hold the bottle upside down.

I did and watched as the liquid arrived at the needle and started to run out. Harry doubled the pipe over and then plunged the needle into Thrifty's rump. She didn't stir.

'Will she be alright?' I asked.

'Don't know boy. She's pretty far gone. Just hold that bottle up. This is a subcutaneous injection which places the calcium solution under the skin where it's absorbed into the blood stream,' he explained. 'She's been giving more milk than she has calcium.'

I changed arms and held the bottle up and waited while the fluid made its way into Thrifty. After about five minutes the bottle was empty, and I could see a slight swelling where it had gathered under her skin. Harry removed the needle and gave the area a gentle rub to help disperse it.

And then we stood and waited. I went round to Thrifty's head and stroked her under the chin and behind her ears – her two favourite places.

'Well it's a good job you came down here early today boy. I don't think she would have still been with us if you'd been much later. Looks like we have the vicar to thank for that.'

It was good news of a sort, but there was still no sign that Thrifty was going to make it.

Harry looked at his watch. 'Look, I'd better get up to the farm and make sure the cows haven't gone visiting. With a bit of luck Alice will have seen them and sorted them out. Anyway, you stay on here with her and I'll be back as soon as I can.'

And with that he climbed into the Land Rover and headed back to the farm leaving me alone with Thrifty.

'Come on old girl,' I whispered into her ear. 'Don't go anywhere, not yet, we'd all miss you too much.' Her ear twitched. I swear it did. So I blew on it and it twitched again.

'Thrifty,' I gasped. 'Are you going to be alright? Come on girl.' I ran my hands down her neck and watched as her eyes started to blink and then she was trying to lift her head and I put my arms around her neck and held her.

'Steady old girl, there's no rush. We've all the time in the world. Just take it steady.'

Thrifty had put a leg forward and was now trying to push herself into a position where she could get to her feet. But I didn't want her to rush.

Her eyes focussed on me and I smiled and, while still looking as if she had a dreadful hangover, she snorted in a friendly way and looked around her.

'Are you feeling better?'

She snorted again and then struggled up on to her rear legs, paused to get her balance, and then pushed up with the front legs. She was standing, but only just and she had yet to take a step. But bit by bit the magic of the calcium did its job and slowly, Thrifty returned to us and I welcomed her with a big cuddle.

Harry arrived back with the Land Rover pulling the horse box. 'She's up then,' he said as he climbed out. 'That calcium does an amazing job as long as you catch them early enough. Do you think you can get her to go into the box? We had better keep her at the farm tonight so we can keep a check on her.'

Harry let the rear ramp down and then gave me a hand to gently push Thrifty into the box. 'Come on girl, let's find you a room for the night,' he said as she wobbled her way up the ramp.

'I'll stay in here with her,' I said. 'She's still a bit unsteady on her feet and she might enjoy the company. But go steady.'

The rest of the herd were in the collecting yard, thanks to Alice who had spotted them down by the house and persuaded them that they might be going the wrong way. We put Thrifty in a freshly strawed pen with some hay and a supply of water; a five-star treatment for a five-star patient.

'I'll have to milk her out by hand,' Harry said. 'She's too much milk in her to last until morning and I'll leave the other calcium bottle in the dairy if she needs a second dose.'

Chapter twelve

Harvest festival

It was getting on for ten to seven when I finally finished milking and made it into the house. Harry said he would take the hay out so I could get ready for my visit with Pedro to the Harvest Festival.

'You don't think I shall be too late, do you?' I asked.

'You'll be alright. Pedro's ready to go as soon as you are,' Harry replied, holding up his hand for me to be quiet and pointing to the church. 'Can you tell there's no one pulling the base bell? It's not the same, is it?'

To me, it didn't sound any different at all; just the usual tuneless clanking of bells accompanied by the furious barking of dogs. There seemed no going back now so, having washed and changed into some clean clothes, I went across to the paddock and untied Pedro's rope and led him down the slope into the street.

'Come on,' I said to him. 'Let's get this over with.'

After walking along the street for a hundred yards we turned right and headed back up the slope along the path to the church.

The bells stopped ringing as I lifted the latch and pushed the big wooden door open and we were met by a wall of noise. Far from being the gentle muttering of a congregation awaiting the start of a service, these people were yelling their heads off at each other.

'If you're wondering what all the noise is about it's the

organist up to his tricks again,' said a man sitting close to the door.

'And what's that?' I asked.

'He starts off playing very quietly and everyone talks normally. Gradually though, he increases the volume and, to be heard, everyone starts talking more loudly and because everyone is talking loudly everyone has to start yelling at each other. Meanwhile the organist keeps turning up the volume until you reach the level he's at now. But the best is yet to come. You wait, he'll suddenly stop playing but the shouting and screaming will carry on regardless. That's the best bit.'

Not to miss out, Pedro joined in and started braying as loudly as I've ever heard him and when the organist suddenly stopped playing, as the man had predicted, it was Pedro who made everyone look round as he continued to bray even though the shouting and yelling quickly subsided.

I smiled back and Pedro gave a half-hearted bray just to show that he too had finished. Looking up the aisle I could see that each of the pews had been decorated with bunches of vegetables – radishes, carrots, swedes, turnips, onions, freshly dug potatoes, a couple of marrows, a net of Brussel-sprouts and an assortment of several other colourful vegetables. And Pedro had seen them too. I thought about finding another route to take but the vicar was beckoning us to make our way up the central aisle to the front of the church.

'Come on, old chap. Our moment has arrived,' I whispered into his ear. 'And keep your eyes and mind off the vegetables and your gob shut.'

We moved off together and, at first, all went well; he was managing to resist the goodies which were being displayed so temptingly as he walked by them. But then I realised Pedro had been saving himself for the carrots, a huge bunch which would have been the pride and joy of a local gardener who, no doubt, had spent weeks on his hand and knees nurturing and cossetting their development.

I tried to stop him, but he outsmarted me by taking a quick double step which gave him the slack in the rope to lunge forward, mouth agape. And as his teeth closed around them, parents gathered their children up into their arms, fearing Pedro's sudden attack on the carrots might escalate into something worse.

And my concerns grew when I spotted other bunches of carrots placed at intervals along the pew in front of them, but I wrestled Pedro back and with him chewing victoriously on a mouthful of award winning carrots, we resumed our walk to meet the vicar at the front of the church.

'Hello, John,' he said. 'Glad you could make it. I suppose Harry is up to his arms in a cow, or something?'

'Yes, something like that,' I said.

'Well, if you could take Pedro over there.' He pointed to where more vegetables had been stacked in a display and added: 'I should try and keep as far away from the vegetables as you can, and then we can make a start.'

I stood there holding Pedro's rope hoping he would at least stay still. But while his head remained still the rest of his torso did not and it was the gasp from the congregation followed by a loud cheer, which told me what was happening; that and the foul smell.

'Oh Pedro, there was no need for that.'

But there was it seemed, because he then decided to have a wee which brought more cheers from everyone watching as it gushed and steamed its way across the tiled floor.

Sensing that the meaning of the service could be drifting away from its central cause, the vicar stepped forwards and raised his hands for quiet.

'Let me first welcome you all to this year's harvest festival service,' he said, instinctively ducking as Pedro let go a rasping passage of wind that echoed around the church. 'I would like to thank all those who contributed to the wonderful vegetable display and the decorations but I'd particularly like to extend our thanks to John here for bringing back to us a great favourite of all the children: Pedro the donkey.'

He paused as a rather muted round of applause accompanied by some cheering emerged from the congregation. Many of those at the front of the church and nearest to Pedro were holding handkerchiefs over their noses and were finding it difficult to applaud, even if they felt like they wanted to.

'You know, I think it is very appropriate that John and Pedro are here this evening,' continued the vicar. If there had been any chatter among his flock before he uttered those few words, there wasn't any now. The church had gone very quiet as everyone waited to learn what was lucky about having an incontinent, noisy, donkey with an uncontrollable passion for raw carrots and an audible, prolific flatulence problem in front of them.

'You see, it occurred to me that what Pedro has just done is to display his out-going approach to life – the carefree attitude which all animals in this world are blessed with. And it's because they can freely demonstrate this, there have been generations before us who managed to grow food for society to feed on and for this, we have to thank the natural fertiliser which is so generously donated by animals, both wild and domesticated. Yes, we are so lucky to have Pedro here with us on this important occasion.

'We'll begin our service with hymn number seventeen, 'All things bright and beautiful' and, while we sing can I suggest we all walk up to Pedro and say thank you to him. You might even want to scoop up some of his gift to us and anoint yourselves as you tender your thanks.'

The organist played the opening line and paused briefly to allow the congregation to begin the hymn together. And I waited to see what would happen. By the start of the

121

second verse no one had made a move in our direction. Truer to say that there were now fewer people near us than there had been at the start of the hymn, due to a mass retreat by the occupants of the first two pews closest to Pedro's recent deposits.

But the vicar was not going to be ignored and, clasping the hands of two elderly ladies he led them over to where we were standing. Smiling, he raised his hand and extended a finger before bending down and dipping it into the steaming donkey poo. Raising it up, he positioned his finger on the forehead of one of the ladies and slid it across to leave a brown smear. He then did the same to the second lady and they both turned, beaming, overcome by the event, before returning to their seats.

At that point the whole church went sort of quiet causing the organist to believe he was playing a verse too many. So he stopped too.

'Wonderful,' said the vicar. 'Just wonderful. What better time could there be to come so close to nature and savour what it has to offer, first hand.' He wiped his hand on his surplus. 'Let's continue our service of thanks with a traditional hymn at this time, 'We plough the fields and scatter.'

And as the organist played the introduction, I grabbed Pedro's rope and led him back down the aisle and out into the graveyard beyond.

***

'I don't think I'll be doing that again,' I said, when I had returned Pedro to his paddock and made my way into the kitchen. 'That vicar is barking mad.'

'Oh, I wouldn't be saying that, boy. He may be a bit strange but by all accounts, he doesn't do a bad job,' Harry said.

'What? You would have had to be there to see what a disaster it was. He even daubed the foreheads of two old ladies with donkey poo. And that's not to mention the organist playing tricks with the volume so everyone was screaming at each other.

'Anyway, that's over for another year. Next year we can just send a bunch of carrots and a bucketful of donkey poo and leave them to it.'

'I wouldn't be so sure,' Alice said, peering out of the kitchen window. 'From where I'm sitting I can see two old ladies leaning over the paddock gate giving Pedro some bread to eat.

'Oh, for pity's sake,' Harry said.

Chapter thirteen

Dogs and sheep

First thing the next morning, while Harry was bringing in the cows, I went to see how Thrifty was. I'd seen her last night and she was lying down but not showing a lot of interest in life and I had wondered whether I should give her another bottle of calcium. Today, though, she was on her feet and idly pulling mouthfuls of hay from the rack. She looked a lot better and I gave her a tickle under her chin.

'Welcome back, old lady,' I said. 'I guess you're ready to join the rest of the girls.'

I opened the gate and let her out and she wandered out to the collecting yard, her udder leaking milk and clearly in need of a milking.

'How is she, boy?' asked Harry.

'I think she's more of herself and on the mend.'

'Well, keep an eye on her.'

A good deal of Harry's time was taken up with the sheep and through July and August one of the weekly tasks was sorting out the fat lambs which had been weaned from the ewes so that there was a steady flow of lambs to market.

All of which meant the lambs needed to be run through a race and over a weighing scale to see which ones were considered fit to go. In a corner of the field where the lambs were grazing, Harry had set up some hurdles to create a holding pen and then a funnel feed into the race and the weigher. When they left, a shedding gate was used to separate those lambs that were staying and those that were off to market.

It was a task which Harry could do quite comfortably by himself but there were occasions when he asked me to give him a hand. And it was on these days I got to see his dogs working.

Ross, a long-haired collie with an enormous tongue and the ability to run all day long, was about seven years old when I arrived in his world and we became good friends to the point he would, for something to do, come with me to get the cows in for milking, not that he ever had to do any work as far as the cows were concerned.

While Ross was a splendid companion to be with, he did have two rather annoying traits. One was to bark and howl whenever the church bells were being rung and the other was to roll in everything he could find that was smelly and horrible. For him to chance upon a fresh cowpat was happiness complete; he'd lower his shoulder and slide blissfully into it before rolling back and forwards until he was matted with the stuff.

When it came to working with sheep though, he was in his element and he used to tremble with the excitement of it all. Like all good sheepdogs he was always one step ahead of the sheep, anticipating their next move before they had even thought about it. With Harry gently shouting the commands, the sheep were driven onto the collecting yard and the hurdle swung shut and tied.

'He's working well today,' I said, as we walked towards the race.

'More than you can say for Bob,' Harry scoffed, pointing at his other dog. 'Don't know why I bother with him. You ask him to do something and half way up the field he's sitting down licking his arse. No sense of urgency; either that or his forgotten why he's going there.

'Mind you, a good dog's worth his weight in gold. A farmer I once knew spent a lot of money on a dog when he bought it from a shepherd somewhere in the wilds of the Scottish Highlands. The dog had won some local championships and came from a family of successful trial dogs.

'Anyway, not long after the dog was with him he asked a few of his friends to come over and see it working. So, it was one Sunday morning so we all turned up to see this wonder dog, which I have to say looked pretty sharp and lively. There were about fifty ewes out in the field and the chap had set up some hurdles so he could show how the dog could drive them into it.

With his dog walking to heel, he walked out to the hurdles and untied one of them and swung it open. And then he gave his command to the dog: "Away!" and the dog shot off but not to the sheep in that field. He headed for the far fence, jumped that one and then across the next field and the next and so on until before long, he was just a black dot moving about on the horizon.

And then, after about fifteen minutes, we saw all these sheep coming towards us and I'm not sure there weren't a few bullocks among them. I asked the chap what had happened and he said that back in his home in the Highlands, the dog was used to working at a longer range than in a five-acre paddock. As far as the dog was concerned, those sheep were already here; he was going after the others in the county. Good dog though, just wanted a bit of reigning in and a couple of mountains to run about on.'

We spent the next hour pushing the lambs through the race. Each one was weighed and those that were considered heavy enough were exited into a pen and the others were allowed back out into the field again.

'It's not just that they are heavy enough,' Harry said. 'They have to be finished, have a good confirmation and that means feeling to see how much fat there is and the finish of the muscles on the loin legs and shoulders. Come and run your hands over this one and see what you think.'

I moved down the side of the race and ran my hands over the back and sides of the lamb.

'Now do the same to this one,' Harry said, moving along to the next lamb.

I did as he asked.

'Do you feel the difference?'

I said I could but I wasn't sure which one was finished and ready for market.

'Don't worry, you'll get it after a few thousand lambs,' he said. 'Now let the first one into the market group and this one back into the field.'

We loaded the dozen fat lambs Harry had picked out into the horse box so they could spend the night in the orchard with Pedro and be close by to load up in the morning. Ross, who had found something nasty to roll in, ran alongside the Land Rover.

A couple of weeks later, some of Harry's ewes that had been grazing rough pasture on a neighbour's farm broke through a hedge and ended up in the local sewage treatment works.

We took Ross down with us and rounded up the ewes and pushed them back into the field before repairing the hole in the hedge. It was while making this repair though, Harry noticed Ross had disappeared.

'Oh no,' he said, looking around.

'He wouldn't have done what I think he shouldn't have done, would he?' I asked.

Harry whistled and Ross sauntered around the corner of a concrete structure; his tongue hanging out and looking incredibly pleased with himself. I could see by the stain on the concrete wall where he had brushed against it, our worst fears were confirmed. There was some indescribable mess hanging off his neck and shoulders and the rest of him was matted with other horrors.

'You should be alright for tomatoes next year,' I said.

'There must be a hose pipe around here somewhere,' said Harry. 'You hold him while I have a look.'

But before I could get a hold on his collar he ran off after Harry and, because the Land Rover door was open, piled in and sat on one of the front seats.

'We'll have to sort this out when we get back,' he said, sliding carefully into the driving seat as I climbed into the back. 'And when we do get back home just pray the kitchen door isn't open.'

***

'How do you fancy a bit of rabbiting?' asked Harry, as we tucked into a slice of creamy sponge cake Alice had made that afternoon.

'What's that involve?' I asked, already wary it may require me to perform some dreadful task.

'We take the Land Rover out across the fields and catch them in the headlights and then Alice makes us all a rabbit stew,' he said. 'You can drive. It will be good practice for when you take your test – next week isn't it?'

I thought about it. Careering around a large field in the dark chasing rabbits did have its fun element and Harry was right. With only days to go before my test, I could do with the practice. 'Alright,' I said. 'When were you aiming to go?'

He leaned back in his chair and picked up a cup of tea. 'We'll give it another hour,' he said, glancing up at the clock hanging on the wall. 'If you want something to do, you can fetch Pedro a bale of straw and bed him down. He's been a bit loose since he dined out at the Harvest Festival. And while you're out there, just slip the latch on the hens' coup, they should have all gone in for the night by now.'

I pulled on my boots and set off for the rick yard before Harry could think of any more jobs I could do. There always seemed to be something to fill the time and recently, I had felt myself falling into the same mind set. Even now I could think of more than a few jobs I could be doing; washing the dog, collecting eggs, filling the cows' feed hoppers in the bail... The list was endless but then, that was the joy of it all and at that moment, as I walked up the yard catching the scent of the evening air, I knew this was what I wanted to do.

And then I met Elizabeth.

'Hello,' she said. She was wearing jeans and a large cream-coloured woollen jersey, and she looked terrific.

'Elizabeth. I didn't expect to see you today. I was just going to get Pedro a bale of straw.'

'I know.'

'You know? How can that be?'

She moved closer and put her arms around me. 'I spoke to Harry earlier and he said you would be coming this way at about this time. So here I am.'

'The scheming old... I would never have believed he would have done that.' I wanted to say more but Elizabeth's lips closed on mine.

'Come on,' she said. 'We've the whole evening in front of us. You can take me out for a drink or something.'

'Yes, but...'

'Don't worry,' she said, holding up a pound note and waving it about. 'Uncle Harry gave me this and I've something important to tell you.'

'What's that?'

'It's just that, next week I'm off to University to start a biomedical science degree course. But I'll be back for Christmas.'

'Which University is that?'

'York.'

'But that's miles away. I shan't be able to see you for weeks.'

'I know but it's something I really want to do and I'll write to you every week, I promise.'

'We had better go and have that drink and you can tell me all about it,' I said.

As we walked through the churchyard I could sense

there was something else Elizabeth wanted to say to me; there was a tension in her hand and try as she might, she wasn't her usual outgoing self.

'What's the matter, Elizabeth?' I asked when we arrived at the gate which led out of the other side of the graveyard.

She sighed and looked at me and drew breath. 'There's something I think you should know,' she said.

'And what's that?' I replied. 'I hope it's not bad news.'

'Follow me, and you'll find out.'

She turned around and we walked back along the path until we came to the opening which marked the entrance to the new section of the graveyard. 'This is the acre of ground Harry donated to the church when the old graveyard was full,' she said.

'That was very generous of him,' I said.

'Well yes and no.' Elizabeth said. 'Come with me and you'll see what I mean.'

We walked along the path until we reached the far wall and then I followed her for a few more yards before we stopped by a grave which had some fresh cut flowers on it. Unlike most other graves in that area which were bordering on the unkempt, this one was pristine, the grass mowed and neatly edged.

'Look what's written on the head stone,' she said.

It was small and I lowered myself onto one knee to read the inscription and my stomach churned. 'It says, Henry James Wilcox.'

'That's right. Now read the date.'

'19th April 1955.'

'Go on, read it all.'

'Henry James Wilcox killed by accident 19th April 1955 aged six,' I read. 'Beloved son of Harry and Alice Wilcox.'

I stood up and looked at Elizabeth. 'That's awful,' I said. 'What happened?'

'I'm not really sure. No one has ever talked to me about it but I thought you should know, just in case you inadvertently said anything that could upset them.'

'Yes, well, that's very thoughtful of you. But I have to say it all seems so sad because he would have been about my age by now and...' It was difficult to continue, too many thoughts began racing through my mind. 'When did he give them the land?'

I think you can work than one out for yourself,' Elizabeth said as she hooked her arm into mine. 'The important thing is that you know, and I think Alice and Harry will be relieved that you know too. Come on, let's go and spend Harry's pound.'

Chapter fourteen

The driving test

'Now are you alright with the Highway Code?' questioned Harry as I drove into town in the Land Rover. 'I mean, what are you supposed to do if you meet some horses being ridden along the road?'

'I would slow down,' I said.

'Yes, but how much?'

'Well, if it's you driving it's usually seventy miles an hour down to about sixty-five, and that's on a narrow country lane.'

Harry scoffed. 'They shouldn't be riding them if they can't control them. Anyway, they should be in fields where they belong, not holding up traffic all the time. You know, boy, it always baffled me what sort of an animal it is that allows you to nail metal shoes on their feet, fasten them up with unfathomable tangles of leather straps and then push a metal bar into their mouth. And if that wasn't enough, strap a saddle on its back and let you sit on it. I ask you, why do you think they gave us cars and lorries for?

'And horses are such fussy eaters. You don't see them putting up with a handful of ground barley and a wad of straw. Oh no. It has to be some expensive mixture of oats, la-de-da minerals and proteins and a hay net full of green, dust-free hay and shredded paper in their bedding.

'And do you know the bit that really gets me going is

that if one of my dogs craps on a path I can get nasty looks from everyone but if a horse dumps a bucketful in the middle of the road, that's alright. Horses are just a one-way soak. Spend a fortune on them and nothing ever comes back.

'Oh, I could go on. Vets bills, cosy little heated stables, tack rooms, dressage rings not to forget the fortune you need to be seen wearing the right clothes at the right events. Just don't start me off about horses, boy.'

'I think we're here,' I said. 'There's a notice which tells us where to park. I'll just reverse into a bay so I'm facing the right way when the test starts.'

'What do you want me to do while you're having the test?' he asked.

'There's probably a waiting room in there somewhere. Come on let's go and book in.'

In the reception area I followed the signs to a small frosted glass hatch which slid open a few inches as I approached it. A hand appeared and I fed it with the papers I had been asked to bring with me. Not long after that, the papers along with my provisional licence reappeared and the hatch slid shut again.

'Sociable sort of people in here,' Harry said as we wandered over to the waiting area. 'Doesn't cost a lot to say something, even if it's only thanks.'

And there we waited until a man who introduced himself as Mr James appeared from somewhere and told me to follow him.

'Good luck, boy,' Harry said.

We walked out into the car park and as I unlocked the passenger door I just knew I should have made an effort to clear out all the junk which was spread across the floor. When the examiner climbed in I could sense his annoyance at having to place his shiny brogues in such an accumulation of spanners, feed bags, bits of machinery and bale string, lots of it.

'You didn't have time to clean out the vehicle, then?' he

said, trying to find somewhere to put his feet.

'Well, I was a bit late finishing the milking today and I just sort of ran out of time. I can place some of it into the back if you like.'

'No time for that. I'll just have to put up with it. Right then, drive off and I want you to take the first turn on the right and then you need to take the second left.'

Half an hour later and we were back and it was Highway Code knowledge test.

'You're driving down a narrow country lane and you meet a horse being ridden. What action should you take?' asked the examiner.

Oh, please don't let me say what I'm thinking. Why can't I get seventy miles an hour out of my head? But he needed an answer. 'I would, having looked in my mirror, braked gently to bring the vehicle to a walking pace and then move over to provide the maximum space available for a pass,' I said, mechanically.

'You mean you wouldn't have wound down the window and shouted out for the rider to get back in the field where the flaming horse belongs. Or slowed down to seventy, or something like that?'

I looked at him and could see the twinkle in his eye and the smile which slowly spread across his face.

'Don't answer that one,' he said holding out a piece of paper. 'Congratulations, you've passed your test. Take this piece of paper to the licensing office and you will be issued with a full license.' He then shook my hand and left the vehicle mumbling something about being in a shit-pit.

'Well done, boy,' Harry said when I met him coming out of the waiting room.

'Oh, so you know, then,' I said.

'Yes, Bill James told me, the examiner bloke - known him for years.'

'Well you didn't say anything when you saw him.'

'That's right. I didn't think it would be proper.'

I sighed. It seemed adult life had a complicated edge

which I had still to get to grips with. We headed for the Land Rover and when I went round to the passenger door Harry insisted I drove home. 'No good having a dog and barking yourself, is it?'

'Not if you say so.'

'Thought you would have spent a bit of time clearing this mess out before we set off this morning,' he said, trying to clear a space for his feet. 'I don't suppose that went down too well with Bill.'

'It didn't. He called it a shit-pit.'

We drew into the yard about mid-day and I took the Land Rover down to the house expecting to park it where it normally resided. But there was another vehicle there, a small pick-up which looked as if it belonged to one of Harry's friends; it had that look about it. I left the Land Rover by the dairy and walked down to the house where I was met by Alice.

'Do I congratulate or commiserate?' she said.

'I passed.'

'Oh well done, John. That's terrific.' She gave me a hug and a kiss on the cheek. 'Didn't I say he'd walk it,' she said to Harry.

'Can't say I remember those exact words. But it probably meant the same.'

Alice ignored him. 'Anyway John, I think it's time to give you these.'

I looked up and saw a bunch of car keys. 'What? Are they for the...?' I pointed to the pick-up and Alice nodded. I was lost for words.

'That's right boy. Don't say anything. We just thought that if you're going to have any future with young Elizabeth you should have something you could take her out in rather than wandering down the Vine pub whenever she makes it up here.'

'That's very thoughtful of you. Thank-you.'

'Alright, be a way with you. It runs on diesel which doesn't mean you can empty the Derv tank every week, if you get what I mean, or the locks will go on.'

***

From that point on nothing quite seemed the same. I hadn't realised it but being able to drive had placed me in another zone which, on one hand gave me less reliance on others, and on another, had taken away from me my youth and innocence. It was as if I had moved from one school into a more senior school where decisions had to be made, decisions for which I would be answerable.

That the year had moved into September hadn't helped. This was the month when school restarted after the summer break and my mother sent my two brothers and me off to catch the bus in blazers, shoes and trousers which were invariably several sizes too big. Her plan was that we would grow into them and the cost of purchasing replacement clothing would be delayed.

There was also that dreadful 'back to school' feeling at this time of the year. Depressing memories which haunted and would remain with me even in the years to come. They were activated by cooler, darker mornings and swinging my feet out of bed at some unearthly hour of the morning to place them on a slab of ice-cold lino. Then there was the hunt for a sock which had gone absent during the night along with a pair of underpants, and the delicate task of removing a drip-dry shirt from a clothes' hanger clinging to a rail over the bath.

My spirits were slightly raised at breakfast time this morning when Alice gave me a letter which had been sent to me. I recognised the writing immediately – it was from Elizabeth.

'Good news?' inquired Alice.

'It's from the Elizabeth. She said she would write to me and she has.'

'Oh, that's good of her,' Alice said. 'I hope she's well.'

Harry cleared his throat. 'I think we should make a start

on some fencing down in Badger Close.'

'Right,' I said, not knowing quite what fencing entailed.

'If you make your way down to the fence which runs along the grass side of the field, not the one around the piece we combined, you can take the wire off the posts and roll it up.'

'How do I get the staples out?'

'Take a hammer and an old mower finger down with you and don't forget to put the staples in a box or something, we have enough punctures as it is without leaving a carpet of staples across the field. And on your way down there, have a check on the cows – I've let them onto a new area of grass and clover and it may be too much for them.'

'Do you want another cuppa before you go, John,' asked Alice, teapot in hand.

I was so tempted to ask for 'just half a cup', but my nerve failed me. 'No, I'm fine thanks, Alice.'

'Well, if you're sure. Harry, how about you?' I heard his cup sliding down the table as I pulled my boots on.

Up in the tractor shed I rummaged about for an old mower finger, one with the long sharp point that pushed its way through the grass and cut it with a blade which moved from side to side through the centre of the finger. They seemed to be in big demand; everyone I found had a bent point which I thought would not have dug under a staple to remove it, but then, that was why they were in the workshop scrap box.

With the best one I could find, and a hammer, I grabbed an old canvas bag to carry them in and set off down the track towards Badger Close. As requested I took a slight detour to see how the cows were on their new grazing area and all was not well, far from it.

At least three of the cows were lying on their side, their sides swollen and taught and they were breathing in short gasps. Oh no, not more trouble, I thought turning and racing back towards the farm. Harry was just coming out

137

of the house when I arrived and told him what I had seen.

'Quick, boy. Get the Land Rover while I get the trocar and cannula. I'll ask Alice to ring the vets and get him over here.'

I wanted to ask him what it was he was fetching and why but thought better of it. This was an emergency.

He jumped into the passenger seat and told me to drive, fast. 'Which one shall we go to first,' I asked as the Land Rover bucked and rolled across the fields at a speed I hadn't driven, even on the road.

'The nearest,' Harry said.

The wheels locked up as I tried to bring the vehicle to a stop but Harry was already out by the time it came to a halt. 'It's the gas in the rumen,' he said. 'It builds up too quickly for the system to release and that puts pressure on the diaphragm and she can't breathe.'

While he was talking he had the trocar cannula out of its case, a metal tube about five inches long and half an inch in diameter having a removable inner core. He held it as if it were a dagger and with his other hand felt for the hip bone and then flattened his hand to measure one hand's width down and one across.

'This is the spot, boy. Here we go.'

He plunged down and pushed the trocar cannula into the cow's flank and then removed the central core and at that moment there was a loud hissing as the trapped gas was released.

'You stay with this one and I'll move onto the next one. And whatever you do, don't strike a match.' He jumped into the Land Rover and tore off. And one by one I watched him treat the cows which were lying down. As he completed the task, the vet drove into the field and pulled up beside me.

'How many has there been?' he asked, leaning out of the window.

'Three, I think.'

'This one seems to be recovering but I don't know

about the others. Harry's with them now.'

'I'd better drive over and have a word with him,' he said. 'Try and keep the wound clean, it'll need cleansing and a stitch or two inserted into the rumen wall before she gets up.'

I watched him cross the field to where Harry was. Harry looked up and shook his head as he got to his feet. It didn't look like good news, at least for that cow. He climbed into the passenger seat beside the Vet and together they went to take a look at the other cow before heading back to me.

'It's not good, boy,' he said. 'We've lost two – didn't get to them in time. How's your patient?'

I could hear the sadness in his voice and felt for him. While I loved these cows dearly and was mortified at their loss, Harry had seen them as calves, young girls, who he had fed and nurtured into adulthood. And now two of them lay dead.

'She's going to be alright, I think. Her breathing has returned to something like normal and she's not in so much pain.'

'That's good,' Harry said. Stay here with David and get her fixed up and I'll take the cows out of the field onto something that's less flush and doesn't have the clover.'

'If you put them in Badger Close I could keep an eye on them,' I offered. 'And the grass is a bit tight in there; could even let them run onto the stubble.'

'I think that would be for the best,' he said turning away to start gathering up the herd.

The vet returned from his car with his bag. 'Hi, I'm David White,' he said, offering me his hand. 'You've been working for Harry for a few months now, I gather?'

'That's right. I moved in at the beginning of July.'

'Enjoying it?'

'Well, apart from today.'

'Yes, well that's to be expected,' he said. 'Could you hold this bottle for me and we'll make a start stitching this old girl up.'

I watched as the needles were threaded and David lent over the cow's flank to place the stitches and in about five minutes he was tying off the last one and trimming off the excess thread with a pair of scissors.

'There we go. All finished,' he said, splashing some disinfectant over the wound.

'Was there anything we should have done to avoid the cows getting blown?' I asked.

He thought about it as he packed up his bag. 'It's a job to say but it is well documented that lush grass leys with a high proportion of clover can cause cows to become bloated. You see, normally, the gas produced in the rumen is belched out – the cows are doing it all the time at a rate of about two litres a minute, would you believe. At the top of the rumen there is a sensor which recognises the gas and allows the cow to belch. The problem comes when the gas is held in a froth which the sensor doesn't recognise and won't allow it to be belched out.'

'And that leads to a build-up of the gas and the problems we've had today,' I said.

'Correct, but as you see, it's not all cows which are affected but I think the way to approach it is to fence off a small area – no bigger than an acre for this number of cows – and let them graze that down first before giving them anymore. Spoon feed them for a while and keep a close eye on them and always have the trocar cannula to hand.'

David gave his hands a wipe and climbed into his car. 'Good to meet you John and good luck with the rest of the year,' he said as he drove off towards the gate.

I waved and headed over to where Harry had left the Land Rover and couldn't avoid seeing the two dead cows on the way. Harry was on his way back from Badger Close when I stopped beside him.

'You'd better leave the fence wire where it is for a day or two,' he said. 'Instead, we'll slip into town and pick up some electric fencing so we can hold the cows on a smaller area of the field, moving a few yards every day.'

He opened the passenger door and climbed in. 'These things happen, boy,' he said.

**

Before we left for town, Harry made a call to the hunt kennels and asked them to come and pick up the two cows – it was a service they offered in return for the opportunity to feed the meat to their hounds. To me, it sounded like a pretty awful business but I accepted there had to be some means of disposing of carcasses.

'Right then, boy. Let's go and see if we can pick up some electric fencing. You drive and I'll keep my eyes shut.' The cup of tea provided by Alice before we left seemed to have revived his spirits.

'I'd prefer it if you could keep them open. I haven't a clue where the dealer is.'

'Oh, you'll be alright, boy. Just keep following the signs for the cattle market. They have premises just across the road from it.'

Singleton Jones Ltd occupied a large site at the bottom of Bridge Street and, as Harry had said, was across the road from the cattle market which was held on Wednesdays and Saturdays. Its frontage was mainly glass behind which were tractors, ploughs and what must have been a full range of the latest agricultural machinery. I couldn't wait to get closer.

Harry led the way through the doors and we walked up between the machines to the counter at the other end of the display area.

'Good morning, Chris,' he said to a man wearing brown overalls. 'And how are you today?'

'Fine thanks, Harry.' The man spread his arms along the counter and drummed his fingers. 'What can I do for you today?'

'We're here to pick up some electric fencing gear – wire, stakes, and the all the gubbins that works it.'

Chris pulled a pencil from behind his ear and extracted a notepad from his pocket. 'How much wire do you want?'

Harry turned to me. 'How far do you think it is across that field, boy? I didn't think to step it out.'

I thought about it and tried to visualise the distance. 'It has to be about three hundred yards,' I said.

Harry scratched his ear. 'Alright, we'll go for that.' He turned back to Chris. 'Give us three hundred yards,' he said.

'It only comes in two hundred-yard lengths, so I'll give you a couple of rolls. How many stakes will you need, most people place them at about twenty yards but if the cows are pushing you might need to place them a bit closer, what do you think?'

'We'll do every twenty yards so what's that?'

'Fifteen,' I said.

'Really? That doesn't sound enough. Let's make it twenty stakes.'

'You'll need the two end strainers to keep it taught, unless you have a post to tie the wire to.'

Harry was getting impatient. 'Alright add in two end strainers. But what about the box of tricks which powers it?'

Chris finished his list, slipped the pencil back behind his ear and leaned over the counter pointing to some electric fencing units leaning against the wall.

'If you go over there and have a look at what we have, I'll get your wire and stakes collected up,' he said.

We wandered over to the fencers and looked at what was on offer and to be fair, they were all very much of a likeness.

By the time we had made a choice Chris had another customer to serve and Harry and I stood and waited at the end of the counter, checking over the model we had selected. 'These two leads must go to the battery,' he said. 'Like that battery over there. Just slide it this way and we'll give it a test.'

I did as he asked and watched him clip the leads onto the battery's terminals and then push the wire, which would have been attached to the fence, under the long brass ruler running the length of the counter.

Chris had adopted his authoritative, spread-hand stance which placed both of his hands firmly on the brass ruler. Meanwhile, his customer was counting out some hay tedding tines, a few of which, I noticed with some alarm, were also touching the ruler.

'Switch her on, boy,' Harry whispered.

'Are you sure?'

'Yes, yes boy. Do it now.'

The result was amazing. Chris jolted and his hands shot forwards and struck the customer with such force he toppled over backwards, taking a display of screws with him while the tines, which had been thrown in the air, clattered down around him.

'I suppose you think that's funny,' Chris said, after he had pulled the lead away from the brass ruler and held it up for all to see.

Harry did his best to reply but was still fighting off a fit of giggles which brought tears pouring down his face. It was an infectious laugh and I couldn't help joining in.

'Dear oh dear,' Harry said at last, mopping his face with a handkerchief. 'I don't know what to say. Come on, boy. Let's help the man to his feet.'

***

'Well, I think we chose the most powerful one they had,' Harry said, as we drove out of the carpark.

'It certainly looked like it. Do you think you really will be hearing from that customer's solicitor?'

'Shouldn't think so. Anyway, it was you who switched it on.'

'Thanks, Harry.'

We drove home and as we left the outskirts of the town, the rain began to fall; not much to start with but within a few minutes it was a deluge which hammered down on the Land Rover's metal roof and made conversation next to impossible.

Harry reached for the windscreen wiper switch seeking out a faster speed but there wasn't one and what with the rubber on the wipers about perished and an annoying wad of straw trapped underneath one of them, visibility was not good.

'I should find somewhere to pull over, boy,' Harry shouted.

A good suggestion but a bit of a non-starter bearing in mind it was next to impossible to see the side of the road, let alone anything that looked like a layby. We motored on, the water laying inches deep over the road. And then, just as it had started, the rain stopped and the sun came out.

'The sun shines on the good people of this world and rolls thunder and lightning over those who wander off the path of righteousness,' Harry said. 'Someone up there just made a big mistake.'

'I don't know but I would think it was more of a split decision.'

'Yeah, well they put it right in the end.'

Chapter fifteen

Tupping the ewes

'It's time to put the tups in with the ewes,' announced Harry at breakfast.

'When will they start lambing,' I asked.

'Probably when it's the wettest and coldest few weeks in March, if the last few years are anything to go by.'

We'd had this conversation before; Harry was convinced he was jinxed when it came to suffering spells of cold wet weather when he was lambing. He had even tried changing the dates when he put the tups in but to no avail; the cold wet weather always arrived at the wrong time.

'Well, what's the date today?' I asked.

Harry grabbed the newspaper and checked the date. 'Today is the eleventh of October which means we should start lambing about the second week in March. The gestation period for sheep and goats is usually put at one hundred and forty-seven days, which is about five months, give or take a few days.'

'I don't suppose they do long range weather forecasting?'

'Not that far ahead and anyway, I know what it's going to be like; wet cold and windy.'

There wasn't a lot more to be said on the subject. We would have to wait until March to see if Harry's prediction was right.

'More tea, anyone?' asked Alice.

'Why not?' Harry said. 'We've a lot of walking and running around to do today.'

I looked up from the paper to see Harry grinning at me. 'I'll have another cup please, Alice.'

Out in the yard we loaded the Land Rover with crooks and a few bags of ground barley, which made sense but I was lost when it came to explaining why Harry was also taking several pots of paint. We then hooked the horsebox onto the back and we were ready to set off down the track.

After I had closed the gate at the top of the yard, I climbed into the passenger seat and put my arm around Ross who sat in the middle seat with his big tongue hanging out, dripping saliva all over the place and not smelling very sweet.

'How many ewes are there to lamb?' I asked, as we rattled and rocked our way along the track.

'Altogether, there are about two hundred and fifty,' Harry said. 'Last week I spent a couple of days trimming their back ends in preparation for tupping, and I've also wormed them and they're now getting a small amount of ground barley to ensure they are in top condition when the tups are put in.'

'So how many tups do there need to be?'

'That's a good question, boy. Most would reckon to use a tup for every fifty ewes, or possibly less but there are those who say that if a tup is fit, active, mobile and fertile, he should manage to serve one hundred ewes. But I think that's a bit risky because if all the ewes come in season at about the same time he could soon be totally knackered, rogered to a standstill and lying down in the corner of the field trying to catch his breath with half the flock standing around him.

'The point is, boy, that successful tupping is essential – no lambs and you've kept a flock of ewes for a year with no return.'

'So what do you do, then?'

'I usually split the flock into three groups – which is what we're going to do now -and put three tups in with each lot and swap the tups around every seventeen days, that's the interval when the ewes come into season. If we do that, any failings in a tup will hopefully be overcome by putting a fresh one in with a group.'

We had come to the end of the track and were now driving down Brier Hill towards the bridge that crossed the brook into the large grass field beyond.

'Got the subsidy man out a few years back to see if I was eligible for a hill subsidy,' Harry said as we bumped our way down.

'Any good?'

'No, he wasn't having it. He said it wasn't exactly Snowden or Ben Nevis, which I had to agree with, but it was still a hill none-the-less. And then he told me he'd seen bigger hills in the Fens and I was wasting his time, so I dropped him off at the bottom and told him to walk back.'

'Did he change his mind?'

'No but he was puffing well by the time he got to the top.'

We crossed the bridge which was constructed from old railway sleepers and drew to a halt about fifty yards into the field. The sound of the Land Rover brought the ewes to us and it wasn't long before there were over two hundred of them milling around.

'What we need to do is to take about a hundred and fifty out of these and we'll take them over to Long Field and leave another eighty there and the rest can stay in Brier Hill,' explained Harry. 'So if you stand by the gate and count them as they go through, you can shut it when you get to a hundred and fifty. Don't have the gate too wide open or you'll never be able to count them. Are you ready?'

I took up my position by the gate, opened it as wide as I dared and waited. Harry had Ross out and he was rounding the sheep up and driving them in my direction, a wall of wool heading straight for me. The first ones arrived and, pushed on by those behind, began to cross the bridge. And I tried to count them but soon lost the plot as they surged across in front of me in a solid uncountable block.

'Close the gate more,' Harry bellowed. 'Do you have enough, yet?'

I didn't know. There was no way I could know but I thought it best to close the gate and take stock. And when I managed to stem the flow and pull the gate to, I looked to see how many were left in the field and I think I counted six, but there may have been a couple more I couldn't see behind the horsebox.

'They just came through too fast,' I said.

'If we leave them like that this group will have more tups than ewes,' Harry said. 'And then there will be some awful squabbles going on. Let's see if we can get eighty of them back in this field.'

Harry went off with Ross to round up the sheep and start driving them towards me again. This time I only opened the gate a foot or two and for a start, all was going well. I had just about reached thirty something when the gate gave in to the pressure and fell off its hinges. And then all the sheep piled through across the bridge back into the field, again.

'You're not having a lot of luck, are you boy,' Harry said, as he did his best to lift the gate back onto its hinges. 'Tell you what, I'll look after the gate and do the counting and you have a turn at driving them towards me.'

'Will Ross know what to do?'

'I should think so, he's just done it two times. If he gets too close and pushy tell him to lie down. All set?'

I went off with Ross to round up the sheep again and he soon twigged what was required. And very soon after that they were heading towards Harry at a steady trot which, as they closed in, became a flat-out gallop.

'Don't let him push them too hard, boy,' Harry said.

But Ross was out to impress and came up behind any stragglers and sent them off into the crowd with a growl.

'Call the dog off,' Harry cried as several tons of mutton arrived at the bridge travelling at a speed.

Harry did his best to hold everything together but it was an impossible task and, bit by bit, he was forced backwards towards the edge. 'For pity's sake boy,' were probably the last few words I heard before there was a tremendous splash as Harry was forced off the bridge into the brook.

I called Ross over to me and told him we were now both in deep-mire trouble and even the dog's jaw dropped when he caught sight of Harry approaching, wringing out his cap and making a sort of squelching noise as he walked.

Well, that's three goes we've had,' he said, turning his attention to squeezing the water out of his jacket cuffs. 'How many have we got in this field now?'

There wasn't many. 'I don't know, probably a few.'

'Don't tell me there are too many to count?'

'No, but one may be hiding behind the Land Rover.'

Harry drew breath and took stock of the situation. 'Look, it can't be that difficult to split off eighty sodding sheep from a bunch of two hundred and fifty, can it?'

I didn't know whether he was talking to me or the dog, so I remained silent.

'Let's give it another go,' he said.

'How about if we try and split about two thirds of them off before they get to the bridge?' I said.

'If you think it will work, give it a go.'

I could sense Harry beginning to despair. This should have been a ten-minute job and it was taking half a morning.

'Right then, let's gather them up and see what we can do.'

Harry placed Ross near the bridge and told him to lie down and stay. Which he did while I took the position about halfway between the Land Rover and the bridge, ready to dive in to create the split, and Harry stood in front of them and gradually teased them towards the bridge.

As they filtered past me I tried to estimate what two thirds of them would look like and when I reached that point I ran into them to split them, calling Ross away to give me a hand. It wasn't perfect but I think it worked as well as it could. Those that had been turned towards the bridge continued to run that way and the others in the smaller group dallied about for a few moments before heading off the other way.

'We've cracked it,' Harry said as he closed the gate. 'All we need to do now is take half of these down to Long Field and the job is done.'

'And then we need to sort out the tups,' I added.

'I know, but I thought I'd go and get a change of clothes before we did that.'

***

We didn't make it down to the field again until after lunch. Alice, appalled at Harry's misfortune of being pushed off the bridge into the brook, insisted he had a hot bath as well as a change of clothing. And while he was doing that, she prepared a bowl of hot soup and looked out a hand-knitted scarf to keep his chest warm.

As luck would have it, Ronny made an appearance as we were driving up the yard.

'Ronny,' Harry said, as he slowed to a stop. 'How good to see you. Are you available or are you on a business lunch and need to be back for a crisis meeting with the CEO?'

'Cut the crap, Harry. I just wondered whether you could do with a hand with anything.'

'You'd better jump in the back then.'

Ronny was still clambering over the tailgate when Harry let the clutch in and powered the Land Rover out of the yard. 'Hang on Ron,' he shouted. 'And mind what you sit on.'

We drove down Brier Hill and Ronny jumped out to open the gate so we could cross the bridge. And then, with Ronny standing on the metal light guards and hanging onto the roof we scorched across the largest grass field on the farm to the pens at the far end.

'Right,' Harry said as he stepped out. 'What we need to do is take three tups out to each of the groups of sheep. But first we have to put some marker paint on their chests.'

I looked at him. 'We'll do what?'

'Put some marker paint on their chests,' Harry said. 'Every time they serve a ewe he smears some of the paint on to the back of the ewe so, just by looking at the flock, we can see how many have been served and when they were served.'

'Oh, right,' I said. 'Let's do that then.'

Harry reached into the back of the Land Rover and brought out a bucket. 'What we need to do is mix up some powder with this oil into a stiff paint that will last for a few days,' he said, holding up a bottle of vegetable oil.' He reached over the tailgate and brought out a carton of 'Raddle Powder'.

'Hey, Ronny, come over here and be useful.'

Ronny, who at that moment was blissfully enjoying one of his hand-rolled cigarettes reluctantly clipped the end of it and strolled over. 'Do you want me to mix it, Harry?' he asked, smoke still pouring out of his mouth and one nostril.

'Yes, you do that while we push three of the tups into the back of the box.'

'These are Suffolks,' Harry said. 'You can tell by the black faces and long Roman noses. What do you reckon to them?'

I looked at their tight coats and broad backs and could tell Harry had spent a lot of time ensuring they were in peak condition. 'They look very good.'

'I've kept them well away from the ewes for a few weeks to avoid any accidents, and they've been having some supplementary feed each day. I reckon they look pretty good too. Let's pick three out for Long Field.'

It's not until you get close to a healthy, Suffolk ram whose thoughts were now turning to mating with every ewe in the county and beyond, just how strong and stubborn they can be. With the tailboard down, we pushed and cajoled three of the tups into the box and then lifted and closed the door.

'How's that paint coming on?' Harry asked.

I looked across to where Ronny was kneeling on the ground, furiously mixing a thick, glutinous mass of yellow paint. 'Why have yellow – I'd have thought a red or a blue would have been more noticeable?' I asked.

'You're right but we start with a light colour so if a ewe doesn't take on the first service you can mark her with a darker colour on the second, rather than the other way around which would be more difficult to see,' Harry explained.

Ronny stood up and carried the paint over to where we were standing by the small side door into the box. 'Is it thick enough?' he asked.

'Yes, that's fine Ron, if we had fifty tups to do and the side of a house. Have you got the smearer – the wooden paddle to smear it on with?'

'It's in there. That's what I've been using to mix it up with.'

Harry looked into the paint and saw the top inch of the paddle sticking out. 'Right then, we'll hold the tups and you can smear the paint on,' he said.

We climbed the box and Harry grabbed one of the tups around the neck and shoulders and gently turned him until he was sitting on his bottom, his chest exposed and ready to be painted.

'Alright, Ron. Let's do it.'

Ron dipped the paddle in the pot and brought it over

to the tup Harry was holding. In one deft movement he spread a thick layer of yellow paint over the tup's testicles and before Harry could say anything, continued north, applying the paint across his stomach.

'What on earth are you doing?' asked Harry incredulously, looking down at Ronny's handiwork. 'Why are you putting it there?'

Ronny looked at him. 'Well that's the bit he uses, isn't it?'

'Oh, for goodness sake, Ronny. It might be the bit he uses but it's not the bit that… Look, just give me the paddle and I'll do it.'

And that was the start of it. Slowly at first but gaining momentum by the minute, the paint spread from Ronny's hands to his clothes, to his hair, to the sides of the box and then outside to the gate latches, it was unstoppable.

Leaving instructions for Ronny to stand still and not touch anything, Harry and I took the first three tups down to Long Field and by the time we opened the door to let them out they only had to lean on a ewe to mark it, let alone serve it.

'Oh well, we might as well carry on now we've started,' Harry said. 'Let's do the next three before we put them in the box.'

But the damage had been done. Despite Harry's attempts at staying clean, the yellow oily paint moved onto his jacket, trousers and then to the hand-knitted scarf Alice had been so keen for him to wear.

I thought I was doing rather well until Harry pointed out it was across the back of my coat where I had leaned against a pen rail. By the time we set about applying the paint to the last three tups Ronny had stopped caring and Harry wasn't far off doing the same.

'How come you've avoided the worst of it?' Harry asked.

'I don't know, I guess I'm just lucky,' I told him.

On the drive home I had the front of the Land Rover

to myself with only Ross to keep me company. Harry and Ronny were confined in the horsebox and when I let them out in the farm yard they looked as if they had contracted some dreadful disease.

'Hope you're not planning on going out tonight, Ronny. Because no one will have to look too hard to discover just where you've been, who you've been with and a closer look will probably reveal what you were doing as well,' I said.

Ronny loped off down to the village while I set off to fetch the cows in. I didn't want to be about when Alice caught sight of Harry and what remained of the hand knitted scarf.

Chapter sixteen

Lifting fodder beet

November, and I was now in my fifth month at Church Farm and it had been an enlightening experience. I think, by now, I had realised that Harry was not the most progressive of farmers; he had been brought up in a time when to spread the risk of volatile market prices or the effect of poor weather, his income was derived from having numerous projects on the go at the same time. Should one fail due to poor weather, low market prices or for any other reason, there was another one which could flourish.

Hens, milk, beef, sheep and pigs just about covered the livestock side of the job while barley, grass along with crops of kale, Lucerne, fodder beet and the odd row of potatoes was a fair spread on the arable side.

The farming press was increasingly reporting on farmers who had moved away from this style of farming and had chosen to specialise. There were those who were now majoring in larger dairy units as there were those who had sold all their livestock and had embarked on growing continuous cereals.

Little did they know the problems they were stacking up for the years to come; uncontrollable grass weeds, fungal diseases, impaired soil structure and soil health, and an increasing reliance on chemical pesticides, to name just a few.

Harry's mixed farming approach was a fail-safe way of farming that ensured that whatever happened, deluge or drought, there would be some revenue from the business. Not an enormous income but a living income and, importantly, one which also ensured land was retained in a good working condition.

Working on a mixed farm was also good for me in that I had a taste of so many different farming systems which was to be a valuable education for the years to come.

But all that was in the future and I will always wonder if the industry, knowing what it does now and could turn the clock back, would have embarked on the route it did or would it have maintained a more mixed approach with all the benefits it has to offer.

***

I didn't recognise the car that drove into the yard this morning as I prepared to take the last three churns of milk down to the ramp. It was a dark red Mini Cooper driven by a middle-aged man wearing a light brown suit. I watched him as he headed down the yard to the house and heard the knock on the door.

By the time I had returned to the dairy, the man was standing outside the house talking to Harry who waved me over to join them.

'This is Mr Jackson, he works for the local fire prevention and control company which provides a range of hand-held extinguishers.'

I smiled at him and he nodded his head.

'He says he's had a look round and we should have fire extinguishers at key points around the buildings.'

'That's right,' interrupted Mr Jackson. 'We can supply extinguishers for a wide range of different fires – diesel fires, wood fires, oil fires and fires caused by electrical problems and several more besides.'

'Anyway,' Harry continued. 'I've decided to give Mr

Jackson a chance of supplying us with an extinguisher if he wouldn't mind giving us a demonstration.'

Mr Jackson was now nodding his head enthusiastically with some vigour and I was beginning to wonder if he had a muscular disorder which prevented his head from staying still.

'Just put together a few things we can set fire to and I'll show you what our extinguishers can do,' he said.

'Well, we haven't the time to do it today but perhaps you could call back on Tuesday afternoon next week,' Harry said. 'We should have something ready for you or we'll soon find something to burn, I'm sure.'

'Oh, that will be fine. I look forward to that.' And with that, Mr Jackson walked back to his car and drove out of the yard, his head, I noticed, still nodding.

Harry was looking pleased with himself as we walked into the kitchen. I waited for him to finish washing his hands before I asked him what was that all about. Normally when a company representative calls without an appointment they were sent on their way with a few choice words ringing in their ears.

'What was what all about?' he said.

'Mr Jackson and the fire extinguishers.'

'Oh him; I just thought we should all become a little more safety conscious and the idea of having a few fire extinguishers could be prudent, what with Ronny and his rollups. We might get a reduction on the insurance too.'

There was that look on Harry's face and I knew he was stalling, so I just smiled. I would find out soon enough, Tuesday afternoon was only a few days away.

I worked my way through the boiled bacon slices and read the newspaper – unemployment had just topped one million people, was the headline which was a sobering thought.

'We'll start lifting the fodder beet today,' Harry said.

I looked up and tried to make sense of what he was saying. It was the first time I had heard of any fodder beet, whatever that was, and even less why we needed to lift it.

'Fodder beet,' he repeated. 'We grow it to feed to the sheep and beef cattle during the winter and they do very well on it.'

'Where about is it growing?'

'There's about eight acres of it at the bottom of Samuels Lane.'

There are some parts of this farm I still don't know about, it seems. 'So, what do we need to lift the fodder beet?'

'A knife to cut the top growth off as you pull it out of the ground, a trailer and a beet fork to load the beet onto the trailer,' Harry said. 'And if you can find Ronny, we'll take him too.'

'And if you think you're going to take any of my knives from here, you are going to have to think again,' Alice intervened.

I looked at Harry. 'They'll be alright and we'll bring them back,' he said.

'That's what you said last year and every year before it, but they didn't come back and nor will these. And I'm fed up getting gift-wrapped carving knives for Christmas too.'

Now I thought that was a pretty convincing argument and if it had been down to me, I would have conceded defeat.

'If that's the case, I don't suppose you will be interested in having these, then,' Harry said, moving his chair back so he could slide the table draw out and reach in to retrieve a couple of fine looking knives with ivory handles and fearfully sharp stainless-steel blades.

'Oh Harry, what are you up to now?' Alice said. 'Pass them down here and let me have a look at them.'

Harry did as he was asked and Alice picked them up and inspected them. 'These are too good for beet lifting,' she said. 'They're almost too good for slicing boiled bacon.'

And there's me thinking that most knives were too

good for slicing boiled bacon.

'Alright,' she said at last. 'I'll do you a swap. You can take the calving knife and the bread knife and I'll have these. Now, more tea anyone? Oh, and there's a letter from Elizabeth for you, John. I've put it in your room.'

***

I hooked the tractor onto a two-wheel trailer and, with two knives and a sharpening stone wrapped in a sack and two beet forks on board, I set off down to Samuels Lane. Harry said he would meet me down there.

There was a keen wind blowing when I arrived, one I hadn't noticed when I was milking. But now it had a penetrating feel about it and I pulled the edges of my jacket together so they overlapped and tied a length of bale string around my waste. It looked as if it was going to be a testing sort of day.

Harry rolled into the field and climbed out of the Land Rover. 'Bloody hell, boy, the wind cuts in a bit. It's us thin ones that tend to really feel the cold.'

I looked at him and while I wouldn't say he was fat – an active farm life does not allow that – he was not exactly thin either. He pulled a length of bale string out of his pocket and tied it around his waist.

'My father used to say that a cord around a waist was as good as wearing an extra coat,' he said.

There didn't seem to be anything to add to that so I reached into the trailer for the knives and the beet fork – a fork which had about a dozen, close spaced tines with small balls at the end of them to prevent the tines damaging the beet.

'We won't be needing the fork for a while,' Harry said. 'The first task is to lift the headland rows so we can get the trailer into the field without running on any of the beet. We'll each take two rows and put the beet into piles as we go. Then they can be loaded onto the trailer. All clear?'

It wasn't clear at all but I felt it was not going to be too difficult to achieve. I stood, knife in hand and let Harry make a start. Bending down, he took hold of the green leaves with his left hand and pulled the beet out of the ground and then, with a gentle swing towards the knife cut the tops off. The beet, which was about the size of a football, carried on to where a pile was to be started and he let the tops fall onto the ground.

'It's all in the swing,' he said. 'Get that right and the beet goes towards the pile while you let the tops fall onto the ground. But you have to be careful; have the knife blade too high and it will scythe into you knuckles.' He pointed to the scars he had on his left hand. 'Too low and you'll just stab the beet and achieve nothing.'

I had a go and it wasn't easy. The best I could do was to hold the beet steady when I had pulled it from the ground and then saw away with the knife until the top came off and the beet fell to the ground.

'You'll get it, boy. It's just a matter of practice. Work on creating a smooth lift, swing and a slanting cut, all in one sweet movement,' he said. 'And don't forget to keep a check on how many fingers you still have.'

From that point on my back became stiffer, my hands became colder and the knife blunter. It seemed to take an eternity to make one circuit of the field.

'If we go round the other way we can throw the beet on to the piles we've already started,' Harry said. 'You're getting better but just try and slice as close to the crown of the beet as you can. We don't want any green in the clamp if we can help it.'

I hadn't bothered to straighten up. I remained bent double and just grunted a reply before shuffling round and beginning another row of fodder beet. But before I did, Harry asked if I wanted my knife sharpening.

It was a chance to take a short break so I hobbled over to the Land Rover and slowly pulled myself upright as Harry worked the blade of the knife across the sharpening stone.

'There, that should get you going at a much faster rate,'

he said. 'But mind your fingers.'

I straddled the row, adopted the position and started pulling beet, trying to mimic the smooth effortless swing and cut technique Harry had mastered. Sometimes I made it and others were a complete disaster as I just sawed away at the tops. It seemed I needed to move the knife across the tops as I swung into it and once I had realised that, I was firing on all cylinders.

But then I became a little over confident and on one swing I felt the blade graze across my left knuckle. It was a timely warning and it is one which I should have heeded. Twelve beets later and I was bleeding, the blade had gashed straight into the flesh just above the knuckle on my index finger.

'And it's first blood to John,' announced Harry. 'Let's have a look at it boy and see if we need to take it off at the nearest joint or give the undertaker a call. No point messing about.'

I removed the handkerchief covering my wound and Harry had a look. 'Just a scratch, boy,' he said. 'You'll live.'

And with that assessment, I re-wrapped the handkerchief around my finger and carried on pulling, swinging and cutting. By lunch time we had just about finished the headlands and there was now room for the tractor and trailer to do a tour of the field so that the piles of beet we had made could be forked into it.

When we made it back to the farm and into the kitchen, I let the water pour over my cut to clean it and then, at Alice's suggestion, held it up in the air to help stop it bleeding. By the time it had stopped she had found the first aid box and a suitably sized plaster to cover the gash.

'What you need is a reinforced glove, like they wear in the butchers when they're carving meat up,' she said. 'I wonder where they get them from. Do you know, Harry?'

'No idea. Probably the best thing to do is to pop up the butchers and see if they'll let us have one, a left hand one. Failing that, a good dunk in iodine should do the trick.'

'Well you have your lunch and I'll go and see,' Alice said. 'I need to pick up next week's bacon joint anyway.'

The thick meaty stew Alice had prepared went down well, as did the apple crumble and custard and I was beginning to think I'd never be able to work doubled up all afternoon with that lot inside me.

By the time we reached the tea course, Alice was back and she had some good news. 'They only had two sizes, small and large, so I brought one of each. And it's a good job you're right handed because they don't have any right-hand gloves.' She reached into her bag and pulled them out.

'They certainly feel tough,' I said, feeling the chainmail covering which was designed to prevent soft flesh and sharp knives coming into contact. The small one was too small and the large one was a comfortable, generous size. 'I'll have the large one, thanks Alice.'

Back in the field we began to fork the lifted beet into the trailer and it was amazing how quickly the trailer filled up before we had made it half way round. 'Time to fetch another trailer, boy,' Harry said. 'Bring the one with the high sides. It holds more than the others.'

'Where do you want me to drop this one?'

'The rick yard will do for now.'

Chapter seventeen

The impossible bonfire

Fodder beet lifting dominated the next five days – days which were hard and gruelling. The beet were stored on the ground under the eaves of the large stone barn and when the last load had been forked off, we covered them with straw to keep the worst of the frost off but to also allow some ventilation. Harry pointed out that they could heat up without it and start to rot.

With the beet safely harvested Harry suddenly seemed keen to tidy the farm up and insisted I spent a day taking all the rubbish out into the middle of the paddock.

'I want everything that can burn out there,' he said. 'And that includes old tyres, sacks with holes in, paper bags, the odd railway sleeper, rotten wooden doors, gate posts and, before you start, put a good layer of dry straw in the base.'

'Don't tell me, today's the day Mr Jackson and his fire extinguishers are due to arrive.'

'That's right, boy. And if it had escaped your notice, today is the fifth of November. I thought we'd have a bit of a do with a few fireworks and some hotdogs.'

'Now that sounds good,' I said.

By lunch time the bonfire in the paddock had grown into something quite enormous. I just carried on building it with everything I could find and, bearing in mind there was the best part of a century of accumulated rubbish to choose from, finding sufficient fuel for this monster bonfire was not particularly difficult.

'I think that might just about be enough,' said Harry as I threw the last piece of rotten door up onto the pile. 'You've done a good job. Now we need to fill a few tins with diesel and give it all a good drenching.'

Alice had been busy in the kitchen cooking bread rolls, sausages, and mountains of other nibbles which were now temptingly laid out in trays that covered every available surface.

'You can just try one,' she said, as I came in to get the bucket of hot water I used to wash the cows' udders before they were milked. And then she asked me if I knew where Harry was.

'No, I don't. I think he said he was going into town to get some fireworks at some stage, but I'm not sure.'

'Well if you see him before I do, tell him Mr Jackson rang to say he was going to be a little later than he expected. He thought he would be here about half past six.'

'No worry, I'll tell him.'

It's strange how cows can sense there's something going on. I mean, I know they had just walked past a bonfire that was as high as a house, and more, but that in itself wasn't what was disturbing them. I held out the usual handfuls of ground barley for some of the girls to get their tongues round but today they were not interested. Instead they just looked at me.

And when I had milked Horns, the last cow, I looked around the collecting yard and noticed it was covered in slurry, a sure sign something was upsetting them. I was beginning to have bad vibes about the bonfire and if Harry was planning on letting off a shed full of fireworks, that could really upset the girls.

'Do you think we could put the cows in the orchard tonight?' I asked him when he arrived back from town.

'Why's that, boy?'

'Well, with all the fireworks going off tonight and one thing and another, I thought they might be more settled in there with a few bales of hay to chew through and Pedro to keep them company.'

Harry thought about it. 'You don't think putting them in the orchard would upset them anyway?'

'Not if they had some hay and we could always keep an eye on them.'

'Alright. I'll bring some bales of hay round and then we'll set about putting them in there. Has anyone seen Mr Jackson yet?'

'Alice said he'd called to say he wasn't going to make it here until half past six.'

Harry looked at his watch. 'Well I hope the little bugger turn's up after all the work we've done for him.'

Mr Jackson and his dark red Mini Cooper drove into the yard fifteen minutes later and walked down to the house. We had put the cows in the orchard and left them to pick their way through a generous amount of hay which I hoped would keep them settled.

'Come in, Mr Jackson,' said Alice. 'I think we're all ready for you.'

Sitting at the table with a cup of tea, I tried to contain a smirk and received a reprimanding stare for Harry.

'Yes, come in Mr Jackson,' he said. 'Sit yourself down and have a cup of tea.'

His head was already nodding. 'I'm really sorry for being late. It's been one of those days when everything seemed to go wrong.'

'Yes, well we all get them,' said Alice passing over a cup of tea to him.

'I was just wondering if you thought it would be too late for a demonstration seeing as its now dark.'

'No, don't you worry about that. It's probably the best time of the day now we've finished milking and all the other jobs we have to do.'

'Oh right,' Mr Jackson said.

Just then the door burst open and in trooped Rose Hill Farm and Elizabeth was with them.

'Hello everyone,' said Kate. 'We've left the truck in the street and walked up.' She looked around the table. 'Hi John, you alright?'

'Yes, thank you, Kate. Good to see you again.' My eyes turned to Elizabeth and she returned the stare and smiled. 'Does anyone want to sit down,' I said, standing up. But I don't think anyone heard me, such was the level of babble going on.

Out in the yard I looked up at the sky and saw that the clouds had disappeared, and the moon and stars were shining down on what was going to be a frosty night.

'You got my letters then,' said Elizabeth.

'Yes, and I hope you received mine?'

'Of course I did and they were wonderful.'

I took her hand and pulled her to me. 'I've missed you so much,' was all I could say before her lips met mine. It was a kiss to make up for all the weeks when she had been away at university.

There was some activity down at the house as everyone came out and started walking up the yard. 'I'll take the Land Rover with Mr Jackson and his extinguishers,' I heard Harry say. So as everyone walked by, Elizabeth and I tagged on behind.

Out in the middle of the paddock, Harry had parked so the headlights shone onto the bonfire and as we approached it I could see him emptying a tin full of petrol. We all assembled at a safe distance.

'Well this is the moment, Mr Jackson,' Harry said. 'You have your extinguisher and we have our fire.'

I looked at Mr Jackson holding his extinguisher and then at the bonfire we had built, and felt he was probably on a bit of a loser. I also noticed his head had stopped nodding.

'What I suggest, Mr Jackson, is you stand well back while I light this trail of petrol and then wait a little while for the fire to establish itself before you put it out. How does that sound?'

Pretty impossible, I thought but he seemed game enough to have a try. I gave Elizabeth's hand a squeeze as Harry struck a match and dropped into the petrol which instantly flared and headed for the bonfire. There was a pause when it arrived but suddenly the straw was alight and then the diesel caught and we all had to take a step back as the whole bonfire quickly became a mass of flames and black acrid smoke.

'Over to you, Mr Jackson,' said Harry.

Mr Jackson did not hesitate and raised his coat collar, pulled the pin out of the extinguisher and with the water spraying in front of him stepped closer to the fire, his form silhouetted in the bright flames. It was not long before he retreated and grabbed another extinguisher and rushed forward again.

After emptying five extinguishers he tried a different approach and slid forward on his front towards the fire but with no luck he retreated and then started to move around the fire darting in and out to apply quick bursts of water. But it was a lost cause. Very soon all his extinguishers were empty and he conceded defeat. Far from reducing the amount of flame, the ferocity of the conflagration had continued to increase.

'I think the tyres are burning,' I said to Elizabeth. 'That's what the smell is.'

'I thought it was the boiled bacon,' she replied.

There was nothing more for Mr Jackson to do. He had tried and he had failed, and as he collected up his empties Harry put his arm around his shoulders. 'You're not going, are you?' he asked.

'Well, there's not a lot more I can do.'

'Stay a while and enjoy the evening. I'm just about to set off the fireworks and Alice has spent all day cooking sausages and things. We've even got some beer and don't worry about the fire, it will go out when it's ready.'

'In about a week's time, I would think,' Mr Jackson said.

Elizabeth and I each grabbed a hot dog and a bottle of beer and slunk off to a quiet corner of the paddock and settled down to watch the fireworks. Even though we were over a hundred feet away, we could still feel the heat of the fire.

Harry had returned from town with a large box crammed full of fireworks and he worked his way through them – rockets, jumping jacks, penny bangers – he had them all, and when they had all gone he reached into the Land Rover and fetched out a string of pigeon scarers – giant bangers attached at intervals along a rope. As the rope smouldered slowly along its length, it set fire to the bangers which exploded with a deafening explosion, not that Harry waited for the rope to burn.

'I think we should go and check on the cows,' I said. 'I would hate to think they're all getting stressed out with the noise and everything.'

Elizabeth rested her head on my shoulder. 'That's what I like about you, John. You always put the cows first.'

'Before what?'

'Before this,' she said, reaching out for me.

Chapter eighteen

Cutting kale

If I had been surprised by the effort required to harvest fodder beet it was, by comparison, an easier job than cutting kale. Yet another crop I didn't have any knowledge of, Harry had nearly ten acres of kale in a field I didn't even know was part of the farm.

'Jump in and I'll show you where it is,' Harry said one cold December morning when a white covering of frost spread out across the countryside. 'It's a field I rent from Jo Parker, the chap with the giant bale sledge and the dislocated shoulder. It's too far away from his own farm to be of much use to him so I took it on about five years ago.'

We drove along the main road for about half a mile and then turned off through a gateway to be faced by a mass of vegetation in which I thought it was quite possible to get lost in.

'It's tall,' I said.

Harry smiled. 'Kale is a brassica, a member of the cabbage family. This is a variety called Marrow stem which, as you can see, grows really tall and has a tremendous amount of leaf on it. It's also winter hardy which means it will withstand the frost and we can use it as a winter feed for the cows.'

We walked into the crop and gave it a closer look. Everything about this crop was big, its height, the leaves and most impressive of all, the thickness of the stem which, at its base was nearly as thick as your wrist.

'How do you feed it?'

'Well, it has its challenges,' Harry said. 'Some run a tractor across it to flatten a couple of rows at intervals across the field so an electric fence can be used to control how much the cows eat and others choose to cut a quantity, load it on to a trailer and feed it out to the cows back at the farm.'

I had an inkling that the cut and load option was going to be the method employed. There was no way the cows were going to strip graze this field, it was too far away and short of walking down the main road there didn't seem to be a route they could take to get here.

'So, we cut and cart, then,' I said.

'You got it one, boy. The only thing is that kale needs to be cut fresh, it won't keep beyond a day before it wilts and then the cows don't like it.'

'It needs to be cut every day, then. And how much do I need to cut?'

Harry looked out across the field and thought about it. 'We need to fill a trailer and I would think that if you cut and load a couple of rows each day, you'll be about there. We'll have to monitor how much they eat and see if we need to increase or reduce.'

We drove back to the farm and walked down to the house for breakfast. 'You will need to take a sickle with you to cut the kale. Try and cut it about six inches off the ground. Below that, the stem is too woody to be any use. And you'll also need a fork to load the trailer.'

'What sort of fork?' I asked.

'Oh, I should try the four-tine muck fork and see how you get on. I used to find scooping it up in my arms was the best way, providing you have a good coat.'

I washed my hands and sat down wondering how long it would take to cut and load a trailer with kale.

'Have you been given the kale cutting job?' asked Alice.

'Yes, it would seem so,' I said.

'Well, if you take my advice, you'll take a waterproof coat with big collar.'

She looked at me in a knowing sort of way before passing over a cup of tea.

***

I turned into the kale field with some apprehension. This was something new and I hadn't a clue how it was going to work out. I thought it made sense to cut an area I could park the tractor and trailer on before I started cutting rows across the field.

Taking the sickle in hand I bent down beneath the closest kale plant and struck the stem and the next thing that happened was a shower of ice cold water pouring down on me. It trickled down my neck and as I stood up it carried on down my back. Now I knew why Alice said I should take a coat with a big collar.

Making matters worse was that I had actually failed to cut the stem. There was a slight nick and nothing more. I took another swipe at the stem only this time I aimed to cut it at an angle and this seemed to work, it toppled over to my left, helped by a push with my hand. There was nothing for it, other than to carry on cutting.

Feeling increasingly like a wet rag I cleared an area which I hoped would be large enough to manoeuvre the tractor and trailer, and the set off up the rows, cutting four of them at a time and stacking the cut stems on top of each other.

After half an hour, I thought I may have cut enough and went back to the trailer to start loading. But it was deceiving. After I had loaded everything I had cut, I could still see the bottom of the trailer. So much for Harry's suggestion I cut just one row.

Two hours later I was driving back to the farm with a load of kale on board and as I rumbled over the cattle grid at the end of the top road I met up with Harry.

'Looks as if you've a tidy load on there,' he said.

'Should be enough for a couple of days. What we'll do is take it down to where the cows are and you can drive as I fork off about a quarter of it for them to tuck into.'

Harry parked the Land Rover and climbed aboard the tractor with me. 'Bloody hell, boy. You're soaked,' he said, when he saw the back of my jacket. 'You want to take one of the plastic, hooded coats out of the garage.'

The smell and sight of fresh kale coming their way had the cows milling around the gate before we arrived. Harry jumped off the tractor to open it and pushed them out of the way so I could drive through. He then climbed onto the trailer and I drove out to the middle of the field where he started to fork the kale off.

I've never seen the girls so pleased to see something before. They formed a long line and munched into the stems and leaves. I could see it in their eyes, the absolute happiness and pleasure and it was a joy to be part of it.

'That's enough, boy,' Harry said. 'They can have another lot this evening after milking. You had better park the trailer in the rick yard.'

Once I had the trailer parked up I ran down to the house for a change of clothing and tried and failed to avoid Alice who sighed and said she had told me to wear some suitable clothing. I said I would next time.

When I had changed into some dry clothes I met up with Harry in the workshop mending a puncture in one of the horsebox tyres. He had the inner tube out and was just putting some air into it to see if he could find the puncture by holding the tube to his face to feel any escaping air.

'No, it's no use,' he said, having been around the tube a couple of times. 'The hole's too small. We'll have to put it in the trough of water.'

He reconnected the airline to increase the pressure in the tube and then took it over to the trough and plunged it in. And there he spotted a trail of air bubbles coming from a position which was about opposite the valve.

'There it is,' he said. 'The little bugger looks like a nail in the tyre. You feel round inside the tyre to see if you can find it while I get this mended.'

I'd done this before with my bike tyre and I had managed to rip my finger apart on a nail which I scraped over, so I set about the job rather more gently than I think Harry would have. After three careful rounds of the tyre I found it, a nasty spike of metal just poking through the tyre's tread. I was just about to mark it with a piece of chalk when Harry called me over to give him a hand.

'I just wanted to show you how this is done,' he said and went on to explain how the rubber around the puncture was roughed up before the fluid was applied. The patch was placed over the hole and then it was placed between two heating pads so that the rubber was vulcanised to make it stronger and more elastic.

When I saw the vulcaniser I had my doubts it would work. It looked more than old and well past its shelf life. The timing system which controlled the duration of the process seemed to depend on the life of a fuse-like insert designed to melt after a set period of time and switch everything off.

Harry grabbed the handle on the top with both hands and started to wind the two oval-shaped heating pads together with the inner tube and patch pressed between them. 'Alright, boy it's ready. Switch it on.'

The switch was on the wall on the far side of the work bench, so stepping over some plough shares, I leaned across and pulled the switch down. And as I did so there was sort of strangled cry from Harry who then began rocking back and forwards, his face screwed up in a terrifying tangle, an expression I'd never seen before.

Something wasn't right and the obvious action was to switch the machine off. In my haste to achieve this I stumbled over the shares and only just prevented falling onto the bench vice. But eventually I managed to reach up for the switch and push it up.

My timing wasn't perfect, far from it. Harry was on a

backswing as I turned the electricity off and the release of his hands from the wheel was followed by a backward tumble across the workshop floor.

'Bugger that! Did you feel it?' he asked, climbing onto his feet.

'No, I think you had all there was to feel. That machine wants to be taken down the tip and buried. It's lethal. If I hadn't been here you would have been electrocuted.'

Harry was recovering fast. 'If you hadn't been here you couldn't have switched it on and I would have been alright,' he said.

All of which I thought was a little ungrateful seeing as I had pulled him back from the brink, even if he was going backwards at the time.

'Whatever you say, Harry,' I said.

'Let's slip this tyre round to the garage and have them mend it and then we can take the box down to the sheep after lunch. It's time to move the tups round and change the paint colour.'

'Oh no, not all that again,' I said.

'Should be better this time.' He held up his hand and started counting. 'Number one is that I've been feeding the tups every day so they will come up to us without any trouble. Number two is that I've mixed up the paint already. Number three is that I now have a paddle that has a longer handle and number four is Ronny won't be with us. Four good reasons for a smooth and successful operation. What do you say?'

'We'll see.' I put the tyre, the hub and inner tube into the back of the truck and climbed in. The garage, Bill Hargreaves & Son, was down a pot-holed single-track road and was one of the last places you would choose to go for fuel.

But for repairs and spares it was second to none. Peter Hargreaves, who had taken over the business from his father, was a big chap who it was said, could fit tyres with his bare hands and bend metal bars around his waist.

A couple of boots were sticking out from beneath a car Peter was working on when we walked into the workshop.

'Just put it all over by the door and I'll sort it out when I've finished this job,' he said.

That's no good we need it being fixed right now. We've some tups to move,' Harry said. 'What sort of business is it you run around here?'

Ronny pulled himself out from under the vehicle and got to his feet, wiping his hands on a rag. 'It's always the same with you Harry Wilcox. Tomorrow will never do, will it?'

He strolled over to where we had placed everything and picked up the inner tube. 'Well, this is buggered for a start,' he said. 'You've made a right pig's ear of trying to mend this.'

He then grabbed the tyre and felt round the inside of it until he found the nail and then, finding the head of the nail in the tread, reached into his overalls for a pair of plyers and pulled it out. 'I'll get you a new inner tube.'

Less than ten minutes later we were on our way back to the farm with the wheel ready to be put back on the horsebox.

'He's alright is Peter,' Harry said. 'You just need to talk to him right.'

While I put the wheel back on the horsebox, Harry set about modernising the vulcanisation kit with a sledge hammer. And then we stopped for lunch.

Chapter nineteen

Sally

Cutting the kale soon became a routine job for me, one which was hard but all the same, enjoyable as row by row, day by day, the crop was cut and carted out of the field.

To make things easier, I was now working it so the trailer became empty after they had been fed in the morning, which meant I had more time to re-load it after breakfast.

It was also interesting to see the effect the kale had on the milk yield, which at this time of the year, would have been falling as the dependency on conserved feed took the place of grass. But the kale put the brakes on this decline and yields were sustained, if not actually increased.

The kale, though, was not an inexhaustible supply, and after about four weeks, the field was finished and we started using the fodder beet to supplement the bales of hay they received.

At this point, I had no idea about animal nutrition and, I wasn't sure whether Harry had; a lifetime of livestock feeding must have resulted in him knowing, almost instinctively, what the feed value of different products were and how much should be fed.

Generally, though, the cows were milking well and I was proud of the way they all appeared to be relaxed and easy-going. I was, however, becoming increasingly concerned about Sally, the big Friesian. Despite me ensuring she had her rations, she was losing weight and condition and her milk yield had dropped alarmingly over the last few weeks.

Harry dosed her with everything he had available and the vet was called to have a look at her. He gave some anti-biotics and vitamins but I don't think he was too optimistic for her recovery. Every day I was keen to see if she had started to improve but it didn't happen.

After one evening's milking, her condition had deteriorated to the point I decided to keep her in for the night. I thought a warm box and a deep bed of straw would be better for her but when I went to look at her later that night she had gone down and was clearly in some discomfort.

I went and fetched Harry to see what he thought about it, and as I knelt down and stroked Sally's ears he told me he thought she was on her way home.

'Isn't there anything we can do for her?' I asked.

'I don't think so, boy. We've tried our best and now it's probably time to say good-bye.'

'I'll stay with her a bit longer,' I said, as Harry got up to leave.

'That's alright, boy. I'll leave the yard light on for you.'

I don't know how long I stayed with Sally but I talked to her and told her over and over again she was a wonderful girl and I carried on stroking her as her breathing became shallower and more intermittent until she gave a final snort and died.

The cows were still finishing the last of the hay when I left Sally and walked over to them. I couldn't bring myself to go down to the house, it was too soon. I just wanted to be with the girls for a few minutes and spend a short while hearing them pulling at the hay, settling down for the night to await the arrival of a new day.

***

'She didn't make it then,' said Harry, as he poured out the first cup of tea of the day.

'No, she died while I knelt down beside her.'

'Well, that's farming.' He turned to take a cup of tea up to Alice but paused. 'These things happen but always remember, it's the way livestock are looked after when they are alive that really matters. They serve you and they always deserve to be treated well in return.'

I went over to the dairy to get the bucket for the udder washing water which I carried up to the milking bail. It was a sub-zero temperature start to the day and the cows came into the collecting yard with frost on their whiskers.

Cold weather also meant the Lister engine took a bit of cranking over before it kicked into action and, for the first time that winter, the pulsators started to ice up. The pulsators alter the pressure in the teat cups causing the rubber liner to rhythmically squeeze the teat and then release it so that, in many ways it mimics the action of the calf suckling. Without them, the milking machines do not work.

Tempting as it is to put a warm wet cloth around the units to de-ice them, this was not a good idea because after only a short while, the moisture from the cloth will freeze them up again.

The only way to solve the problem long term is to use the heat from the cows which stand immediately below the pulsator unit. It takes a little time but once working it usually carries on working, however low the ambient temperature might be.

For me though, the cold soon started to penetrate the layers of clothes I had managed to pull on and the bucket of washing water became ice cold along with it my hands

'A bit chilly today,' Harry said, as I rolled the churns across the yard to put them on the trolley. 'You need to get yourself a length of bale string around your middle – good as an extra coat.'

'So you say. I should think the water trough across the paddock will be frozen up so I'll have to sort that out as soon as I can.'

178

'Don't worry about that just now, boy. We can have a look at it when we take the fodder beet out. Just get the milk down to the ramp and go in for breakfast and get yourself warm.'

It was when I was unloading the churns off the trolley onto the ramp I saw the hunt lorry go past and by the time I had walked back up to the dairy it had driven along the top road and was coming down the yard to collect Sally. And then I realised why Harry has told me to go into the house for breakfast.

It was thoughtful of him but I also realised that this was a commercial farm and if I was to have a future in farming I had to come to terms with the down side and the upsets that inevitably occur.

I didn't go in for breakfast but stood quietly and watched as the knacker man did his job, using a cable to winch Sally's carcass up on to the bed of his lorry. I felt an arm around my shoulder, it was Harry.

'You didn't have to see this, boy,' he said.

'I know but I can't keep avoiding it. Sally was a wonderful cow; kind, obedient and loving. She had a good life and now it's ended and I'm just so glad she didn't have to see the inside of an abattoir.'

He turned to face me. 'Let me tell you this, John. No old and loyal servant of mine has or ever will see the inside of an abattoir. On that, you have my word. Now let's go and have some breakfast.' And as the lorry left the farm we turned and headed down the yard to the house.

'Winter's arrived,' Alice said. 'And the forecast is snow.'

Judging by the number of dogs and cats that now lay under the table, it seemed reasonable to assume that they too had worked out what was coming.

'We'd better clear a space for the cows in the barn, boy,' Harry said. 'Just in case it really sets in.'

'How about the sheep?' I asked.

'They should be alright. They've plenty of shelter and they are a tough lot. I took hay and barley down to them

179

this morning and they look alright for now but if it looks like setting in, it might be worth taking some bales of straw down and building a few windbreaks for them.'

'And how are the tups working?'

'That's the other thing. I see there's a lot of yellow and red marked ewes, which is good, and there's some with both yellow and red which means they haven't conceived on the first time round. We'll leave them for another week and then sort them out into lambing groups. There's bound to be some barren ewes among them too and they will have to be weeded out.'

'Don't want to alarm you but it's starting to snow,' Alice said, looking out of the window.

I looked out too and saw the first flakes falling. Every so often there would be a gust of wind that drove them across the yard and made me shiver. I looked away and set into my slices of boiled bacon and noticed that Alice had cut the bread a little thicker this morning.

'Right,' said Harry. 'If you load up the trailer with fodder beet, I'll be with you to fork it off in the field and while you're loading I'll have a go at sorting out the water in the paddock, not that there's much chance of getting it running.' He looked out of the window. 'It's coming down heavier.'

I pushed my chair back and got up to leave but Alice insisted on making me another cup of tea. 'You will need the warmth inside you today,' she said. 'Are you going to have half a cup, Harry?'

By the time I had hooked the tractor up to the trailer and hauled it round to the fodder beet the snow was blowing almost horizontally and I could barely see the cows in the field. This was more of a blizzard and I assumed, and hoped, they had taken shelter behind the stone wall which divided the paddock from Farm Close. I started to fork the beet into the trailer but Harry, head bent low, walked around the corner.

'Change of plan, boy. I think we'd better get the cows

in now. They'll do no good standing out in this. Let's get the barn sorted out. Leave the trailer here and bring the tractor.'

I put the fork down and hurried after Harry. We needed to move a few pieces of machinery and then try and find the gate which was used to close off the front of the barn. The last time I had seen it, the gate was in the orchard to make a holding pen for some fat lambs. I told Harry and we went and retrieved it.

'All we need now are some straw bales for the bedding,' Harry said.

We went to the rick yard and made several trips back to the barn carrying a bale in either hand before we had enough. I noticed the wind had now really picked up and the snow was causing almost a white out and was building up in drifts against the barn walls.

With the straw spread we set out to bring the cows in and struggled across a paddock I barely recognised. All the wheel ruts and undulations had been filled in and the field was flat and featureless, the snow swirling about in eddies across its surface.

We found the cows standing in the lee of the stone wall and had to cajole them to walk out into the wind and the snow. They thought they had found the best place to be, but we knew there was better.

'Come on girls!' shouted Harry. 'Let's go and get warm in the barn.'

I could hardly hear him, the wind was howling so much and the snow stung when it hit my face. Eventually we managed to take then back to the farm and steered them into to the barn.

'There,' said Harry, as he shut the gate. 'At least they are in some shelter.'

The snow that had built up on their coats started to slide off them and one or two were already thinking of lying down. Yes, I thought, at least you lot are in the right place.

'Still need to sort them out some water and we'll have to take them hay and beet,' Harry said. 'Can I leave you to do that while I just go and check on the sheep again? I think I might have to move them closer to home.'

A few minutes later I heard the Land Rover fire up and Harry drove up the yard. The windscreen wipers were doing their best to clear the snow but they were not making a good job of it.

Finding a suitable trough for the cows to drink out of was not easy if only because most of the yard was now covered in a deepening layer of snow. I finally located one in the orchard – it seemed all things migrated at some time to the orchard for one reason or another – and I tied a rope to the ring on the end plate and pulled it with the tractor around to the barn with the cows in.

To deter them from walking out while I manoeuvred it through the gateway, I took them a couple of bales of hay and spread it along the back wall. Once I had the trough where I wanted it to be I looked for some hose pipe I could use to fill it up.

And that is where life became more difficult. I found the hose but it was now blocked by ice and nothing would run through it. I guess I spent two hours unblocking that pipe, just because the last time it was used no one had bothered to drain it. At last though, after immersing it in a bath of hot water, I managed to free the trapped ice and water started to flow and I made sure it kept flowing until the cows had each drunk their fill and the trough was full to the brink. I then took it away, drained it and then buried the hose pipe under a heap of straw.

More hay along the front of the barn and good layer of fodder beet and the job was done, at least, for the moment.

Chapter twenty

Harry and the big freeze

I pulled my jacket tightly around me and, with head bowed, walked up to top of the yard to see if there was any sign of Harry returning. But with no success. The blizzard was still blowing and the snow was as deep as I had ever seen it.

As I returned to the shelter of the tractor shed, Alice appeared. 'Have you seen Harry?' she asked.

'No, I was just looking but there's no sign of him.'

'Well, do you think he's alright?'

Alice was worried and the more I thought about it, I began to think she may have had good reason to be. Every vehicle has its limits and it might just be that the Land Rover has become stuck and if Harry is trying to walk home in this weather it could be dangerous.

'I don't know but I think I should try and find out.'

'What will you do?'

'Well, I'll have to take a tractor down and see if I can find him. The trouble is, I don't know which field he will be in. There're three groups of sheep in three different fields and he could be any of them.'

The thought of driving down the field in this weather on tractor which offered no protection from the wind or the snow didn't fill me with too much enthusiasm but there wasn't any choice.

I looked around the tractor shed and spotted a couple

of extra-long length coats which, with Alice's help, I managed to squeeze into, and she also found me a pair of gloves. Feeling increasingly like a Michelin Man I strode over to the tractor and, with some difficulty, climbed aboard and started the engine. And then I thought I had better take a tow-rope with me in case Harry had the Land Rover stuck in a snow drift or something.

The drive up the yard wasn't too bad but as I set off across the paddock the full power of the wind and the snow hit me, stinging my face and making my eyes water so that I had to hold a hand in front to try and prevent the snow hitting me.

Thankfully, Harry had left all the gates open down the track so I could stay put on the tractor seat. In Badger Close the snow had already drifted so that it was almost at hedge height and I was forced to drive in the shallower snow further out in the field.

At the top of Brier Hill I stopped briefly to see if there was any sign of the Land Rover but the driving snow meant that anything beyond a few yards was obliterated. There was nothing there – no Land Rover, no sheep and no Harry. I slipped the tractor into gear and drove on down the hill until I came to the bridge over the brook. Here, the wind had not allowed the snow to settle and I looked for any tyre marks there may have been.

The situation seemed pretty hopeless and I was getting colder. I drove into the big field over the brook with the intention of driving round it but as I drove away from the gate I wondered if I would ever find it again; the wheel marks made by the tractor were soon wiped away by the wind and the drifting snow.

I returned to the gate and the bridge and stopped the engine, aware that if it failed to restart I would be in serious trouble, but I thought I might be able to hear the Land Rover if it was nearby. I listened and all I could hear was the screaming of the wind as it hurtled across the fields and tore through hedges and fences.

I started the tractor and drove along the field boundary and stopped when I reached the other side of the field and had another listen, standing up on the gearbox to gain more height above the hedge.

And then I heard it, the Land Rover's hooter, a faint cry of help which, try as I might, I couldn't work out which direction it was coming from. The sound was carried away on the wind mixed in with the endless cacophony of screams and wailing as the snow swirled within it, sometimes seeming to be from behind me and then shifting around to any number of different directions.

The gate into Long Field was open and I looked at it, wondering what that could mean, my mind numbed by the cold. If Harry had driven into Long Field he would have closed the gate when he came out – the sheep would have been too interested in being fed than leaving the field.

I started the tractor and drove through the gateway. If Harry wasn't in here I was going to have to make my way back to the farm, alone.

Long Field was, by its name, long and mercifully thin, but it was also a long way round and I had made it to the third corner before I found the Land Rover. It was in the ditch almost laying on its side and going nowhere. I drove up alongside it and the passenger door opened and Harry struggled to climb out.

'It's good to see you, boy,' he said.

He sounded weak and drawn. The last few hours had clearly taken its toll on him.

'Do you want to try and pull the Land Rover out?' I asked.

He shook his head. 'No point, I've used all the fuel there was trying to keep warm.'

Harry had only his normal jacket on and while it was alright for a heated Land Rover cab, it was not enough for these artic conditions. I took one of my coats off and helped him put it on before wrapping a length of bale twine around him.

And all this took time, time I didn't feel we had to spare if either of us was going to make it back to the farm.

I climbed up onto the tractor and helped Harry to find room beside me. I just hoped he would be able to hang on.

The journey back seemed to take for ever. This time I had to keep stopping to close gates and the wind and snow was straight into us. It was only because I knew the way after we had made it up Brier Hill, we managed to keep going. Harry's condition was worsening and he kept leaning across me as he appeared to fall asleep.

'Come on Harry!' I yelled at him, digging my elbow into his ribs. 'Not far now.'

At last, we drove into the yard and I took the tractor down and parked it close to the house. I didn't think Harry was going to be able to walk too far. Alice came out to meet us and looked at Harry.

'Help me get him down,' I said. 'He's about all in.'

She put her arms up and held him as best as she could while I jumped down from the other side and came round to help ease him down the two steps. It wasn't easy but we managed to get him into the kitchen and sat him down at the table.

'What do you reckon? Do you think we should call the doctor?' asked Alice.

'I think that would be a good idea,' I said.

Alice went off to make the call while I tried to pull off the coat he was wearing. There were chunks of ice in the folds and I noticed that his hands were white.

'The doctor is on his way,' Alice said. 'How is he now?'

'Much the same. I think he must be suffering from hypothermia. We need to get him warm.'

'What's the best way?'

'I was thinking along the lines of a warm bath,' I said. Since he had arrived in the kitchen Harry hadn't uttered a word. He had leaned forward in his chair and with his head on his arms looked as if he had gone to sleep. I didn't think sleeping was a good idea and I shook him and talked to him until he started to lift his head.

'How would we get him upstairs to the bathroom?' Alice asked.

'I didn't know but I think we should try.'

And tried we did but it was no use. Harry was just too heavy for us. We were considering our options when there was a tap at the door and the doctor walked in.

'Hello. Alice,' he said. 'What's Harry done now?'

'He went down the fields to check on the sheep and got stuck with the Land Rover,' I explained. 'When, after about three hours he hadn't returned, I took the tractor down to find him and bring him back. But the cold seems to have got to him.'

'What do you suggest we do?' Alice asked.

'What I'd really like is for Harry to go to hospital where they can do all sorts of things to increase body temperature and keep a check on his progress, but with the roads impassable that's not going to be possible. 'A warm bath would be a good start. If you go and run it, I'll give the young man here a hand to get him upstairs.'

It was never going to be an easy job but with Harry adding some help, we eventually managed to get him into the bath after pulling off his now soaking clothing.

'We need to keep an eye on him,' said the doctor. 'There's a danger that when the really cold blood returns from his hands and feet it will have an adverse effect on his heart, so you must stay with him.'

'How long do you think he needs to stay in the bath?'

'As long as he wants to. He should soon start being a little more proactive but keep an eye on the water temperature and top it up as it cools down. I'll be off back to the surgery now but give me a call in an hour's time and tell me how he is – or sooner if you feel it necessary.'

The doctor left and I looked across at Alice. 'Oh John,' she said. 'Was he really that close to not coming back?'

I could see the tears brimming in her eyes as the realisation of the enormity of the situation landed with her and how close she had come to losing Harry. Rightly or wrongly, I stepped closer to her and put my arms around her and gave her a comforting embrace. 'It's going to be alright,' I said.

'Thank you, John, you're very kind and I haven't thanked you for what you did.'

Before I could answer there was a splashing noise behind us. 'Are you two going to stand there all day? I usually have some privacy when I'm in here.'

Alice's face lit up. 'Harry,' she said. 'How are you feeling now?'

'Cold, tired and tingling,' he replied.

I was closest, so I turned the hot tap on and swished the water about to mix it in.

'Good God, boy. I employ you to work on the farm, not the bathroom, and I'll end up being cooked if you don't turn that tap off. Sort him out Alice.'

'I think it's time for you to leave,' Alice said. 'Go down and make yourself a cup of tea.'

***

It took the best part of two days for Harry to recover and several days more before I considered he was really back to his normal self. During that time I did my best to keep the farm going. Mercifully, the snow storm blew itself out on the second day but it left a legacy of snow drifts which were ten feet high in some places and temperatures which didn't get above freezing from one end of the day to the next.

Looking out across the paddock and into Farm Close and beyond was to not recognise a single feature; it had become a new landscape carved out by the wind and the snow it had carried.

Putting the cows under the barn had been a good decision and I dread to think what would have happened to them if we had left them outside but milking them on that first morning after the storm was not easy. Before I could even think about it I had to shovel the snow out of the stalls and scoop it out of the feed boxes.

I like to think the cows understood the difficulties I was having though and they did their best to behave although the bright glaring snow brought some strange, nervous reactions from some of them.

In the engine compartment, the Lister engine was covered in several inches of spindrift that had found its way in through the small gaps around the door but when I swung the starting handle it burst into life, just as it always did.

One of the biggest concerns was whether or not the milk lorry was going to arrive. Being in the village, the roads became reasonably passable after a few hours but I knew there were outlying farms which would be impossible for the lorry to visit or worse, get stuck trying to visit.

If the churns of milk were not collected it meant we had no empty churns to milk the cows into and the milk would have to be poured away and I'm not sure the villagers would appreciate a river of frozen milk. But there was no way I could pull full churns up the steep slope to the dairy. They would have to be emptied in the street.

When milking was finally over, I set about doing Harry's pre-breakfast jobs which involved feeding the calves, pigs, hens. I really wasn't too sure just how much to give the pigs and the hens but I reasoned that if they had something in front of them and some water to drink they would at least stay alive.

At this time too, I realised that ensuring the water supply did not freeze up had to be a priority and I took time out to drain hoses, and stack piles of warm muck around the pipes which fed into water troughs.

Through all this though, there was one overriding concern regarding the ewes and how they had fared during the storm. There was nothing more to do other than to load some hay bales and bags of ground barley onto a trailer and try and haul it down to them with the tractor.

After what had turned out to be a late breakfast, I set out through the snow drifts to forge a way down to the lower fields and discover what had happened to them. The first field I drove into, the one across the bridge appeared to be totally empty – there was not a sheep to be seen and I feared the worst. But then, about a hundred yards along the hedge I saw a flash of red, the red left by a tup and I headed that way.

I know sheep are not renowned for their survival capabilities but these ewes had found a sheltered area and had gathered as a flock and kept warm and alive, treading down the snow as it fell around them.

They were hungry though and as I pulled some bales of hay off the trailer I was surrounded by them as they pulled the hay out of my hand. I also gave them some ground barley which they devoured with similar fervour.

Difficult as it was, I attempted to make a head count and convinced myself they were all present which was good news and I wondered if it would be the same when I went to see how the other two groups were coping.

Back on the tractor I left the sheep to it and went off in search of the rest of the flock and, when I came across them, these too had managed to find shelter and survive. I was elated and couldn't wait to give Harry the news.

Not such good news when I found the Land Rover which looked to be in a sorry state. One of the windows had been open a crack and spindrift had found it way in to cover everything in a layer of icy snow. The exposed back had several feet of it.

I prized open the door and it was like looking into a fridge and Harry must have had a tough time trying to keep warm even before the fuel ran out and the engine stopped. There was nothing I could do on my own to retrieve the Land Rover, it would have to wait until Harry was up and about.

Back at the farm Harry was sitting in the kitchen when I walked in, his hands cupped around a mug of soup, which was good to see.

'How's things out there?' he asked.

'Well, the good news is that the all the sheep appear to have survived. I found them under the hedges as groups and gave them some hay and barley. I don't know what they are doing for water.'

'That's a relief but I'd feel happier if they were closer to home where we could keep an eye on them. There's no telling what this weather is going to do.'

I looked at him and wondered whether he was going to ask me to bring them up. I'd have a go but I wasn't sure if I could manage it. Just walking down there and back again would be a taxing exercise let alone trying to bring two hundred and fifty sheep back home with me.

'If we took the tractor and trailer with a few bales of hay on it the sheep would probably follow us without anyone having to do a lot of pushing,' he said. 'You could stay on the trailer for most of the way just dropping out the odd handful of hay, and they would have the track made by the tractor to walk in.'

'Well, do you feel better now?' I asked.

'Better than I did a couple of days ago. I'll be alright.'

At that point Alice put her head around the door. 'And what are you planning to do now? I hope it's not going out of the yard, you know what the doctor said.'

'We're just going to bring the sheep up to Farm Close,' Harry said. 'I'm only going to sit on the tractor.'

Alice sighed. 'Well just be sure you have some warm clothes on this time.'

So, with Harry driving and me sitting in the trailer on a bale of hay we set off back down to the lower fields. It was now a bright sunny day and the bright glare of the snow made me squint. Perhaps I was going to get a bout of snow blindness.

We meandered along over virgin snow and it was, if the sound of the tractor was ignored, so quiet and it seemed as if the snow was soaking up all the usual sounds of the countryside. In all, when compared to the weather we had endured, it was a pleasant day to be outside.

As I was earlier, we were met by the sheep at the gate and after Harry had turned the tractor and trailer round, I opened it to let them stream out after him. And it was the same when we went to the other fields – it seemed the sheep were just so pleased to be going somewhere, anywhere was better than where they were.

Before long there was trail of sheep about a hundred yards long behind us walking in the wheel marks of the tractor in two columns.

'This is the way to do it, boy,' shouted Harry.

'They know where they want to be,' I said, dropping another handful of hay off the back of the trailer.

In less than an hour, we had all the sheep in Farm Close, just one field away from the farm. Harry wanted to try a head count when they ran through the gate but they were going too fast to make any sense of it.

'We'll let them settle down for a bit and then see if we can get them through a race,' he said. 'It will give us a chance to see how many have yellow and red marks on them.'

I spread out the bales of hay we had and left them to it. Compared to the other fiascos we had had moving sheep about I thought this one had gone remarkably well. All we needed to do now was see if we could retrieve the Land Rover.

'Get the jump leads out of the workshop and fill a can with Derv – not the red diesel – and don't forget the funnel,' Harry said. 'And you'd better bring a tow rope and the tool box in case we have to bleed the fuel through.'

It had occurred to me, although I didn't say anything, that when I had run the tractor out of diesel a few weeks ago, Harry had made me carry a can of diesel down to the tractor – if only to remind me to check the fuel before I left the yard. Running the Land Rover out of fuel albeit in an artic blizzard didn't count it seemed, even though, unlike the tractor, it had a fuel gauge.

This was the third time I had been down to the lower fields this morning and for most of the way I could take my hands off the steering wheel and the tractor would steer itself down the deep, trench-like ruts we had made in the snow. But only as far as the gate into Long Field. From then on, we were in virgin snow again as I cut across to where the Land Rover was.

'It seems to be more on a slope than I recall it being,' Harry said.

'That could be because it's in the ditch,' I said.

'Good job we brought the tow rope, boy. If you drop the trailer off you can attach the rope to the drawbar and we'll pull it out backwards.'

Harry set off with the other end of the rope to attach it to rear of the Land Rover.

'You don't think we should try and get the Land Rover started first?' I asked. 'It's a pretty dead weight to pull out without some help.'

'We can try,' Harry said. 'The fuel filler cap is on the up side, which will help and I think the jump leads are long enough to reach the battery. Yes, let's give it a go but leave the tractor running.'

The trickiest part was crawling into the cab to find the bonnet catch and then trying to lift it along with a foot of frozen snow. But we did it and with the fuel on board and the batteries connected, Harry settled himself in to the driving seat and pressed the start button.

It was not good. The engine turned over but only reluctantly. I gave the jump lead ends another turn on the terminals and Harry tried again. This time there was more life in the engine and on the third go it started to fire intermittently before all the cylinders decided to play.

'That's good,' Harry said. 'Better than I expected. Now let's see if we can pull her out.'

With the jump leads back in the trailer, I climbed up on the tractor and drove out until the rope was taut and then waved at Harry who had put the Land Rover in four-wheel drive. Together we applied the power and, with wheels slipping on the snow, the Land Rover inched itself out of the ditch, finding more and more grip as it arrived on level ground.

I walked around the Land Rover to see if there was any damage caused by its plunge into the ditch, but there was no sign of any. Just how it came to be in the ditch was still beyond me and with Harry not offering any explanation. I assumed the visibility had been so poor he had just driven out of the field.

'I think I'll attach the tow rope to the front of the Land Rover,' Harry said. 'Those ruts are so deep I'm likely to get stuck again.'

'How about the trailer?'

'Leave it here but put the jump leads and everything else in the front of the Land Rover.'

It was a good decision to use the tow rope. Like two alpine climbers roped together, we made our way back to the farm and there were numerous times when the depth of the snow was just too deep for the Land Rover to cope with and I pulled him through, the snow building up in front until it poured over the bonnet.

Back in the yard I parked up and took stock of things. We had the sheep where we wanted them, the Land Rover was home in one piece and Harry seemed to have recovered. It was time for lunch.

Chapter twenty-one

Fun in the snow

It was a hard winter. Day after day temperatures stayed below freezing and it became almost routine for me to spend time thawing out water pipes which I had spent time thawing out only the day before. It snowed on and off for most of December which meant that the fields were constantly covered with a layer of it.

The cows came in at night but made it clear they would rather be out during the day as long as it wasn't snowing or the wind was too strong. They just spent their time mooching about in the paddock eating the hay and fodder beet I put out for them. Nothing appeared to worry them.

Harry, after he had completed his feeding chores retreated to the workshop, the radio on full blast accompanied by a load of hammering and grinding. One morning, as I brought the milk churns down to the dairy he called me over to have a look at what he had been making.

'What do you reckon to that?' he asked. 'It's Alice's Christmas present.'

Harry had made a sledge, a fine looking one with long, shiny stainless-steel runners that curved up and the front and a polished varnished platform large enough for at least three people to sit on.

'Looks good,' I said. 'Very good.'

'Fancy giving it a test drive?'

'Well, yes. Why not?'

'Let's get breakfast out of the way and we'll take it down to Brier Hill. I thought we could take the tractor down to save having to pull it back up ourselves. But not a word to Alice.'

'And what are you two up to today?' asked Alice as she poured me out my first cup of tea.

I looked at Harry and wondered what he was going to say.

'Oh, we've a few jobs to be getting on with,' he said, as he carved the week's boiled bacon joint. 'But we'll start by checking on the fencing in Brier Hill.'

'Brier Hill? I thought that was due to be ploughed up next year.'

Harry looked flustered. 'You're right it is. I just wanted to check if we could take any of the wire off the posts and use it again.'

Alice looked hard at him. 'Harry, if you're up to something, I think you should tell me about it,' she said. 'I haven't forgotten that episode with the hovercraft yet. And I shouldn't think most of the people in the village have either. I mean, how did you expect to stop it when it wasn't even touching the ground?'

Harry sighed. 'Well boy, if you hook the tractor to the trailer and collect up what you think we'll need from the workshop, I'll see you out there.'

I did as I was asked and backed the trailer up to the work shop door and waited. If Harry was intent on taking the sledge out it would take the two of us to lift it on to the trailer. Harry hadn't scrimped on the metal or the wood; it weighed a ton.

'Already, boy?' he asked.

'Well, all but for the sledge. I think it needs both of us to lift it on to the trailer.'

Harry bent down, tried to lift one end and groaned. 'I think you're right. Come on, you take that end and we'll see how we get on.'

It wasn't easy and an attempt at a straight lift failed without the sledge getting halfway there. After we had lowered it back down to the ground again, Harry suggested standing the sledge up and leaning it against the back of the trailer. If we could get one end over the back of the trailer we could lift the other and slide it on to the trailer.

And just as we prepared ourselves for the lift, Ronny wandered into the workshop.

'Bloody Hell, Ronny, you must be a genius. How did you know we needed you to help load this sledge?'

Ronny took another drag on his roll-up and peered at the sledge. 'What have you got there, Harry?' he asked, smoke trailing out of his mouth and interestingly, on this occasion, from both nostrils. 'And where are the wheels?'

'Like I said. It's a sledge,' said Harry.

'A what?'

'Oh, for pity's sake, Ronny. Just jump up there and pull it onto the trailer as we lift it will you.'

Ronny clambered aboard and did just that and, between the three of us, we managed to heave the sledge on board and secure it with a length of rope.

'Right then, have you anything to do this morning like making another skin cream commercial or modelling Woolworth's latest swimwear range?'

'No, I don't think so, Harry,' Ronny said, jumping down off the trailer.

'Right then, get back on and we'll head off down the field.'

I joined him on the trailer and we both sat down on the sledge. Ronny rolled himself another cigarette, an operation he performed quite skilfully and the finished product looked to be a neat job. It almost seemed a pity to set fire to it but that was what he proceeded to do.

After a couple of weeks of snow lying about, the novelty of it all had long past and I yearned to see some green fields and hedgerows, but the way things were going we were some time away from that.

Harry brought the tractor to a halt on a piece of level ground at the top of Brier Hill and between us we grappled with the sledge to lower it to the ground. I have to say, it looked entirely at home in the snow and I gave it a little push and was surprised to discover just how easily it glided, despite its weight.

'Who's having first go?' Harry asked.

I looked down the hill and although I had driven up and down it on numerous occasions, today it looked particularly steep and long, and I stepped back away from the sledge.

'Oh, come on,' Harry said. 'Ronny, you can have the honour of being the first one to try it.'

Ronny thought about it. 'How do you steer it?' he asked.

'That's simple. You just head straight down, there's no need to steer it.'

Ronny's self-survival instincts were working well this morning. 'And how do you stop it?'

'You just put your feet down in the snow,' Harry said.

And on that detail, I thought Harry was being particularly optimistic. You don't bring a sledge travelling at thirty miles an hour and weighing a couple of hundredweight to a halt by dangling your feet in the snow.

'Everything clear, then? Any more questions?'

Ronny shook his head.

'Right then. I think you should sit somewhere in the middle to keep the weight evenly balanced,' Harry said.

'There isn't much to hang on to,' Ronny said after he had placed himself about halfway along the polished boards, his boots just about reaching the ground.

'Just lean forwards and put your hands on the woodwork. You'll be alright. We won't let you go too fast.'

Ronny wasn't answering and stared ahead, a grim expression on his face.

'Alright, boy?'

We pulled the front of the sledge round so it pointed

downhill. At this point, Ronny began making some sort of primitive whining noise and he looked wide eyed and fearful.

'I'm not happy about this, Harry,' he said.

He began to stand up to leave but he was too late. Harry gave the sledge a firm push and Ronny was on his way. As we looked, the sledge dropped away from us as if we had dropped it off a tall building, rapidly gathering speed as it careered downwards until it arrived at the flat land below and continued without any perceptible sign of slowing.

Very soon, it was approaching the far hedge, a hedge with an enormous snow drift stacked against it and I think I saw Ronny dabbing his boots into the snow, but it might have been wishful thinking. Either way, with only yards to go, Ronny bailed out as the sledge piled into the snowdrift, a cloud of spindrift thrown into the air to mark the point of entry.

'Wow! Did you see that, boy?'

'I think we should take the tractor down and see how Ronny is,' I said. 'I don't think he's moved yet.'

He was still lying in the snow when we arrived and I ran over to him, fearing the worst. 'You alright?' I asked, looking round for any sign of blood or twisted limbs.

Ronny then started laughing. 'Did you see how fast it went? That was terrific!'

I turned my attention to Harry who was peering into a sledge-shaped hole in the snowdrift. 'Do you think it's gone straight through?' he asked. 'Have a look from the other side.'

I trudged along to the gate and climbed over and walked back along the other side of the hedge. I was just about to shout to Harry there was no sign of it when I spotted two shiny, stainless steel runners poking out.

'It's over here, at least the front half is,' I yelled.

'Perhaps if we put a rope on it we can pull it out from your side then,' Harry said.

'Worth a try.'

Harry brought the tractor round, Ronny was sitting in the trailer, and we tied one end of the rope to the sledge and the other to the trailer axle. I was expecting the extraction of the sledge was going to be a drawn-out affair with the tractor slipping all over the place, tow-ropes breaking and tempers rising.

But with just a little hesitation as a few branches were swept aside, the sledge came straight out and looked none the worse for its journey.

'Oh, that's great,' said a jubilant Harry. 'Let's tow it back up the hill and give it another run only this time we'll launch it from halfway up. How do you feel about having a go, boy?'

'Alright, I think.'

And so the morning passed with successive runs with Harry's new, home-made sledge and it was terrific, exhilarating fun. When it came round to my turn I just let the sledge go and hung on as best as I could. A firm, well intentioned push from Harry and Ronny set me on my way and it went as straight as an arrow at some impossible speed stopping just short of the snow drift.

Harry had a nasty moment when the sledge veered off to the right for some reason and headed straight for the bridge. 'I think you had too much weight on one side,' I suggested, as we pulled the sledge out of the brook.

We tried running it with two of us on board and then, as a final run of the morning, with all three of us, which was a mistake when we realised that someone now had to the task of walking all the way back up the hill to get the tractor.

'Do you think Alice will like it?' Harry asked, as we waited for Ronny to arrive.

'She'll adore it,' I said. 'Might take a bit of wrapping though.'

***

The last letter I received from Elizabeth said she would be

returning home from university for the Christmas break today and after I finished milking and feeding the cows I took the pick-up down to Rose Hill.

It had been dark for some hours when I arrived at the entrance to the track which would take me across the fields to the farm buildings. As usual, the gate was tied shut with bale string and someone had tangled it up so it was difficult to release but I managed it and pulled the gate open and drove through.

With the gate secured, I drove on into the darkness trying to avoid the worst of the potholes and avoid leaving the track where the snow and the field merged into one. After about ten minutes, I arrived at the buildings and turned the engine and lights off.

I couldn't believe how dark and quiet it all was. There was just one faint light from one of the down stair windows and that was it; no yard lights, no sound, nothing but darkness. I grabbed the torch out of the glove compartment and climbed out. So quiet, so dark, so spooky.

It was the first time I had been here by myself and there had never been a need to knock on the door before but on this occasion I thought I better had – not that I expected a reply. It would take more courage than I possessed at this moment to open the door to an unexpected visitor at this time of night.

I knocked and waited and heard nothing until, just as I was about to retreat to the pick-up a light came on and I heard a bolt being slid back and the door swung open. It was Kate.

'John,' she said. 'What a surprise. Come on in. We're all down in the back room so we didn't hear you arrive.'

I stepped into the kitchen and followed her along the dimly lit passageway which led to the room where I had first met Elizabeth. There were sounds of people talking and I listened hard to see if I could recognise Elizabeth's voice among them, but I couldn't.

Kate was in front of me and as she pushed the door open she announced that they had a visitor: 'It's John from Harry and Alice's,' she said.

I looked around the room. Grandfather William was sitting on one side of the fire place and Grandma was on the other looking for all the world like two book ends. They must have been brought in their chairs from the kitchen because both of them were asleep.

Directly in front of the fire, which was well banked up with logs so that it was crackling and roaring and sending great tongues of flame up the chimney, lay two dogs which seemed oblivious to the sparks that landed on them. Further back and arranged in a half-circle sat dour William in an armchair next to an empty chair I assumed was Kate's. Spread out on the sofa lounged young William and further along reading some tired-looking books were Elsie and Emily. But there was no Elizabeth.

'Sit yourself down and I'll make you a cup of tea. I could even make you a sandwich, if you want one.'

'No, that's very kind of you Kate, but a cup of tea will be just fine.' I looked for somewhere to sit down and chose a seat at the table, the thought of asking William to move over was not one I wanted to embark on. I wondered what everyone was doing here. There was no television or radio on and conversation was hardly flowing. No wonder Elizabeth was so keen to get out on an evening if they were all a dull as this appeared to be.

'How's it all going up at Church Farm?' asked young William. 'I hear you had an entertaining session with Pedro at the Harvest Festival service.'

There were chortles all round and William, with an open-mouthed grin soaked up the admiration from his family; the highlight, in conversational terms, of his week, no doubt.

'Well, it could have gone a little better but that's the unpredictability of donkeys. But I guess you already knew that,' I replied. 'What's everyone doing this evening?'

Young William looked questioningly over towards his father for a response. 'What do you mean?' dour William asked.

'I just wondered if anyone was going out, or anything.'

'No, I don't see any reason why they should. Anyway, what brings you down here? Harry thrown you out or something?'

'No, nothing like that I was just wondering how Elizabeth was. I gather she's back from college. Is she alright?'

'Yes, she's fine.'

I waited for more but it was not going to happen. I was about to inquire further when Kate walked in with my tea.

'There you go, John. I've put a slice of cake in the saucer for you.'

'Oh, that's great. Thanks.' I took a sip of tea while Kate settled back down in her armchair.

'Kate, I was just asking how Elizabeth was.'

She half turned and looked at me. 'Elizabeth? She's fine, thank you.'

This was going nowhere. 'Well can you tell me where she is, please?'

'I think she's in her bedroom.'

'Oh right.' I munched on my cake, wondering what these people did on a Saturday night.

'I can tell her you're here, if you want,' Kate said.

'That would be good if it's not too much trouble.'

I waited and listened out for the sound of feet approaching. And I didn't have to wait long. Elizabeth burst into the room and headed straight for me.

'John!' she screamed. 'How long have you been here?'

'Only a few minutes. I just thought I'd call in and see how you are.'

'Didn't anyone tell you, I arrived back yesterday? I asked enough people to tell you.'

I shook my head. 'No one said a word to me but how are you?'

'Would you two like to retreat to the kitchen?' asked Kate. 'That way we can get on with our evening.'

'Sorry Kate, I should have realised,' I said and took Elizabeth's arm and headed for the door. Halfway down the passageway I could wait no longer and pulled her to me and kissed her.

Chapter twenty-two

Christmas madness

In the week before Christmas the temperature suddenly rose by about ten degrees and a rapid thaw set in. Almost overnight, piles of snow that had become a permanent feature on the landscape melted away and poured water into the ditches, brooks and caused rivers to burst their banks, with the result there was large scale flooding across acres of low lying land.

I stood on the top of Brier Hill and looked out on what had become an enormous lake with only the trees and some of the hedgerows visible.

It would be a day or two before that lot sorted itself and I was relieved Harry had taken the decision to bring the sheep up when we did.

Meanwhile, back at the farm, Christmas-fever was setting in. Alice spent most days in the kitchen mixing ingredients and cooking, filling the air with mouth-watering aromas of spices and warm pastries.

For my part, I began the task of making stock piles of hay and ground barley around the yard so that, come Christmas morning, time spent feeding could be minimised, and Harry set out to find a Christmas tree with firm instructions from Alice that it wasn't to be too tall. 'We're not in Trafalgar Square,' she told him.

'I know, but we don't want one of those tiddly things

with a couple of branches and gets stuffed in a bucket the cats crap in, do we?' he said.

Alice hadn't answered and I thought this was probably a conversation Harry and Alice had at this time every year.

Anyway, fired up with the rise in temperature, I soon had piles of feed placed at key points around the yard. I had even placed a few bags of 'Layers mash' alongside the hen house. With the retreat of the snow, the yard looked as untidy as I had ever seen it and that was after I had found and collected every shred of combustible material a few weeks ago to help build the bonfire.

There was nothing for it but to get the brush out and sweep it from top to bottom. It took some time, but I think it was a job well done and I was shovelling the last of the sweepings into a barrow just as Harry arrived.

'You found a small Christmas tree then,' I said, looking at the long bushy spruce tree that extended about ten feet off the back of the Land Rover and as far again out at the front. 'How did you see where you were going?'

'I just looked out of the window every few yards. Wasn't too bad but I don't think the postman will be riding his bike for a few weeks. You'd better give me a hand getting it off.'

We untied the ropes and then swung the base of the tree off to the side and then drove the Land Rover backwards so that the rest of it slipped onto the concrete.

'Good job you swept the yard, boy. Don't want to get the branches dirty.'

'Yes, but where are you going to put it? Could struggle to fit in the house.'

'Well I thought it would look pretty good just outside the kitchen. We could cover it in lights and things and it would be a sort of focal point. What do you reckon?'

'I reckon you're in for a mega bollocking,' I said, having spotted Alice walking up the yard, her arms folded and a look of displeasure on her face that could probably be seen from the moon.

Harry followed my view and turned to see. 'Ah, I see what you mean,' he said.

I left them to it and took the tractor and trailer round to load it with fodder beet which would be taken out to the sheep along with some ground barley. Finding somewhere clean to place it was becoming increasingly hard. All those feet were turning the field into a mud bath.

For the cows, the change in the weather had created a new set of problems. They obviously preferred to be outside – perhaps the barn was just too warm for them – but the field was too wet to carry them. The only way to manage it was to have a 'sacrificial area' where they could be fed and splash about as much as they wanted during the day and then to house them at night. Cleaning their udders after a day in the field was now becoming a major operation and required several buckets of water.

'Harry, if you're ready we can take some beet out to the sheep,' I said, expecting to see him still in conversation with Alice. But he had moved on and was now digging a hole in the lawn outside the kitchen window.

'Ah, John. Just the man. Let's see if we can get the base of the tree in the hole.'

Somehow, he had dragged the tree down the yard so that it now lay with its base just a few feet away from the hole he had dug. He had also tied some ropes near to the top of the tree to use as guy ropes.

We lifted the end of the tree and tried to 'walk' it up right while pushing the base end towards the hole. I felt like a pole-vaulter measuring up before making an attempt to get over the high bar.

'Push, boy,' Harry said.

I pushed.

'Hold it there.'

And I held it there.

'Right then, that looks good. Pull the rope and raise it.'

And I pulled the rope and raised it.

'Good. Nearly there. Don't let it topple sideways.'

And it toppled sideways.

The kitchen window, with its leaded panes of hand blown glass had been a feature of the farmhouse for many years and one which more than a few visitors had commented favourably on. The panes rattled a bit and the window was far from being draught free but all in all, it was an attractive part of the house which neither Harry nor Alice had had any immediate plans to change.

To be fair, not all the glass panes had smashed. The damage was confined mainly to the top two rows where one of the larger branches had pushed its way in so that it now hovered, just below ceiling level, over the kitchen table.

'We could hang some coloured lights on it,' Harry said but Alice was far from being amused.

'Are you going to get the chainsaw, or shall I?' she demanded.

'Come on, boy. Let's sort this out. I thought I said not to let it topple...'

It took a couple of hours but by lunch time the tree was standing tall and upright, held up by the three ropes which had been anchored with metal poles we had hammered into the ground.

'There,' Harry said, giving the tree a shake. 'As safe as houses. All we need to do now is put the decorations on. But let's have a bit of lunch first.'

Sitting in the kitchen with a broken window was an interesting experience if only because no one wanted to acknowledge there actually was a broken window, although I noticed that Alice had taken to wearing her long coat and that the cats now entered and departed the kitchen through the gap created by the missing glass panes. As a result, long muddy foot marks covered most of the remaining lower panes.

During lunch, there was a visit from Sam Jones, Smith's farm manager who, out spoken as ever, congratulated Harry on his Christmas tree and then inquired whether they had decided to have double glazing installed.

'These old leaded windows are so flipping draughty,' he said. 'And the rattling noise they make never stops and can keep you awake all night. You're doing the right thing, Harry; rip them out and be done with them. You won't regret it. I would if I had the chance but you don't have the say in a tied cottage. The old man is as tight as a squirrel's arse.'

'And how is George these days, I haven't seen him for ages?' Harry asked, looking to steer the conversation away from windows.

'Oh, I wish I could say the same. He's in a right old mood today – he's been round the barn three times looking for me. I've been four times.'

'Are you going to have a cup of tea while you're here,' Alice asked. 'I've only just made it.'

'No, I won't thanks, Alice. I shall have to get back before the old man blows his top. I just called by to see if you had any spare land I could drop some ewes onto. Our ground's just about chewed up what with the flooding.'

'Not really, Sam,' Harry said. 'I would if I could but we're in the same boat. I've brought them all up from the bottom fields where they should be and they're taking Farm Close to bits as we speak.'

'No worries, Harry. I just thought I'd ask.' He turned to leave. 'Anyway, if I don't see you before, have yourselves a good Christmas and you'll really enjoy your double glazing – it will go with your automatic washing machine.' And with that, he turned and marched up the yard to his pick-up.

'That was Sam Jones,' Harry said. 'Never stands still for a minute.'

'So I gathered,' I said.

'Have you called the window man?' asked Alice.

'Yes,' he said he would be here about three o'clock and he would probably have to board it up while he makes up some new leading. I suppose if you talked to him nicely, he could put a cat flap in it. Now, does anyone want another slice of bacon?'

With lunch over, we walked up to the workshop where Harry said he had stored all last year's tree decorations. And he was right, although I wouldn't have used the word 'stored'. In a cardboard box was a tangle of lights and wiring that took me the best part of an hour to sort out.

When I eventually had it laid out on the concrete, Ronny walked down the yard. Harry, who was trying to place a ladder against the tree, looked up.

'Ronny, that's timely. We were just wondering whether you wanted to be this year's fairy. How are you fixed?'

'Oh no. Sorry Harry, you know what happened the last time you wanted me to go up a tree.'

'That was entirely different. This is a Christmas tree – you know, the one you and your brothers used to pinch all the chocolate off in the doctor's waiting room.'

'It wasn't as big as that one,' Ronny said.

'That's why we have the ladder but there's not a lot to lean the ladder on.' Harry looked up into the branches. 'I reckon if it slips, it will take out the bathroom window.'

'How about loading a trailer with straw bales and using the top as an operating platform? We could do with some straw for the pigs fetching round,' I said.

Harry considered the plan for a minute and glanced at the bathroom window which, like the kitchen window below, was also leaded, rattled and draughty. Perhaps he was thinking a change to double glazing wouldn't be such a bad idea after all, but I doubted it.

'Alright then, if you think that will be safer, let's do it that way. Take Ronny with you and put a load on. I would guess you will need to go six courses high. I'll try and sort out more of the decorations. There should be another couple of boxes somewhere.'

It would be good to report that from then on, everything went smoothly but alas, no. The bales put Ronny at the right height but the tapering of the tree's branches meant he couldn't reach across to the all-important central point.

To give him credit, he tried and actually managed to get a hand around it but when he pulled it towards him, he lost his footing and he ended up swinging on the top of the tree.

'He makes a bloody ugly fairy,' Harry said, looking up through the foliage. 'How are we going to get him down now? He'll break every branch if he tries to climb down.'

'I'll go back up and throw him a rope so I can pull him back onto the bales,' I said.

'Tell him if he snaps just one branch I'll do the same to his neck,' Harry said, as I climbed the ladder.

Up on the bales, rope in hand, I tried to throw an end across to Ronny who was still swinging back and forwards and coming perilously close to the bathroom window.

'I don't think I can hang on much longer,' he said.

'You're alright. Just catch hold of the rope.'

I threw it across to him and he very nearly caught it but he was on the back swing before he could close is hand around it. I needed to time it so he was coming towards me.

'This time,' I shouted to him, and threw the end at him.

'I've got it,' he said.

I must confess I hadn't really thought this through. If he lets go of the tree he'll crash through the branches as he swings towards the trailer. I wouldn't be able to haul enough rope in to prevent it.

'You're going to have to stay where you are for a little longer,' I said to him. 'Just wrap a length of rope around the tree and tie it off so you can relax.'

'What's going on up there?' Harry shouted. 'Have you got him off the tree yet?'

'Well, not exactly,' I said. I'm just working out how to do it. At the moment, he's used the rope to tie himself to the top of the tree, so he's safe.'

'Never mind him. How's my tree?'

'Fine, fine, just fine with no damage to report. I'll tell you what, though, Harry, Ronny's in a good position to attach the top lights to the tree. We'll never get a better opportunity.'

'Oh right. I'll bring the end with the first light up to you.'

'If you could find a long pole it would be useful for passing the lights over to Ronny.'

'How am I going to get out of this tree?' Ronny asked while we waited. 'This rope is starting to cut into me.'

'I really don't know now but if you could just stay there for a little longer so we can fix the top lights that would be good. Then we'll get you down somehow – I'm sure you have better things to do than spend the whole of Christmas tied to the top of a tree.'

'What?'

Harry brought up the first light, the cable trailing behind him down the side of the straw bales.

'Cop hold of the wire,' he said and then reached down over the edge of the bales to bring up a long piece of wood. 'This is the best I could find – it's the top rail of a ten-foot gate.'

Harry then produced a piece of string, tied the wire to the rail and then pushed it over to Ronny. 'Tie the wire to the top of the tree so the bulb sticks out at the top,' Harry instructed. 'It'll provide a warning for aeroplanes.'

And when Ronny had done that he asked him to start to spiral the lights around the branches. 'That's right Ronny, tie the wire to the branches.'

Harry fed the wire across to him and Ronny did as much as he could reach. 'That's all I can do,' he said. 'Can I get off now?'

'Yes,' Harry said, picking up the rope. 'You untie yourself from the tree, tie the rope around you and then we'll pull you across to us. You'll probably hit the side of the bales and then we'll lower you to the ground. Alright?'

I couldn't look. Just how Ronny was going to tie the

rope around him while swinging around in the top of a tree was beyond me. And by the sound of the breaking branches I could hear behind me, it was also beyond Ronny. Turning to look, I reckon he had dropped at least ten feet and broken every branch he met on the way. It was only when he encountered the older and stronger lower branches his downward plummet was arrested.

'Bloody Hell, Ron. Look what you've done. That's just what we didn't want to happen.'

But Ronny wasn't listening. He was more intent on making his way down the last twenty feet to the ground. Which I thought was understandable.

A combination of lassoing, twirling and something that was not too dissimilar to a maypole dance saw the rest of the lights being attached to the tree, once we had pulled the trailer of straw out of the way. And at that point I left Harry to put the rest of the decorations on while I set about milking the cows.

Chapter twenty-three

More Christmas madness

On Christmas Eve we attended Midnight Mass, the one service of the year when it seemed the entire village turned out. It was also the one service of the year when the church was lit by hundreds of candles and it was just so impressive.

Alice's Rose Hill relations had descended on Church Farm earlier in the evening and I was pleased to see Elizabeth was with them. When the time came to leave for the church, we all trooped down to the street and joined others making their way to the service.

I stayed close to Elizabeth and we held hands as we walked along the street and then up the steep slope to the church. I could hear the organ playing as we approached the entrance and I wondered if the organist was going to work his party trick with the volume increase.

Just as we set foot in the church I could hear Pedro braying. 'Can you hear that?' I asked Elizabeth.

'Afraid so,' she replied. 'And I think everyone else can too.'

She was right. People were leaning out to have a look behind us to see if we had brought Pedro and most of them looked relieved when they discovered we hadn't. Some were even flapping their hands in front of their noses, which I thought was a little unkind.

We found a vacant pew near the back of the church

and settled down for the service which started off well with a carol but seemed to lose its edge when the vicar gave the first reading accompanied by Pedro's braying which echoed through the church with quite amazing volume.

And it wasn't only once. With uncanny timing, every time the vicar drew breath to speak Pedro started bellowing. The vicar even tried starting and then stopping but Pedro had him every time.

As for congregation, what started as a polite sympathetic smile soon descended in to unstoppable hysterical laughter. I looked along the row to Harry and he was laughing along with the rest of them.

After the service had ended, the vicar stood at the door to wish everyone a Merry Christmas. 'Nice one, Harry,' he said when we were leaving. 'Perhaps you could wish Pedro a happy Christmas for me and thank him for making it a memorable service.'

Back to the farm and Harry switched the lights on the tree while Alice brought out a plate of sausage rolls and glasses of warmed mulled wine.

'How did you get the light on the top?' Elizabeth asked.

'Well, how long have you got?'

'All night,' she said.

'Do you think Pedro would like a sausage roll?'

She took my arm. 'Let's go and find out.'

***

Christmas day arrived as a bright frosty morning; a blue sky, white fields and a sun which, still low, cast long shadows across the cows as Harry brought them into the collecting yard.

'Happy Christmas girls!' I shouted. 'Today, the fodder beets are on me.' Not a big response but I received a long sideways look from Thrifty.

I started the engine, put a scoopful of ground barley in each feeder box, opened the gate for the first four cows and we were milking. Took a moment out to give a handful of barley to Thrifty and felt her big rough tongue rasping across my palm as she licked it clean, and then did the same for Horns but she insisted on having the backs of her ears stroked as well. I don't know who's soppier, me or her.

And then, surprise, surprise, Alice brought me a mug of tea. 'Happy Christmas, John,' she said, leaning over the gate to give me a kiss on the cheek.

A Happy Christmas to you too,' I said. 'It's a beautiful morning.'

'It is that. Don't be late for breakfast.' She turned and made her way back across the collecting yard.

'Well,' I said to the girls. 'This is a first – a mug of tea.'

I managed to meet the milk lorry driver as I took the churns down to the ramp and wished him a Merry Christmas.

'What's merry about it?' he said as he heaved the churns onto the lorry. 'I'm still getting up at four o'clock, driving a lorry with a dent in the side and mauling churns about all day. And now I'm having to put up with people wishing me a Happy Christmas and then, when my back's turned calling me a miserable old sod.'

'Oh, I'm sorry to hear that,' I said. 'But listen, you have a wonderful day and make a really big effort not to be a miserable old sod.'

I loaded the empty churns on to the trolley and pulled it back up the slope to the dairy and ran into Harry.

'That milk lorry bloke isn't very festive,' I said.

'Oh him, he's just a miserable old sod,' said Harry.

'The Land Rover's loaded if you want to take the feed out to the cows now or after breakfast. It's up to you.'

'I think I'll clean up the bail and get the milking machines down here for Alice and then take the feed out afterwards. There will also be the fodder beet to take out for them and the sheep.'

Somewhere along the way, someone had managed to decorate the kitchen with paper chains and sprigs of holly and beside each bowl of cereal there was a glass of warmed mulled wine. Harry had put a Father Christmas hat on.

'What do you reckon, boy?'

'I think you make a very good Father Christmas, Harry,' I said and raised my glass to him. It was then I noticed there was an extra place setting.

'Are we expecting guests at breakfast?'

'No one you don't know,' Alice said.

Then, on cue, it seemed, the kitchen door opened and in walked Elizabeth.

'Happy Christmas everyone,' she said. 'And a special Happy Christmas to you, John.'

I thought she looked wonderful and stood up to give her a kiss. 'Happy Christmas,' I said. 'But I would have thought you would have been with your family.'

'Well Uncle Harry called round this morning and I cadged a lift with him. It's alright - everyone's going to be here for dinner, anyway.'

'And it's lovely to see you,' Alice said. 'Sit yourself down and tuck in. I don't want to hurry you guys but I need to get the turkey into the oven.'

'I can give you a hand if you want,' Elizabeth said.

'No, there's no need. I think I'm just about organised, thank you.'

Harry cleared his throat. 'If you really want something to do, you can give John some help with the fodder beet,' he said.

Elizabeth turned and looked at me. 'Oh, that would be fun, wouldn't it John?'

'If you drive the tractor, I can fork it off,' I said. 'If that's alright with you?'

'Of course it is,' she replied.

'Right then, that's that sorted,' Harry said. 'Now who wants another slice of boiled bacon – one more for Christmas?'

***

Rose Hill drove into the yard shortly after two o'clock,

young William, and two of the girls squashed into the front of a pick-up driven by Kate, and grandma, grandad, in the back of a car driven by dour William.

Harry and I wandered out to greet them. 'That's the end of peace in our time,' he muttered as the girls thundered past us. 'They breed like rabbits.'

'Happy Christmas everyone,' Kate yelled, hefting a huge sack on to her shoulder which I assume held a load of presents.

'Happy Christmas,' I replied, wondering if I should offer to carry the sack, but thought not.

'Morning Harry,' said dour William, as he strolled past us. 'Nice tree, pity about the window.'

'And Happy Christmas to you too,' said Harry.

Young William swaggered towards us, clearly experiencing discomfort in the nether regions due to an ill-fitting pair of jeans that had either shrunk in the wash or had been in the wardrobe since last Christmas. And it could have been that the sports jacket he was wearing fitted marginally better at that time too.

'Happy Christmas,' he said, pausing to look at the tree. 'Nice tree, pity about the window, though.'

Meanwhile Grandma and Grandad had made it out of the car, gathered up their walking sticks and were on their way towards the house.

'Give Grandma a hand and I'll give Grandad a push,' Harry said. 'It'll be time to go home before they get in at this rate.'

'Nice tree... pity about the window...though,' Grandad stuttered, his walking stick trembling. 'Could be a good opportunity let go a bit of money and double glaze it, you tight bastard.'

Harry sighed.

Inside there was bedlam as presents were exchanged and paper wrapping lay strewn across the floor. Alice had brought in a big plastic bag to place the paper in but it remained largely unused.

For my part, I slipped away up to my room suddenly feeling strangely alienated. This was their Christmas and just at this moment downstairs wasn't the place for me to be. I sat on the bed and stared out across the grave yard and tried, as I always did, to work out which one of the grave stones was responsible for casting a shadow on to my curtains at night.

It was a problem I didn't get much of a chance to work on because there was a tap on the door and Elizabeth came in.

'What are you doing up here?' she asked.

'Oh, I don't know. It just didn't feel as I should be with you all while you were doing the present thing – and I didn't think anyone would notice if I wasn't there.'

She sat down on the bed and wrapped her arms around me and stared into my face. 'John,' she started. 'I love you so much I want this to be our Christmas too, so please don't run away from it. Let's enjoy it together,'

'I love you too,' I said. 'Yes, let's do just that.'

She got up and took my hand. 'Come on then. I'm not sure Alice will be too approving if she knew where we were.'

'I don't know what she will think if she sees the wet patch where you've been sitting,' I said.

'What! That's your wet tractor seat,' she gasped.

'But before we go I want to give you this.' I pulled open the top drawer of my dressing table and removed her present.

'Oh, John, you shouldn't have. Shall I open it now?' she asked her hand already pulling at the red strings.

'Of course, it's Christmas day.'

With the wrapping removed, she opened the box to reveal the bracelet.

'It's wonderful. Thank you,' she exclaimed, kissing me madly.

I stood back. 'Try it on. I'll give you a hand with the clasp.'

'There,' she said holding her wrist up when I had managed to make the two ends stay together. 'It's perfect. Shall I keep it on?'

'I'd like that,' I said giving her another kiss. 'But we'd better be getting back down there.'

'Not before I give you your present,' she said.

And for me that really was the highlight of Christmas although the dinner came pretty close to it. Held in the front room around a table big enough for everyone to sit up to, crackers were pulled, jokes read out and silly hats placed on heads. The turkey, too heavy to carry from the kitchen, was wheeled in on a trolley and calved ceremoniously by Harry. Alice passed him the plates which soon became piled up with sprouts and all the trimmings of a traditional Christmas dinner.

'If you're good, you can have my boiled bacon,' I whispered to Elizabeth sitting beside me.

From then on, after a glass or two of red wine and a generous helping of port, it was all a bit of a haze and I was almost relieved when, at about four o'clock I walked up the yard with Elizabeth to fetch the cows in for milking.

'It's good to get some fresh air,' I said.

'Yes,' she replied. 'But you have to say Alice put together a tremendous dinner.'

'She's amazing.'

The cows were waiting by the paddock gate and all I had to do was open it and watch them walk across to the collecting yard.

'You've got them well trained,' she said. 'Our lot make a point of retreating to the farthest end of the field when they know it's time for milking. I've watched them do it.'

'Ah, you haven't got cows like old Thrifty here,' I said as she walked by. 'She's as placid and friendly as a cow can be.'

By the time we had the churns in the fridge and the cows fed, the sky had cleared and a hard frost had set in.

Even as we spread the hay, the grass we were walking on had a crisp sound to it.

When we made my way down to the house there was hardly a sound to be heard; everywhere was just so quiet and, as I looked upwards, the sky was full of stars, as many as I had ever seen. 'Love you, Elizabeth,' I said.

'Love you too, John.'

Two strides away from making it into the house the kitchen door opened and we were met by Alice holding a jug.

'I need some more milk, John if you wouldn't mind fetching it,' she said.

'Not at all,' I replied, taking the jug from her and heading back to the dairy leaving Elizabeth to make her way into the kitchen. I pulled open the fridge door, stepped in and lifted the lid of a full churn and noticed that the cream was already on the top – not just your top of the milk cream but the really thick cream that sticks to the top of your mouth.

I grabbed the scoop with it long handle and dipped it into the top inch of milk and let some flow into the scoop. I couldn't resist it and took a long swig of the rich cream – delicious. Alice though, just wanted milk so I dipped the scoop into the churn and gave it a good swirl round before taking a couple of scoopfuls and filling the jug.

Back in the house I slipped off my boots and overalls and washed my hands before putting the jug of milk in the fridge. Harry emerged from the front room.

'We're off down to Rose Hill for the evening,' he said. 'Kate's prepared a feast for us and there will be a few frolics so if you fancy coming, we'll be leaving in about half an hour.

'Has everyone gone then?'

'Well, not quite. Young William and his father left to do the milking just after you did and Kate, Grandma and Grandpa and the two girls left a little later, all squeezed in the car.'

'And Elizabeth?' I asked.

'She wanted to stop a little longer and go down with us. I don't remember why though.'

I smiled. 'Oh right. I'll go and have a quick bath and get ready then. Tell Alice I've put the milk in the fridge.'

Chapter twenty-four

Ploughing lessons

'What did you reckon to last night?' Harry asked, as he poured the boiling water from the kettle into the teapot.

'It was very good, too much food, but very good. I still don't quite understand why you were wearing a pair of green tights and the Father Christmas hat, but there you go. And I thought the lights-out game of hide-and-seek was a little over played with you hiding behind the bath panel. I mean, what were you doing with a screwdriver anyhow?'

'That's nothing,' Harry said. 'Young William climbed on top of the wardrobe and discovered his mother was already there.'

I could have added that Elizabeth and I sneaked off and found a comfortable part of the airing cupboard until we were found by dour William using a long cane to prod everywhere he looked.

'Anyway, it was all a bit of fun,' Harry said as he left to take Alice's cup of tea up to her.

It was my cue to fetch the bucket in from the dairy and fill it with hot water. Harry set off to fetch the cows in and the day could begin. It was bitterly cold day though and even though I had wrapped up with everything I could find, my feet and hands were soon painfully cold.

The ruts across the paddock were frozen hard and the

cows picked their way carefully over them, clearly not enjoying the experience. Their difficulty was also noted by Harry who put his head over the gate to tell me to keep the cows in today.

'We could end up with a lot of foot problems,' he said. 'And a lame cow soon goes off her feed and milk yields plummet like you've never seen.'

Halfway through milking, the bucket of water was cold and dirty, so I ran down to the house to get some more hot water, if only to try and keep my hands warmer. I think the cows appreciated a nice warm wash of their udders. If you do it right she will let her milk down a lot more quickly and not need so much milking out.

'I think it's about time we started turning over a bit of soil, boy,' Harry announced at breakfast time. 'Next week will be the New Year and before you know it we will be in to spring and there will be ewes lambing and crops which will need drilling and all the rest of it. I'll help you put the plough on the tractor and we'll take it down to the Forty Acre field and see how we go.'

He turned to Alice. 'Can you make some lunch for John, there's no point him coming all the way back here for half an hour.'

The plough was under the machinery shed, as it had been since I started work on the farm and while I had given it a cursory once over there was still a lot of handles and adjustments for which I hadn't a clue what they were for.

I reversed the tractor towards the plough having lowered the two linkage arms which, if I get it right, would connect with the plough's cross bar.

'Keep her coming,' said Harry, beckoning me with his hand. 'Another inch and you're there.'

Harry pushed the ends of the linkage arms on and inserted lynch pins to prevent them slipping off again.

'Now we need to attach the top link which is an extendible bar that connects the tractor to the plough and creates the three-point-linkage – two arms down here and the top link up here.'

With all the pins in place I pulled the lift control lever and raised the plough off the ground.

'Right then, make sure you've a full tank of fuel and then set off down to the Forty-Acre and I'll see you there. You'd better find something warm to wear too.'

I think I had already worked that out and I had doubled up on coats and bale string to the point it was becoming difficult to climb on and off the tractor. But here I was setting off for my first go with the plough, the task I had read so much about; the task which dated back to biblical times and beyond; the task by which all tractor drivers are judged. I was excited at the prospect.

'The point is that the top of the ground is frozen and the wheels will get so much more grip,' explained Harry when we met up in the field. 'That is until it starts to thaw and then you'll be skating around all over the place and looking for grip from the furrow.'

'Not much chance of that today,' I said. 'Or for the coming week, if the forecast is correct.'

'Right then – the basics. Good ploughing is straight, the furrows are level and even, and all the surface rubbish is buried. You'll note, if you haven't already, that the mouldboards turn the soil only one way and so we can't plough up and down the field, we need to mark the field out and plough in lands.'

I nodded. Already I was feeling apprehensive about all this. It had occurred to me that this was a job in which it was possible to make a horrible mess. And I couldn't see Harry being very forgiving if or when I did.

'I've some marker poles in the back of the Land Rover so we'll put those out first so we at least start with a straight furrow,' he said.

I joined him in the cab and felt the warmth but not for long. We drove over to a point which was a short distance away from the hedge line and stopped. 'Walk over to the hedge and step out thirty-five yards towards the Land Rover and stick a pole in the ground,' he said.

We then drove about fifty yards down the field and did my stepping out again and placed a second pole in the ground.

'The third pole wants to be in line with the two you've already placed,' Harry said. 'And now you'll wish you had put them upright and not leaning over.'

He was right. As I held the pole and squinted to try and line it up it was difficult to know which bit of it to use. But I managed, I think.

And so we worked our way down the field until there was a string of marker poles stretching from one end to the other. Harry took me over to where we had left the tractor and I followed him to the where the poles began.

'Now reverse back to the hedge and relax, sit square in the seat and line the tractor and your eyes up with the poles. You should only be able to see one pole with all the others lined up behind it. Keep it like that as you move down the field and you will be straight.'

With a bit of shunting I felt I was about in the right position.

'Now comes the tricky bit,' Harry said.

And you think what we've just done wasn't tricky, I thought.

'Lower the plough and drive forwards a few yards – keeping the poles in line.'

I needed eyes in the back of my head.

'Alright, stop and jump off the tractor.'

I did as I was asked and joined Harry looking at the plough.

'What we want to do is draw out the first furrow with only the back mouldboard so it leaves a just a shallow turn of the soil you can use to drive in when you plough back up the field.'

Harry started turning handles and adjusting linkages muttering about shortening this, lengthening that and levelling probably everything else. 'Right try that,' he said.

I climbed onto the tractor and began to drive forwards until after a few yards, Harry shouted for me to stop so he could make a few more adjustments. After numerous other stops and starts I was allowed to keep going, concentrating hard on keeping everything in line. Harry drove down beside me and retrieved the poles.

When I reached the other end of the field I dared to turn round and have a look and I was impressed; a single shallow furrow and almost arrow-straight.

'Not bad, boy. The skill now is to keep it straight.'

I turned the tractor round, placed the front right wheel in the shallow furrow I had made and lowered the plough. More stops and starts and more complicated adjustments but eventually I was creating two even furrows at a depth of about eight inches.

'For the next run, you need to create a furrow on the other side so you can go down one side of the land and up the other,' Harry said. 'And match ploughmen take hours on this and it looks terrific but the ground won't grow any more crop for it. We are commercial ploughing so you want to run the plough so it moves the unturned soil which sits below the soil that was moved over by the mouldboard on you last run.

Harry had me there. 'Where do I run the front wheel then?'

Harry scoffed and walked round to the front of the tractor and stamped his boot on the ground. 'Just there, boy,' he said.

The next run with the plough placed extra soil on top to create a ridge and when we had achieved that there was now a furrow to run the tractor wheels in and this called for more plough adjustment.

'All you need to do is get off the tractor and have a look at the plough from the side and ask yourself whether it's level and shorten or lengthen the top link to make it level, and then look from the back and see again if the plough is level – if it's not, wind up or lower a linkage arm,' he said. 'And then you should be about there.'

'How about the discs and these things?' I asked pointing to some miniature mouldboards that hung down in front of the main mouldboards.

'These 'things' are the skimmers which take off the top inch or so of soil with its vegetation and drop it in front of the mouldboard so that it gets buried. They're a right pain to adjust using wedges to angle them and clamps to alter their depth. In some conditions you can take them off but don't forget where you leave them. The discs make a vertical cut in the soil so the mouldboard and skimmers make a clean job of taking the right width of soil.'

I hadn't realised just how complicated a plough could be and at this stage I wouldn't begin to know what to adjust with any confidence.

'Don't worry boy. The golden rule is, if it's ploughing alright leave everything alone to get on with the job. If you start meddling you'll find that one adjustment leads to another and another and you'll get nowhere. Get the plough level and you'll always be about there.'

And with that, Harry walked over to the Land Rover and dug out a bag with my lunch in which he hung on the fence and placed the stack of marker poles alongside. He then drove out of the field and, as he did, the first seagulls appeared from nowhere and settled down on the ground to wait for me to start ploughing and turn up plenty of worms for them to eat.

I set off and had to get used to sitting with the tractor at an angle – the right-hand wheels were in the furrow and about eight inches lower than the left-hand wheels which were on the unploughed land. Looking behind me, I could see the soil being turned by the mouldboards, the skimmers just taking off the top couple of inches, as Harry had explained.

For the next hour or two, I carried on ploughing down one side and up the other and, as the land became wider I began to wonder what I should do when I ran out of ground on the hedge side. I was also very cold.

When I reached the far end of the field I stopped to have a think about it and it dawned on me I needed to start another land and that would mean that I would, at some stage, have to bring two lands together.

It was something that wasn't going to happen today or possibly the day after. The two-furrow plough only took about thirty inches at a time and in a forty acre field, things didn't happen very quickly. There would be time to ask Harry.

My feet felt as if they had died, it was so cold. For the first time, I took one of them off and held it over the exhaust pipe and when I pulled it back on it was just so good, so I did the same with the other one and, for possibly five minutes I was returned to some semblance of normality. But it didn't last and soon I was stopping to warm my feet and hands on the exhaust pipe at the end of every bout.

Lunch time arrived and I drove along the headland to where Harry left my lunch bag. Have to say that when I opened it I was disappointed: a bottle of tea which was ice cold and a boiled bacon sandwich. Hardly the piping hot soup in a flask I had half expected, but at least it was something.

Ten minutes later I was ploughing again and to break the monotony and perhaps work some warmth into my feet, I thought I would have a go at setting out another land using the starting procedure Harry had explained – stepping out the width and marking it with poles so I could create a straight opening furrow.

After I had gone through it all I was feeling rather pleased with myself; the opening was almost straight, and I had ended up with the two furrows to plough off. All I needed to do was plough as far as I could with the first land until I had met the hedge and then start on the new land and hope they met without any horrible triangles.

But that was all for tomorrow but for now, with the light starting to fade, I wished my seagull friends a goodnight and headed back to the farm to milk the cows.

***

The days during the next two weeks became almost a routine. After I'd finished milking, cleaning up and feeding the cows their daily ration of hay and fodder beet, I would have breakfast during which time Alice would pack up a boiled bacon sandwich and a bottle of tea.

I always wondered why she bothered to make it hot because by the time I had refuelled the tractor and checked water and oil levels, it had lost most of its heat and well on its way to becoming ice cold.

But that was the way it had been done for years and it wasn't going to change. I wondered if bottles were used originally to put cider in but then, that might have resulted in some bendy ploughing and that would never do. I had a vision of a ploughman swigging farm brewed scrumpy cider as he walked behind his team of shire horses plodding up the furrow. It might not have been straight but I bet his feet were warm.

On the third day I asked Harry what happens when two lands come together.

'I'd better come down and show you,' he said. 'How long have you got before they get somewhere close?'

'Not until this afternoon, I would think. I stepped out fifty yards so there's a fair bit to go at.'

'Right, I'll be down after lunch,' Harry said.

I set off down the track, took a left turn halfway down Brier Hill and headed on down for the Forty-Acre. From half way up the hill I could see the area I had ploughed and, although it was small, I was rather proud of it – the freshly turned soil contrasting with the dull, weathered stubble of the previous barley crop.

The temperature was still sub-zero but this time I had made an effort to stay at least half warm. I had grabbed a couple of large hessian sacks to place over my knees and squeezed into yet another coat which Harry said had been a fireman's coat. Anyway, whatever it was, it certainly helped keep the cold out and I felt a lot better. There was though, still the problem of my feet which were already starting to give me some grief despite doubling up in the socks department. Oh well, here comes the exhaust pot.

I lowered the plough and within a few yards it was working at full depth and the soil, forced to follow the shape of the mouldboard was turned over. At this end of the farm, it was predominantly a clay soil which needs a lot of weathering to ease the task of creating a seedbed in the spring. At the top of Brier Hill, the soil changed to the much lighter sand, soil Harry described as being 'boys' land'.

I hadn't travelled far down the first bout of the day when the seagulls arrived and this time they had brought all their friends. There were hundreds of them and they all fought and squabbled over the worms the plough brought to the surface.

They came so close I thought it could only be a matter of time before I was bombed when a seagull emptied its bowls over me but, strangely, it never happened. Close, yes, but a direct hit, inverted yogurt carton on the head-type, thankfully no. Well, not so far.

As arranged, Harry arrived in the field after lunch, caught up with me and drove alongside as I ploughed. When he stopped I brought the tractor to a halt too and he asked me how it was going.

'Not too badly,' I said. 'Bit of a job to keep straight but I think it's turning over alright,' I said. 'What do you think?'

'It looks good, boy. I've seen a lot worse. Anyway, Alice has made you up a plate of lunch seeing as I was coming down, so if you jump in the Land Rover and tuck in, I'll carry on ploughing.'

'Oh, that's very kind of her,' I said, heading straight for the cab, wondering if I started the engine there would be some heat on my feet. 'There's some Hessian sacks for your knees,' I told him, as I climbed aboard and began to shut the door, already savouring the heat.

'Sacks? You don't need those. They're for wimps,' Harry yelled as he put the tractor into gear and moved off.

I started the engine, turned the heat to full and unwrapped a plate loaded with hot food – roast lamb, potatoes, sprouts and lashings of thick gravy. Take your time, Harry. I'm in no rush.

All too soon, though, Harry was back round with me again and I left it until the last moment to leave my warm quarters, but not too late to see Harry slide the sacks of his knees.

'Bloody hell that's a bit chill when you get going. It's us thin ones which feel the cold, isn't it boy,' he said, flapping his arms around him and stomping his feet.

'So, you need to know how we bring these two lands together, then?' he said. 'Let's climb in the Land Rover and I'll explain.'

We made ourselves comfortable and Harry began. 'The object is to leave a straight finish which isn't too deep. In an ideal world, you will have brought the two sides together not just parallel with each other but also at set distance which is a multiple of the width of the plough.'

'How on earth do you manage that?'

'Ploughing contestants keep measuring the gap and adjust the plough's working width by a few inches over a series of bouts so that when they meet they do it spot on, hopefully. But this commercial ploughing and we don't have the time to keep stopping and measuring so the usual way is to select the side which you think is the straightest and then plough the other side up to it.'

Harry started fiddling with the heater control and I told him it was already turned to maximum heat.

'On a two-furrow plough,' he continued, 'this means ploughing until the front nearside wheel is just in the furrow of the land side you're ploughing to and once you've done that all the way, you pull out a shallower run which leaves just one furrow width of unploughed land. This is the piece you turnover on the next run and the job is done. Got it?'

'Well not really but if you're staying for a little longer perhaps we could work through it together.'

We both climbed onto the tractor, Harry sitting on the mudguard. 'Right,' he shouted in my ear. 'Which side are going to use as the straightest one?'

'The other one,' I replied.

'OK. Plough down to the end and then set the plough a little shallower and plough up the straight side.'

On the headland I wound down the depth wheel to keep the plough working at about five inches and ploughed back up to the top. We were now left with a narrow piece of unploughed land some narrower than others where the furrow bent a little.

'Keep the plough shallow and plough until you front left wheel drops into the opposite furrow,' said Harry. 'When it does that lift the plough up and lower it again when the wheel isn't far enough over to do that.'

I did as Harry asked and when we reached the end and looked back, it appeared to be a horrible mess, but Harry insisted it was alright.

'Now you'll have to drive along the headland and plough up the other side of the land you've made at a normal depth and then drive back to the other end for the penultimate run.

Ten minutes later I was back at the start of the 'mess clearing run' and set the left wheel in the straight furrow and ploughed at a shallow depth all the way down and then, with just one furrow of unploughed land to turn over, ploughed back up to the other end to remove it.

'It's a result,' Harry said, as we looked back at the completed finish. 'And it doesn't look too bad. You'll need to set another land out now.'

I drove round to where the Land Rover was and

dropped Harry off. 'Feels as if the wind is getting up,' he said. 'I should call it a day when you've marked out the new land and come back and get the milking started.'

And I wasn't going to argue with that. The wind was strengthening and with it came darkening clouds which threatened no good. If there was to be more snow I really didn't want to be down here so when I had the marker poles in place I ran out a single furrow and then headed for the farm.

One day, I thought, all tractors will have cabs, heated cabs and operators will be provided with a comfortable environment in which to work. And they will achieve more work because of the cab – not running off home when there's an ice-cold gale blowing outside.

I needed to thaw out before I started the milking so I retreated to the kitchen and leaned against the Rayburn as Alice made a cup of tea.

'Thanks for the lunch today, Alice,' I said. 'I think it just about saved my life.'

She laughed. 'Well you can't survive on just cold tea in that weather,' she said.

By the time I made it up to the collecting yard there was sleet in the air and, as cows do, they all stood with their tales to the wind which always seemed strange to me but who was I to argue? Cows have weathered storms standing in that direction for centuries.

'Come on then girls,' I said, as I opened the gate for the first four cows to enter. 'Let's get this job over with and then you can all go back to your warm barn.'

This evening though, I had a new girl in the herd. She was a freshly calved Friesian heifer that Harry bought from Smiths. She'd being running with the rest of the herd for a few days before she calved so that she knew where she needed to be and enjoy a mouthful of ground barley.

I decided to call her Lucy and when it was her turn to come into the bale she seemed reasonably calm about it but when I started to wash her udder she took exception and started dancing about.

'Come on Lucy girl. It's only a nice warm cloth,' I told her, giving the top of her tail a scratch. I tried again and this time she half tolerated it but she was tensing up.

'That's it,' I said. 'That's you all nice and clean.'

I moved in with the cluster and offered one cup to a teat and the world exploded as her legs flew out at me and she banged about in the stall. Standing up and seeing if I had any damage, I was relieved to see that apart from a liberal dressing of warm slurry oozing its way down my left leg, I was still in one piece.

I let her stand there and calm down. There were other cows to milk standing in the other stalls and Lucy will have to learn how it all works. Eventually though, I came back to her and rewashed her udder and teats and tentatively brought the cluster to her and tried again to put a cup on a teat.

This time she wasn't quite so bad but I still had three more to put on. 'That's it little girl,' I told her. 'Just one more and you've done it.'

I placed the fourth teat cup and held my breath as I stood up, all the time speaking to her and telling how good she was. I gave her some more feed to keep her mind off other things.

And that was it. When it came to removing the cups I gave her udder a light stroke to let her know I was there and then, bending the milk tube to release the vacuum, gently removed the cups. After a handful of udder cream to stop any soreness I opened the door and she walked out.

Shortly after that, Harry walked across the yard and inquired how the new heifer was.

'Oh, she's fine. Danced and kicked a bit to start with but she settled down and milked well,' I said.

'That's good. I was going to give you a helping hand.'

'No, no need for that. I think she'll soon settle in with the other girls but I'll see how she is in the morning.'

Harry turned to go but received a push in the back by a Red Poll called Greta. 'Are there any of these cows you haven't turned into affectionate monsters?' he asked, wiping snot off his jacket.

I laughed. 'Give them each a handful of ground barley and they'll love you for ever,' I said. 'But you have to love them too.'

Chapter twenty-five

Fluffy pink

In contrast to the Christmas shenanigans, New Year's Eve was a relatively mild affair and it began with me taking Elizabeth down to the George Inn for a drink and a chat. The place was quiet at first but as the evening wore on, it became busier as people decided that this was where they were going to bring in the New Year.

Very soon we found ourselves sharing a table with a couple who, when the conversation moved round to work, instantly latched on to the subject of Pedro, and that tended to dominate the hour we spent with them.

'That donkey is a star,' they said, and then went on to tell us why they thought he was. 'But his got his faults, like all of us, after all, he's only human.'

I thought if they could bray and pass wind like Pedro they would have more than just a fault, more a serious condition, but I just nodded and agreed. Eventually, much as we were enjoying their company we had to say goodbye at which point they insisted on kissing and wishing us both a Happy New Year.'

'They were good company,' Elizabeth said as we made our way towards Doctor's Hill. 'Sort of heart and soul stuff.'

'That's what society is made of.' We walked on a little further. 'When did you say you're back at college?'

'I think I'm due there on the tenth. Will you miss me?'

'Too much and I've been wondering what we can do about it.'

'Mum said you should be looking to go to college too,' she said. 'And I think she's right, if that gives you any ideas.'

There was a long wooden fence in Doctor's Hill behind which was Bill McKinley's coal yard and when Elizabeth stopped suddenly, I found myself falling backwards towards it. And not only did it not stop me falling, it sort of funnelled me into a pit which was full of coal dust.

'John!' screamed Elizabeth. 'Are you alright?'

I was aware of lights being switched on and someone heading our way muttering about, 'Bloody drunken kids and needing to call the police.'

'It was an accident,' Elizabeth said when someone arrived. 'I think he must have tripped up or something. He didn't do it on purpose and he's not drunk.'

'That's what they all say. I suppose you'll be after a bag or two of my nutty slack, or something.'

Meanwhile I was trying to extricate myself from the pit. It wasn't very deep but the sides were steep and it was few minutes before I made it over the edge and was able to stand up.

'Are you alright, John?'

'Just a bit shaken up and very dirty.' I tried to brush off some of the coal dust but it was oily and clung to me. I turned to face whoever it was giving us a hard time. 'Look, I'm very sorry about all this. As Elizabeth explained, it was complete accident, I must have tripped or something.'

'Is that Harry Wilcox's wee lad?' the man asked, as he shone his torch into my face. I squinted and tried to see who was asking. The lights were fierce and all I could see was a dark outline.

'Yes, it is. And who are you?'

'It's Bill, Bill McKinley. Who else would you be expecting now? You'd better come in and get cleaned up,' he said, his Glaswegian accent as broad as ever. 'And if truth be known, I should have replaced that fence years ago. But it's the cost of these things. Do you not agree?'

We followed him into the house and into the kitchen where there was a boiler pumping heat out.

'I think I'm making footprints on your floor,' I said.

'Don't you worry about that, it'll wipe. But if you could keep your hands in your pocket it would be better. Anyway, I can see you now, well at least the bit of you that's not covered in coal dust.

'Well, well, fancy that, Mildred, we've got Harry Wilcox's lad in here,' he shouted. And then he turned to Elizabeth. 'I'm sorry, I'm forgetting my manners. I don't think we've met.'

'I'm Elizabeth, my parents have the farm along the Sulgrave Road,' she replied, as Mildred came into the kitchen.

What, Rose Hill Farm?'

'Yes, that's the one.'

'Well, well, fancy that. Mildred, we've got Will Saunder's daughter in here too.'

'I think we should be going,' I said. 'It's been very kind of you to ask us in and I do apologise for the damage to your fence. Perhaps I could have a look at it in daylight with you and see what can be done.'

'You can't let him go in that condition,' Mildred said. 'Look at him. He looks like his just done eight hours down the pit. What will people think and it being New Year's Eve and all that and Alice won't be very pleased if you walk in with that all over you. She'll not like it one bit.'

Mildred had a point and I thought of the jibbing I'd get from Harry and no doubt dour William would want to chip in with some caustic comment, not to mention William the younger with his new-found oratory skills. 'What do you suggest?' I asked.

'Well, if you slip off your jacket, shirt and trousers, I'll drop them in the washing machine while you pop upstairs and have a quick shower. Bill will show you where everything is.'

'Yes, but won't my clothes be wet?'

'No, bless you. This isn't Harry's, the old skinflint. There's a tumble drier over there which will have everything dry in no time.'

I looked at Elizabeth. 'What do you think?'

'I don't think you have a choice if you don't want two families ganging up on you,' she said.

'I suppose you're right.'

Mildred took Elizabeth's arm. 'Now you just come in here with me and leave them to it. You'll not believe this but your grandad once took me out to the cinema.'

I shut the door and stripped off and followed Bill up to the shower room.

'There're some clean towels in the cupboard and I'll leave you a dressing gown on the door hook,' he said.

Ten minutes and I was down stairs again, wearing an enormous fluffy pink dressing gown.

'Very smart, John,' Elizabeth said as I walked in. 'If I had a camera I could make a fortune and if Harry was here he'd be rolling around the floor.'

'Yes, well. When needs must,' I said, pulling the sash a little tighter around my waist.

'Sit yourself down then,' ordered Mildred. 'Bill's putting some drinks together.'

And that was the start of it. When it came to pouring whisky, Bill had a very heavy hand and he didn't leave a lot of space for any water.

'A man has to let himself go once a year. And where better to do it than with two good friends when it's Hogmanay.' He raised his glass and took a large gulp. 'And John, my old friend, don't you ever be putting water in my whisky.'

'You'll be having a wee top up too,' he said after he had poured another generous amount of whisky into his glass.

'No, I'm fine thanks. Just fine.'

'Come on,' he cajoled. 'It's New Year's Eve just another wee dram to be social.'

There was no saying no so I held up my glass and

watched him fill it up. 'And I think I'll join you,' he said, taking the bottle back to his own glass. 'But only to the top, this time.'

Elizabeth leaned over to me and whispered we should be going but I suddenly found I was enjoying Bill's company.

'Oh, come on Elizabeth. Like Bill said, it's New Year's Eve and we're being social with Bill. Are we not?' I took another large sip of whisky. 'We have so much to talk about, don't we Bill.'

'You're drunk and you're slurring,' she said. 'Come on, let's go.'

I lowered the glass to the table and tried to get up off the sofa but my legs didn't want to go. Elizabeth took hold of my arm and helped me on my way.

'You'll not be going so soon, are you?' Bill said, clutching a fresh bottle of whisky.

I opened my mouth. It moved but nothing came out.

'I'm afraid we have to go,' Elizabeth said. 'We have to be somewhere.'

'That's a real shame. But nay bother we can do it again another day. What do you say to that?'

'That's very kind of you and we look forward to it.'

Elizabeth was edging me towards the door and I did my best to keep up with her.

'Clothes,' I managed to utter, trying to point in the direction of the tumble dryer.

'Don't you worry about those. I'll drop them round tomorrow,' said Mildred, turning to Elizabeth. 'I don't suppose he's capable of putting them on, anyhow, not in that condition. You'd better go out the front door and remember me to your grandad.'

'Thank you, I will and may I wish you and Bill a happy New Year.'

I'm not sure how we made it up the slope to the farm. I was hanging on to Elizabeth's arm all the way. What I hadn't realised was that somewhere along the way the sash on the dressing gown had dropped off and the open folds were just flapping about in the wind.

'So, what do we have here?' asked Harry, when we walked into the kitchen. 'The ghost of fluffy pink, or someone who just lost his trousers at Bill McKinley's?'

I looked up and could see a haze of faces all turned towards me. I tried to smile and raise an arm to them and the folds of the dressing gown parted.

'Oh, my goodness. Not in front of the girls, John. Please!' Kate said.

And then through my drink befuddled mind I heard someone counting the clock down to midnight and the cheer as the church clock chimed the hour. I turned and kissed Elizabeth. 'Happy New Year. S'love you slots,' I whispered.

'Come on, stand up everybody it's time for Auld Lang Zine,' Alice said. And someone linked arms with me and we did our best to remember the words and for most of us, the tune.

***

'How much is there left to plough in the Forty-Acre?' asked Harry at breakfast time, the following day.

'There has to be another three days' work and then there will be the headlands,' I said.

Harry thought about it. 'I think we'll try keeping the tractor going for a bit longer each day,' he said. 'I'll take it down and start ploughing after I've fetched the cows in for you and then, when you've had breakfast bring the Land Rover down and can you plough until milking time. I can get my jobs done when I get back here and then at about half past three I'll drive back down and take over from you for another hour or two. How does that sound?'

'I think it's a good plan but you'll have to bring some diesel down with you in the afternoon. I don't think you'll last the day, otherwise.'

Harry nodded. 'Right then, that's what we'll do. Is that alright with you, Alice?'

'Yes, that will be fine. It will just mean a later breakfast for you. At least it's not so cold today.'

I heard Harry set off as I was attaching the milking cups to Lucy, the new addition to the herd and she had yet to get used to being milked. Apart from a little dance about when I cleaned her teats, she was as good as gold, and I told her so.

All of which was very promising but Lucy still had to fit into the society of the herd where there was a level of membership. In some herds this can lead to bullying and conflict, something I think I managed to avoid by trying to always be the central focus and to treat them all as equally as possible. But if I saw just a hint of any unfair activities I would step in to sort it out.

Alice had been right, it was noticeably less cold today; there was still a frost but the wind had dropped away and there was a warming sun. When I had pulled the last of the empty churns up from the street I was looking to shed a layer of clothing before I set about taking some feed out for the cows.

With Harry not about, it was a laborious process and meant I had to stop the tractor, climb up onto the trailer and fork some beet off and then jump down and drive the tractor on a few yards before repeating.

Breakfast was a brief affair and, with Harry missing, lacked the repartee I had become used to at that time of the day. I also think Alice was concerned about Harry's late breakfast and she wanted me down the field ploughing so he could return. So, with a bottle of tea and a boiled bacon sandwich, I climbed into the Land Rover and drove down the track.

At the top of Brier Hill, I paused to see how Harry was getting on. He took a bit of finding but I eventually spotted him stopped on the headland and yes, he had a boot off and holding it over the exhaust pipe.

By the time I drove through the gateway he was half way down the field so I caught up with him and followed him down to the end of the bout. I noticed there was more wheel slip now that the frost had lifted making the ground greasy and when we stopped Harry said he had needed to engage the differential lock pedal.

'Most of the grip is now coming from the wheel in the furrow,' he said. 'Without the differential lock the wheel running on the unploughed land will just spin but remember to release it on the headland or you'll just keep travelling on into the hedge, however hard you turn the steering wheel. Other than that, it's going well but we'll soon have to change the shares, they're getting worn down; everything alright at the farm?'

'Yes, I think so. The new heifer milked a treat and the rest of the girls are as they ever are although I think the Hereford cross may be thinking about calving. She's been springing up for a few days and her pelvic ligaments are pretty relaxed. Perhaps you could have a look at her in the way up.'

Harry moved over to the Land Rover. 'I'll do that, boy and I'll see you this afternoon.' He opened the door, reached in and pulled out the bag with the bottle of tea and the sandwich. 'Don't forget these,' he said.

'Hang the bag on the hedge,' I said.

'Won't your tea get cold?' he asked.

I didn't trust myself to reply. I engaged high-first gear and set off along the headland, turned into the furrow and started ploughing up the other side of the land, remembering to press the diff-lock pedal down with the heel of my right boot.

The seagulls arrived a little later today and I thought they may have already been for a feed when Harry was ploughing but they set about pulling worms out with their usual squabbling and quarrelling, so it seemed unlikely. Perhaps they had been up late celebrating the New Year; tractor driving does funny things to the mind, it seems.

As lunch time approached I could see the lands starting to come together and the time was approaching when I would have to remember what Harry had told me about bringing them together to leave a shallow, straight finish with all the ground ploughed.

I delayed this operation by setting out another land and then stopping for a drink of very lukewarm tea and an attempt at eating a boiled bacon sandwich. After several consecutive days of eating boiled bacon sandwiches I was unsure which component I found the more difficult to consume; the bread or the bacon. I tried eating them separately but it was still difficult to choose. In the end, I pulled it in half, forced myself to have at least one bite out of it and then threw the rest out for the seagulls which strangely, were keen to get hold of it. Perhaps they were equally fed up with a diet of worms.

So here it comes; the joining of two lands. Choose the straightest one to finish on, had been Harry's first command and looking at these two, there wasn't a lot in it. They both had their share of bends, so I chose one of them and wound down the depth wheel using the huge handle I could reach by leaning out of the back of the tractor, and then ploughed down to the other end.

From that point on, I sort of lost it. I just couldn't remember what and to where I should be doing it, with the result that rather than being a straight shallow finish with the last run just catching the remaining foot of unploughed soil, I ended up with something more akin to a dried up brook meandering across a quarry floor.

I moved on and started ploughing the new land I had created and just hoped Harry didn't choose to dwell too long on this particular part of the field when he returned. I must have a few moments with him and get the closing sequence down on paper.

When I spotted the Land Rover coming down Brier Hill I took the first opportunity to drive over to the gate to meet Harry. There seemed no point having him inspecting and commenting on everything. I know my attempt at finishing was rubbish, I just didn't want to be told so.

'How's it going?' he asked.

'Good. Overall, I'd say pretty good. A few teething mistakes with the finish but practice makes perfect, and I'm sure the next one will be so much better if you could spare the time to show me how to do it again.'

'Jump in, we'll go have a quick look at it now and see if we can sort out a few things. I'm sure it's not that bad.'

We drove along the headland and stopped when we drew level with the finish. Harry pulled back his window and stared out. He seemed to be trying to say something.

'Well, what do you think?' I asked.

He turned and looked at me. 'I'm sorry, boy. I'm just lost for words. What on earth were you doing? I mean, let's just forget about straightness, shallowness and buried crop residues; they would come in the advanced course, but you couldn't have made a worse job if you had used a scuffle. There's bits that haven't been ploughed, there's parts where it looks more like an open cast coal mine and other bits which, well, we could use to plant mature oak trees in.'

He put his head in his hands. 'I'm just so relieved we're not by a road for the neighbours to see,' he said.

'Well if you don't like it, why don't you just come out and say as much,' I said. 'Tell me how you think I could improve it and I'll try and do it better next time.'

'I don't want to appear to be unfair, boy, but I don't think we're quite ready for the word 'improve' or even 'better next time' yet. I would be looking to use 'hope' or even 'prayer'. But let's not get too despondent, not both of us, anyhow. When the time comes to close the next land we'll go through it all again and if you remind me later today, you can take some notes down.'

And with that said he drove back to the tractor, stopped the Land Rover and pulled out a five gallon drum of diesel out of the back. 'This should keep her going for the rest of the day,' he said, inverting the can over the tank's filler. Hang on a minute and you can take the drum back up to the farm. Oh, and by the way, that cow you thought was about to calve, she's had a good strong bull calf which I've left on her until tomorrow. She's in a pen by herself and she looks good.'

Harry dropped the empty drum down onto the ground and I grabbed the cap and screwed it on before storing it in the back of the truck. I started to head for the cab but Harry called me back.

'If you think your first finish with the plough is bad you should have seen mine; it was hardly in the field and the bollocking my old man gave me had people shutting windows in the village,' he said. 'Don't worry boy, you'll get better.'

And with that, he started the tractor and headed off along the headland.

Chapter twenty-six

Dry-stone walling

By the time February had arrived, we'd just about finished the ploughing and I for one was pleased to be doing something else – and having some real lunch for a change.

Elizabeth had left for university and we kept in touch writing letters to each other and there was Easter to look forward to when she would be home for a few weeks.

One of the jobs I hadn't expected to be doing was dry stone walling – building walls using stone and no cement to hold it together. The wall around the old grave yard had been built a century or more using the local sandstone and, at that time, the land would have been level on both sides of the wall.

Since then the ground on the outside had been quarried for iron ore which had left it standing on the top of a slope. And that wasn't too good because every so often the ground would slip a few inches and a length of wall would tumble down.

I was never sure whether Harry repaired the wall because he felt a duty to or he needed it intact to keep the sheep and cattle in the paddock behind it. But whatever the reason, I was seconded to repair a section which had recently collapsed.

While I knew next to nothing about dry stone walling, I was aware it was a skilled job and certainly called for more than the ability to balance one stone on top of another.

Before I even touched a stone, I looked at the standing wall on either side of the gap and tried to work out how it had been constructed.

It would seem there was a taper so the top was several inches narrower than the bottom and the stones were laid in such a way they always sloped into the middle of the wall, which gave it stability, unless it was balanced on the edge of an old quarry. The top had a layer of coping stones which, as luck would have it, were the largest and heaviest stones and these were stacked on their edges.

So, in theory, at least, rebuilding a dry stone wall looked to be a reasonably straight forward operation and I had high hopes of success. After all, all the stones were still here, I had the surviving wall to build against to maintain the correct shape and what could possible go wrong?

I decided to start by shifting all of the fallen stones away from the base of the wall and retrieving those that had tumbled down the slope into the paddock, so I could see the line to take. If I had thought a little more at this point I might have made separate piles of different sizes of stone, but I didn't.

I then pulled a few stones off the wall to create a flat starting level, one that didn't have awkward shaped stones projecting out of it and stretched a length of bale string across the gap so I could tell the height of the course I was about to build.

Easy-peasy so far but now came the hunt for the right size stone and that was the difficult bit because every stone I picked up was either too wide, too short or too thick. And I honestly believe I picked up each stone as many as three times. I found I was continually drawn to the same stone like a magnet and I knew as soon as I touched it I had already tried it for size and discarded it.

Slowly but sort of surely, the gap I was rebuilding started to rise. The courses were reasonably even and I used stones to bind in the lower courses. I wasn't too sure what to do about the middle but it seemed logical to shovel in some of the broken rubbish to make a solid wall of it.

Harry came to see how I was getting on and, although he didn't say as much, he didn't appear to be unhappy with the way it was going. That I had been here for nearly three days and only managed about three foot of wall in a six foot gap didn't seem to concern him.

'Better to take your time and build it once than rush it and have to build it again,' he said. 'There's not much of this wall that hasn't been rebuilt at some time or another. I managed to get a lot of stone from the wall we knocked down when the grave yard was extended into the paddock – I gave them an acre of ground so if you ever want to see what an acre looks like there's the place to go.'

'There's no rush,' I said.

'You don't know, boy. You can never book a plot too early because you know you're going to need it one day. You mark my words.'

'Have you booked yours?'

'I certainly have and so has Alice. Seeing as it was my land, they gave me first pick. They also gave me a bier on which to have the coffin brought round to the church from the farm,' he said.

'Isn't that being a bit macabre? I suppose you've chosen the hymns too.'

'No, I haven't gone that far but really, it's just a matter of having it all planned.'

Aware of my visit to the new graveyard with Elizabeth and what it revealed, this was not a conversation I wanted to pursue. But Harry persisted.

'When you have to take care of one of your loved ones you want to make sure you do the best for them,' he said. 'It's the least you can do.'

We were moving into new territory and I looked at Harry and I could see the sadness etched on his face.

'Is there something you want to tell me?' I asked him, anxious he should know I cared.

'No, not really boy. It's just that life does have it sad times and we have to learn to cope with them.' He took out his handkerchief and blew his nose. 'And sometimes it's hard to always do that.'

Harry was hurting and I felt for him. 'Was it about your son?'

He nodded. 'Yes, how did you know?'

'Elizabeth told me. She didn't want me to say anything that would upset you or Alice.'

'That was very kind of her.' He used the handkerchief again. 'Did she tell you what happened?'

'No, and I'm not sure it's my place to know,' I said.

Harry sighed. 'Well, perhaps not now, boy.'

'That's alright, I understand.' And there didn't seem anything else I could say, so I resumed my search for the right size stone I needed. 'Do you really think there're enough stones here to finish this wall?' I asked.

'Well, there should be. It was all there before it fell down, but I take your point, there isn't that much here that's any good. I think the frost has got to it. If you take the tractor and trailer down to the wall at the end of the allotments you can take some of the stone from there. That wall's been crumbling for years.'

***

Somehow, I managed to put a spurt on during the rest of the day. I likened it to doing a jigsaw, you get to a point when the pieces suddenly all start to fit, and I was now up to the coping stone course. But there were no coping stones to put on the wall, I had used what there was on the way up.

So out came the tractor and trailer and as I started to leave the yard Ronny sauntered out from the tractor shed and, despite it being a warm dry day he was wearing wellingtons and I wondered whether he ever took them off. Not that I was remotely interested in seeing what was concealed within them.

'Where are you off to?' he asked.

'Just going to find some large coping stones for the wall in the graveyard,' I said. 'Harry said there are some down on the old allotment wall. Give me a hand if you want.'

Ronny walked round to the rear of the trailer and sat on the floor, his legs swinging off the back as we drove across the paddock. It was not the place I would have chosen to sit if only because you're sitting directly over the axle and receive all the bumps as a result.

But who was I to tell him? With the weather offering a promise of spring and really quite mild and it was not a day to be rushing about, more a day for drinking in the joys of the countryside and relishing the start of another year.

I drew up alongside the old wall as close as I could. There was a tangle of brambles which had grown over the top and it was not going to be easy to extract the stones without receiving some painful lacerations.

'Should have brought a hedge slasher,' Ronny said.

I teased some of the brambles off the wall to make a start and Ronny, standing in the trailer leaned over and pulled the stones across, stones which were about a foot in diameter and a few inches thick.

'How many do you need?' he asked.

'The gap's about six foot wide so if we say four to a foot that would be about twenty-four and a few more for luck. Let's go for thirty and be sure,' I said.

I thought it only fair Ronny should drive the tractor back to the farm and it clearly cheered him up. I stood beside him, not wanting a repeat performance when we crossed the paddock and drove through the gate into the graveyard.

'What's for the best?' he asked, when we arrived. 'Do you want me draw alongside so we place them on the wall from the side of the trailer or do you want me to reverse up to it and take them off the back?'

Then thought of Ronny reversing into the wall was too much so I asked him to drive alongside and get as close as he could.

'Right I'll do that then.'

Ronny drew out in the graveyard and shunted about until he could position the trailer alongside the wall.'

'Is that close enough?' he asked.

'It will do.'

And then we climbed onto the trailer and lifted the coping stones one by one onto the top of the wall. At last, after nearly four days, my wall was finished.

Ronny drove the trailer away so I could get a better view and, to my mind, it looked wonderful.

'What do reckon? A good job or what?' I asked him.

'Looks alright,' he said. 'Shame about the base though.'

'What do you mean? What's wrong with the base?'

'The tree root, it'll have the wall down again in a matter of weeks. That's what brings all these walls down sooner or later – that and the twenty-foot drop on the other side.'

Chapter twenty-seven

Almost spring

Spring was approaching. It started with the snowdrops in the grass verges and woodlands and then there was colour from the crocuses and, as a tint of green appeared in the hedgerows, the daffodils came into bud.

And when spring arrived there was no stopping it. As February moved into March and with it warmer longer days, the countryside appeared to tremble with expectancy as nature prepared to burst into activity.

Spring was also a busy time on the farm which would see another spate of long days, bottled tea and endless boiled bacon sandwiches.

For the last few weeks Harry had been focussing on lambing which was due to start in about two weeks' time. Using the colour of the paint planted by the tup on the ewe when she was served, he had separated the flock into two groups – an early and late group – and was giving the early sheep slightly more feed. Both groups though were now looked at regularly to ensure all was proceeding well.

We had also been busy preparing an area in the rick yard with pens and an adopter system which enabled ewes with single lambs to be given one from a ewe who may have had triplets.

'This year I'm going to make sure we have the room prepared for them to come under cover if the weather turns as foul as it has in other years,' he said. 'Whatever happens we need the barn the cows have been using.'

With one week to go from the expected start of lambing, the weather was warm and fine and the forecast for the next three weeks was for it to remain so. When I told Harry the good news he scoffed, not wanting to believe it.

'We'll see what we get,' he said. 'The key thing is to be prepared as best as we can for the worst.'

Harry was becoming tetchy, clearly apprehensive about how the weeks ahead were going to work out. The weather played a big part not only in the survival rate of the new born lambs but also in the way the sheep could be managed. And long days working in cold wet weather can sap the enthusiasm from even the hardiest of characters.

I slipped away and began chain harrowing the grassland to pull out the dead grasses and weeds and level out molehills and cowpats. The areas where the cows and sheep had been fed when they were outside also needed some attention.

It was good to just sit on the tractor and create long straight stripes in a field although it was important not to go too fast or the chain harrows with their spikes would start to jump across the ground and not do the raking job required.

But the trouble with chain harrows was that they were such a pain to move from field to field. Sometimes you could just pull them through gateways without a lot of trouble but if there was any distance to travel, they needed putting on a trailer.

And that meant rolling them up and then lifting one end of this sagging, overweight roll of metal spikes on to a trailer bed, giving it a push and then lifting the other end on. It wasn't easy and invariably one of the spikes would catch on my jumper or jacket and make a hole.

The golden rule though, was that at the end of the day the chain harrows needed to be rolled up before the tractor left the field to prevent livestock harming themselves and tractor tyres being punctured.

Before or after the harrowing, the grassland received a dose of fertiliser, or artificial as Harry called it which tended to indicate that the availability of factory-made artificial fertiliser was in some way inferior to non-artificial fertiliser which on Harry's farm equated to mountains of pig and cow manure.

Artificial fertiliser was available as straight nitrogen granules or as a blend with potash and phosphate granules. Early Artificial was delivered in paper sacks and bearing in mind fertiliser is designed to attract moisture – become a solution so it was available to the plant – this mode of packaging did not give the products a very good reputation.

I often heard Harry say that when he went fertiliser spreading an essential tool was a hammer to beat out the big lumps which formed in these paper bags and while the introduction of plastic packaging was a big improvement there were still problems of lumps –usually by the small hole that was left in the bag to allow air to escape when they were stacked on top of each other.

Fertiliser was spread by the farm's disc spreader which was attached to the rear of the tractor, its funnel-shaped hopper could hold about four bags of fertiliser and it released the fertiliser onto a spinning disc through a hole in the base of the hopper.

While its operating manual stated it had the ability to spread granules of fertiliser over a seven-yard width, accuracy was not one of its greatest feature and it was not unusual to see strips of different shades of green where the volume of nitrogen applied was not constant.

Fertiliser came in one hundredweight plastic bags and these had to be carried off the delivery lorry and stacked in the barn on the floor and then, when they were to be used, lifted and carried to a trailer to take them to the field and then finally, carried from trailer to the spreader. To be fair though, the spreader could be reversed carefully up to the trailer and the bags just cut and their contents poured in to the hopper – carefully because if the spreader was too close, the spinner would collide with the trailer and bend. And that was a capital offense.

'There's sixty bags which will be enough to do forty acres at a bag and a half per acre,' Harry said when we arrived at the top of Brier Hill. 'That will do this field and Long Field.'

Like most farmers, Harry always talked in terms of 'bags per acre' rather than the more technical 'units of fertiliser' which was understandable when it is known that one unit represents one percent of a hundredweight.

Together we emptied four bags into the hopper to bring the fertiliser up to just about brim level, and then I climbed on to the tractor and looked at the engine rev counter which also showed the speed of the power take off and the forward speed of the tractor in each of its six gears. According to the spreader's operator's manual, I wanted a pto speed of 540rpm and a gear which would give me six miles an hour at that engine speed. And there wasn't one.

'Just get as near as you can and see how you go,' Harry said.

The best I could manage was nearer seven miles an hour in high second gear.

'Do a couple of times around the field to start with and then using the longest, straightest edge work across the field.' he said.

With everything running, I pulled down the lever on the spreader to open the hole in the base of the hopper the required amount and started off. I could see the fertiliser being thrown out by the rotating disc and all looked to be going well. I tried to calculate how long it would take me to empty the hopper but although the figures were all there to be used, I couldn't concentrate. I'd just have to wait and see.

Harry was still where I had left him when I completed

one lap of the field. He looked into the hopper and then said: 'That's about right.'

Which was encouraging but I really didn't know if he was just guessing or he had used the spreader on this field before. It was, I thought, more likely to be the latter. Anyway, I needed fifteen bags on the trailer to do Long Field and I would work towards leaving that amount. And thinking about it, it would have been better to have started with the smaller field to get a better hold on the amount of fertiliser being applied.

Once we had topped up the hopper with a couple of bags, Harry set off to walk back to the farm having said he would return to move the trailer down to Long Field.

Some hours later when having completed Brier Hill, I refilled the hopper and headed off for Long Field and I had just made a start when I spotted Harry bringing the trailer over to me.

'That was good timing.' I said as he drew the trailer into the field.

'It's all about knowing your fields,' he replied. 'Anyway, I've brought you a blobber.'

'A what?'

'A foam marker which leaves a trail of foam blobs on the ground so you don't have to try and find your wheel marks all the while.'

'That sounds interesting.'

Harry reached over the side of the trailer and lifted out a five gallon plastic drum of soap solution. 'We need to attach this to the tractor somewhere,' he said. 'Any suggestions?'

I looked around and struggled to see anywhere suitable.

'I think the only place for now is to tie it to the back of the seat. When we get a minute we can make a frame for it and put it in front of the bonnet,' said Harry.

Tied to the back of the seat, I have to say it looked a little precarious but I gave it a good shake and it seemed alright. Filled up with soap solution, Harry connected the blobber up to the battery and switched it on.

There was a buzzing and a bit of bubbling but not a lot more. But we were being impatient because there was a sudden spluttering and a dollop of foamy water splatted onto the ground, not unlike a dog throwing up.

'It works,' Harry said. 'I thought we could also fit it to the sprayer, the pipes are long enough to get to the end of the booms. What do you think?'

Conversation halted when there was another violent heaving noise followed by a splat and, it may have just been me, but I thought I heard someone shouting 'Hughie' as it landed.

'I think it's a great idea,' I said.

And it was a great idea and it would have been even greater idea if the sheep hadn't been in the field and left their own white blobs of wool everywhere. Truth is, it was very hard to distinguish between the white blob produced by the machine and the white wool dropped by the sheep.

'That's a bugger,' Harry said when I explained the problem to him. 'I'll see if I can mix some colour into the soap solution but it should be alright for the sprayer in the cereal crops.'

'Unless the sheep have got out on to it,' I said, which was probably a little unfair. Anyway, we now had a blobber and I felt sure it was going to be very useful in most fields.

Harry said he would wait while I finished off Long Field and then, if I left the tractor at the top of Brier Hill I wouldn't be too far away from Badger Close and Farm Close where he would leave the trailer when we had loaded it up again.

But for now, it was lunch time and as I drove the Land Rover back to the farm I was feeling rather pleased with myself having had my first outing with the fertiliser spreader. Little did I know there was something a lot worse waiting for me to have a go at tomorrow.

Chapter twenty-eight

Delivery problems

A sunny morning in March can be a magical experience; it was one of those mornings when the air is fresh and crystal clear and everything has a bright sharp edge to it. A touch of frost, yes, but by the time I had finished milking it was a distant memory.

'I've arranged for thirty tons of basic slag to be delivered this morning,' Harry said as he carved the day's boiled bacon slices. 'When he arrives I should try and get as much of it onto trailers without stacking it on the floor in the barn.'

'It sounds very much as if you won't be here,' I said.

'No, Alice and I have been invited out to lunch by the Milk Marketing Board and I'm certainly not going to be handling bags of basic slag before we go to that.'

I felt a certain unease as I pondered the name basic slag which, as far as a sale's description went may be correct, but seemed to deprive the product of that that 'must have' appeal. Surely someone in the marketing department could have come up with a better name than basic slag.

'So what is basic slag?' I asked.

'It's a bi-product of the steel industry which does wonderful things to the soil,' he said. 'And it's particularly good on grassland – it sweetens the soil and makes clover grow like there's no tomorrow and because clover is a legume which makes its own nitrogen we don't need to spend a fortune on purchasing artificial nitrogen.'

'Yes, but what's actually in it?'

'Phosphate mainly, but it also has a lot of different trace elements including calcium which also makes it a useful liming agent.'

'The calcium helping to reduce soil acidity?'

'That's right, boy. What have you been reading?'

'Oh, only something in one of the farming magazines,' I said.

Harry laughed. 'I hope you're not turning into one of those people who have copies of 'What Caravan' or 'Birdcage Weekly' hidden under their beds,' he said.

'Harry,' warned Alice, coming to my aid. 'Don't start on the boy with that sort of rubbish.' She turned to me. 'Take no notice of him John. You have whatever magazines you want under your bed.'

Which was help of a sort and I like to think it was offered with the best intentions.

'Any way, the first lorry — I've told them not to use articulated lorries because they'll never get out of the yard - is due to arrive about eleven o'clock and while you're waiting for it, look in the shed in the orchard and you'll find the piece of kit we use to apply the slag. Pull it out into the yard and have a look through it to make sure it's a goer.'

There was something Harry wasn't telling me about basic slag, but I could tell by the way he seemed to be distancing himself from it but there was no point in asking.

'Have another cup of tea before you go, John,' Alice said, holding her hand out for my cup.

***

The first job was to sort enough trailers out so that none of the thirty tons of basic slag needed to be stored on the floor of the barn. I had already experienced what it's like having to lift hundredweight bags of granular fertiliser from floor level to trailer and it wasn't much fun.

For starters, the bag was not a good shape to get a grip

on and more often than not it was slimy and this added to the problems of grip; it only took a small leakage to attract what seemed to be gallons of water.

When the bag was eventually heaved on to the trailer it had to be stacked, which called for more lifting and it was always in my mind that the bags would have to be lofted for a third time when the time came to empty them into the spreader. And by that time my jeans and jacket were usually plastered.

The trailers were parked all the way along one side of the paddock. 'You can never have too many trailers,' Harry had told me on many occasions. 'If you can get bales off the field and on to trailers they are in the dry even if they stay unloaded for a few weeks,' he said.

I hooked onto a four-wheeler and took it down the yard and parked beside the dairy wall and then returned to the paddock for a second one and positioned it behind the first. It was at that point I realised that, while there were plenty of trailers, not many of them, if any at all, had any braking systems.

Which was a worry. While an empty trailer can be restrained by a couple of bricks behind its wheels, one with a few tons on board is likely to need greater stopping power. I dragged a railway sleeper out of the workshop and placed it behind the wheels of the rear trailer.

Two trailers were not going to be anywhere near enough though, so I brought another five in to the yard and parked them so they could be accessed by the lorries. Six tons on each trailer or there about, depending on trailer condition.

What happens to the loaded trailers was another consideration and while I could squeeze three or possibly four under cover, I would need some tarpaulins to cover the remaining trailers and these were to be found, along with everything else on this farm, in the shed in the orchard. If it can't be found, always look in the shed in the orchard.

It was as I was dragging one of them out, it was heavy enough to have once been part of a circus, I heard Harry and Alice drive out of the yard and I was on my own.

Half an hour later I was all prepared and ready to take delivery of thirty tons of basic slag and that left only about fifteen minutes to have a look for the spreader, Harry had mentioned. But even that was denied me. There was a hiss of brakes and some intricate gear changing as the lorry drove slowly into the yard and, to my horror, I realised it was an articulated lorry. I had been expecting a rigid bodied lorry. Turning and manoeuvring a long artic in what had become quite a cramped yard full of trailers was not going to be easy. It wouldn't be easy even if the yard had been totally empty of trailers.

It was something which had already registered with the driver who stopped the engine and lowered himself to the ground.

'Good morning,' I said. 'We were expecting a couple of rigid lorries not an artic.'

'I just do what I'm told,' he said, looking around the yard. 'Where's your pallet loader?'

'Pallet loader? Sorry, we don't have one,' I replied, already sensing there were difficult times ahead.

'What? You don't expect me to offload four hundred bags one at a time, do you? You want to catch up with the times mate.'

'Well, I've brought all these trailers into the yard. My plan was for you to drive close to each of them and just pass the bags across,' I explained.

'Do you know how much these bags weigh? They're a hundredweight each and they're in paper bags, like bags of cement and ten times as dirty. I wouldn't even have started coming here if I had known this was the situation.'

So much for a man who just does what he's told, I thought.

'Well, the way I see it is that you're in the yard now and I don't think you have a chance in hell of getting out without unloading first. And even unloaded you'll struggle without a tractor to pull the trailer round.'

'Don't you believe it mate. I can get this outfit out of any yard full or empty.'

But then there was another hiss of brakes and gear changing and the second lorry rolled slowly down the slope and stopped a few feet short of the first one. I wandered what was going to happen now.

'I'd have thought you would have had your load off by now,' said the driver of the latest arrival, leaning out of his cab window.

'You must be joking,' his mate replied. 'They don't have a pallet loader and with you now in the way, we're stuck.'

'Oh, shit.' The driver jumped out of his cab, looked around the yard and shook his head. 'We're stuffed,' he said. And then he walked over to where I was standing.

'So, what's your plan then, sunshine? Do you think these lorries tip or something?'

'As I mentioned to your colleague, we were told that two rigid lorries were delivering, not two artics,' I said. 'That's why the trailers are here, to off load directly onto them.'

'First time I've heard that,' he said. He looked around the yard again. 'This is a right cock-up. If your boss had said he only wanted rigid bodied lorries that would be what he would get. I don't understand this at all but one thing's for sure, I'm not unloading four hundred bags by hand. Do you know how filthy basic slag is?'

Just then I heard another lorry at the top of the yard, a rigid body lorry with a load of basic slag on board. This really cannot be happening.

But it was and as I walked up the yard I could see there was a second one behind it. We now had more tons of basic slag than the farm had ever seen, and a traffic jam of terminal proportions.

'You are meant to be delivering to Church Farm?' I

asked one of the artic lorry drivers. He said nothing but climbed into his cab and reached for his delivery instructions.

'That's what it says here,' he said holding it out so I could see.

'Well, you've the right farm but the wrong name,' I said. 'This says Smiths and the manager's name of Sam Jones. Their farm's at the other end of the village.'

'Bloody hell,' said the driver. 'They haven't made that cock-up again, have they? 'I don't suppose you have a phone I could use?'

I led him down to the house and into the hall where the phone was. 'I'll just give our place a call and see if we can sort this out.'

After a few minutes of verbal crossfire, Jack, as he introduced himself, told whoever he was speaking to that he was as about as helpful as a fart in a colander, and put the phone down.

'No luck?' I asked.

'They don't know their arse from their elbow,' he scowled.

'If I give Sam Jones a call and tell him the situation, he might be able to sort something out,' I said. 'I know they've a pallet loader.'

Jack shrugged. 'Give it a go and see what happens. I'm going to start looking for a taxi.'

It took a couple of calls but I eventually managed to track down Sam. 'Good morning, Sam,' I started. 'It's John from Church Farm, Harry's farm.'

'Yes John?' He sounded curt.

'I think you were expecting two lorry loads of basic slag this morning?'

'That's right and we're waiting for them to arrive so we can start spreading. I suppose you're going to tell me their sitting down in your yard because if they are, send the buggers up to me. I'm just about to give them a call to cancel the order.'

'Well, you're right, they are down here but they've come with two artics and there's no way they're getting back out of the yard with full loads. I was wondering if you could send some trailers down and your pallet loader and off load them where they are? The best of it is that the thirty tons Harry ordered has arrived on rigid lorries and they can't unload the artics because those lorries are in their way.'

'Sounds like a right bugger's muddle and Harry's doing his best to turn into a basic slag distribution centre. Where is Harry, anyway?'

'He and Alice have gone off to some Milk Marketing Board lunch.'

'My arse he has,' Sam said. 'He knew what was being delivered.'

'Oh I think that's a bit unfair,' I said.

'Have you ever handled basic slag?'

'No.'

'Well I just hope Alice has laid in plenty of bath cleaner. That's all I'm saying. But anyway, I'll tell you what we'll do. I'll send down the pallet loader and four of our trailers for our slag to be unloaded on to and, because I feel sorry for you and Harry's pulled a fast one, the chap on the pallet loader will also unload your thirty tons. How's that sound?'

'Brilliant,' I said. 'That's very kind.'

'You won't think so when you start spreading it,' he said. 'And you can tell Harry he owes me one.'

'I'll do that. Thank you, Sam.'

I walked up the yard and, as I did so, the lorry drivers turned as one to face me.

'Any news or are we here for the rest of the day?' asked one of them.

'No, you shouldn't be. I've arranged for the farm where the artics should be, to send down trailers and a loader to off load them and then, while it's here, to off load our thirty tons.'

There was general shuffling of agreement and perhaps also a smattering of relief, as much as you could probably expect from a bunch of lorry drivers. There was certainly not a hint of gratitude.

We weren't quite out of the woods yet though. With the route into the yard blocked by the rigid lorries the artics were unreachable and I suggested that the rigids should be unloaded on to Sam's trailers along with ten tons off the back of one of the artics when the route was cleared.

'Can't do that, old lad,' said one of the drivers. 'These loads are set against each customer, so any problems can be traced. Anyway, who's going to sign the delivery note?'

I was getting tired of it all and these people were testing my patience. 'Sod the delivery note,' I told him. 'There's basic slag on the artics and there's basic slag on the rigids. It's all in hundredweight bags and to me they all look exactly the same. If you would prefer it, I could give Mr Jones a call back and he'll ring your office and cancel everything. And God help you if my boss arrives and discovers a yard full of lorries blocking his way.'

I could hear the loader and tractors coming along the top road. 'Make up your minds, because the loader's on its way here and I'm on my way down to the house to make a call.'

I had made a couple of strides when Jack, who seemed to hold some sway with his colleagues, shouted out. 'Alright, you win. We'll do it your way.' He turned to the drivers. 'I think it's time to unrope and get the sheets off,' he said.

From that point on, everything went rather well. The loader transferred the pallets, each holding thirty bags from the lorries to Sam's trailers and then topped up with pallet loads from one of the now accessible artics— an operation which took only minutes.

And from then on it was back to plan 'A' with the loader off-loading all the remaining bags on to the trailers I had set out earlier this morning. Job done, apart from extracting the artics from the yard.

'How are we going to do this?' I asked Jack.

He sighed. 'It's not going to be easy,' he said. 'I think our only hope is to turn sharp across the space we have and then you to pull the rear of the trailer down with a tractor and chain. Once we've done that and shunted about a bit up I might just squeeze the cab past the barn.

It seemed doubtful to me but he was right, there was no other way out, short of trying to reverse all the way back to the main road, a distance of at least half a mile. It took over twenty minutes to free up Jack's artic with me hooking on to the trailer at various intervals to drag it wholesale across the yard, it's tyres protesting loudly as they left wide skid marks on the concrete.

The other one took less time for two reasons: there was more room available and we knew how to do it. But any way, several hours after they first arrived I eventually saw the back end of the last lorry leaving the farm.

I thought I'd have a spot of lunch. Before she left, Alice said she had made a couple of sandwiches for me.

Chapter twenty-nine

Spreading soot and ghostly lambs

There were two things I noticed when I encountered basic slag for the first time. The first is that it is warm; bags that had been stacked in the lower layers on the pallet and insulated from the outside temperatures were sometimes almost too hot to touch, and the second is that it is filthy, horrible stuff to be near. Crushed to a fine powder, it manages to get everywhere, from your hair down to your toes and after half an hour, or less, any attempts at keeping clean have to be abandoned.

The spreading machine was vastly different from the hoper and spinner I had used to apply granular fertiliser. Using one of those would have covered the county in it. No, this was a wide box on wheels which had outlets a regular intervals through which the slag was metered out onto the ground by a series of horizontal, 'cog-like' cast iron spoked wheels. These scooped up the slag from the hopper and drew it to the outlets at the back.

Application rate was, as standard, half a ton per acre and this could be adjusted, but rarely was, by changing the drive sprockets from the land wheel so the metering wheels turned at a different speed.

It was not the fastest job on the farm; nowhere near. The working width of the spreader was about eight feet which allowed it to be towed along roads and through most gates, which was good, but meant it took for ever to get over any size of field. This generous application rate, combined with a hopper which would hold only five or six bags meant a fair proportion of a day could be spent cutting open bags and filling it up.

But it was the grime that got to you. After just half an hour, I was Friday's chimney sweep and I could taste the stuff. Every time I heaved a hundredweight bag off the trailer and laid it across the top of the hopper there would be flurry of black powder which headed straight for me. And when I cut the side of the paper bag and the contents began to pour out there would be another cloud of dust.

At first I tried to avoid them but after the third or fourth fill up of the day there was no point, I just let it happen.

Once full and the hopper closed, I climbed onto the tractor and drove to the part of the field where I ran out with the last load. It wasn't difficult to see; there was an unmissable dark tinge to the grass. Pulling the lever which engaged the drive sprockets, I started spreading at about two miles an hour. Any faster and the metering wheels would be turning too quickly for the slag to be delivered at the required rate.

In even a light breeze, the direction of the wind was an important consideration in that when travelling into it, the tractor could keep ahead of the black cloud of dust but with the wind behind, the cloud would travel with me and add new layers to my already blackened clothes and face.

I had expected to see Harry at some time in the afternoon just to see how the job was going and enquire where I wanted the next trailer load of basic slag taking to. What I didn't expect, when he arrived, was for him to be accompanied by half a dozen women who followed him into the field. When Harry stopped he was immediately surrounded and, while I couldn't hear what was being said, it was pretty clear they were not very happy and it was some time before they started to leave.

'What was all that about?' I asked, when he had driven

over to where I was.

'Bloody women. They think they rule the place,' he said. 'All they've to worry about is their washing and here we are working morn till night to put food on their plates.'

'Don't tell me. The black dust is landing on their freshly washed sheets.' I said.

'You're right but there was one of them who was painting white gloss around her windows and is accusing us of turning it grey with sooty spots all over it. For goodness sake. Has she nothing else to do?'

'What's for the best then? Do you want me to change fields, or what?'

Harry glanced around the six-acre field I was in – the top half of Slade Close which backed up against the village.

'Well you've only a few acres left in here. Best you carry on. We can't be dictated to by those who have only their own interests at heart, can we?'

I thought about it. If the number of bags left on the trailer was anything to go on, I still had about four acres to do that meant a good hour and a half at least. The thought of being accosted by a marauding army of women did not appeal to me.

'I could come back to this field when the wind is blowing in another direction,' I suggested.

'No,' Harry said. 'We'll end up with half-finished bits all over the place if we start that and waste hours travelling back and forwards. No, you stay and finish it. Anyway, how's it spreading? I ran into Sam Jones this morning and he says his man is having a terrible time trying to spread the lumpiest slag they've ever had. He's planning on sending about thirty tons of it back.'

'Oh well, that's the way it goes,' I said. 'I've not had any problems with ours.'

'Good. Right I'll leave it to you. Oh, and Alice says could you leave your overalls in the dairy before you come in to the house.'

'But I'm not wearing any overalls.'

Harry shrugged. 'Do what you can, boy,' he said as he shut the Land Rover door and drove off.

The wind was getting up and what had been a gentle breeze an hour ago was now gusting with some strength. Already, I had chased after some of the empty bags which had blown off the trailer and were heading towards someone's garden.

But I carried on as requested, filling and spreading until, thankfully, I finished the last bout and knocked off the metering drive for the last time. In terms of application accuracy, I was pleased to note I had used all of the six tons and there was just a sprinkle left in the hopper. Spot on.

Now all I had to do was drive past the houses and get back to the farm. And that was something I was not particularly relishing. It started with one lady standing on the side of the road holding a grubby bed sheet stretched out between her arms.

'See what you've done,' she shouted at me.

She was soon joined by four or five other women who began to shout obscenities, words I wasn't aware until that moment, women knew about.

'You should have had more effing sense you bleeding half-wit,' screamed one of them. 'You wait 'til my George gets back. He'll be round to sort you out.'

I was beginning to wish I could travel more quickly but the metal, spoked wheels weren't built for it. Each time a wheel went over a bump or a pothole it dropped a handful of slag out, which then blew across to where the women were standing. All I could do was weather the storm and keep smiling.

'You farm workers are all the same – all mouth and no balls,' shouted another of them and her supporters yelled their agreement.

Back in the yard I had another problem to overcome in that if I was to comply with Alice's request for me to remove my overalls before entering the house, I would be left in just my underwear. And I wasn't sure that would be too well received. I tentatively loosened a button on my shirt while I thought about it.

'That's right, boy, slip them off,' Harry said. 'And I should have a good swill to get the worst of it off your face and arms. Can't be having that mess in the house, can we? Alice won't like it.'

It was predicament for which there was no solution. There was nothing else for it other than to strip off. The walk from the dairy to the house was not one I would want to repeat and things didn't get any better when I walked into the kitchen.

'Oh, I say,' Alice said, when she looked up from the table. 'You don't think you should try and find some other clothes to wear do you?'

'That would be a good idea,' I said. 'But I think a bath might be a better one.'

She looked at Harry. 'Haven't we some overalls he could be wearing?' she asked him. 'Just to keep the worst of it off his clothes?'

'There's a pair hanging up in the workshop,' he said. 'But Alice is right, you should go and find something else to wear – Mildred's pink dressing gown is still in your wardrobe, if you fancy it.'

***

In all, I spent four days spreading basic slag on grassland and I think Alice probably spent as long trying to wash my clothes and keeping the bath clean. We were all pleased to know we had finished that job.

Which was timely, because the very next day the first lambs were born and it was twins. Carrying the two lambs we led the ewe into one of the pens where we could keep an eye on them and make sure both lambs were feeding.

If all goes well, the routine was then to move them in to group pens for a few days after which, if the weather was being kind, they could go out into the field.

'Well that's a good start, boy,' Harry said, after we had

closed the gate on the pen. 'A good healthy set of twins and good dry weather to go with them. You'd better get her some water and put some hay in the rack while I mark her and her lambs with a number.'

Harry took out an aerosol can of red marker fluid and, after shaking it, sprayed 'zero, zero-one' onto each side of her and then on the lambs. 'It's the only way we can be sure of keeping tabs on whose lambs belong to which ewe,' he said, clipping the lid back onto the can. 'And that leaves two hundred and forty nine to go.'

By the end of the day, five more ewes had lambed; two of them with singles, two with twins and one with triplets. We placed one of the ewes with a single in the adopter unit and then took one of the triplets and put it on her. The adopter unit restricted the ewe with a neck yoke preventing her from pushing the 'incoming' lamb away, the idea being that she would soon accept it as her own and allow it to suckle when she was released.

'It's a system which seems to work quite well and stops all the messing about we used to do,' Harry said. 'I've tried rubbing the lamb with the ewe's cleanse and if she's had a dead lamb, I've skinned it and put it on another lamb. It's all about getting her to believe that the lamb smells like hers so she thinks it actually is hers.'

When I came down into the kitchen the next morning, Harry was already out with the sheep so I made a quick cup of tea before heading out into the yard to see what was happening.

'Morning, boy,' Harry said, when we met half way up the yard.

'How's it going?' I asked.

'Well, we had another six last night, five of which were fine but I've had to put one set of twins under the heater lamps to see if they'll come round a bit.'

'Have you been out all night?'

Harry laughed. 'It feels like it but no, I've been popping out every couple of hours to have a walk round them to keep a check on what's happening or I think is about to happen.'

'Well, if you want me to take a turn, I'd be pleased to lend a hand.'

'It's early days, boy, and the bulk of them have yet to start. What we want is for all of them to lamb in one big bunch so we can get it over with, not that it will happen. Anyway, you'd better get on with the milking.'

Harry headed off to the house while I went in the opposite direction to gather the cows and start milking.

Over the next few days we developed a routine where I would take a look round the sheep during the evening to check on the state of play and make sure all the lambed ewes had feed and water. Very often the ewes lambed without any problem at all but there were those which needed a helping hand and for these, I would fetch Harry and together we would pull lambs out and place them in front of the ewe so she could lick some life into them.

It was, I think, the fifth night of lambing when Harry asked me if I would do the one o'clock, three o'clock and five o'clock visits to check on things but not to hesitate to give him a shout if I needed any help or anything.

I agreed. Consecutive nights of intermittent sleep were taking their toll on him and he was almost desperate for a sleep which lasted for longer than a couple of hours. And who could blame him?

At a few minutes to one o'clock my alarm clock gave a buzz and I slid out of bed, pulled on some clothes and made my way down stairs to the kitchen. Until that moment I hadn't realised just how much noise the stairs and the floor boards make when they're walked on.

The big overcoat was on the back of a chair facing the Rayburn so, after I had eased the cat off the length which spilled out onto the floor, I put it on and could feel its warmth seeping into me. Having slipped on my wellingtons I eased the catch on the door as quietly as I could, took a firm hold on the torch and stepped out into the night.

Although being reasonably mild there was a keen wind which howled through the wires and somewhere up the yard I could hear a sheet of tin flapping about. Somewhere between me going to bed and getting up again, the clouds had rolled in and obscured the moon so it was dark; ink dark.

I made my way to the pens holding the new arrivals and shone my torch over them to make sure they were alright and then moved out into the paddock where the main bunch was. Ewes tend to go off by themselves and lie down when their giving birth so I looked carefully through them for any signs that would indicate a birth was imminent and also shone the torch slowly around the paddock walls.

It was when I arrived at the graveyard wall I discovered a ewe on her side and, as I watched she produced two lambs. I cleared their noses and checked their breathing while the ewe clambered to her feet, anxious to make a start on the task of licking them. I made a note to look out for her when I made my next visit.

And then I remembered Harry had put a small bunch of ewes in the grave yard, something he did as an arrangement with the vicar to help keep the grass down. I climbed over the style and instantly registered a drop in temperature as I stepped down into the grave yard and saw and heard nothing, not a sheep or anything.

It all seemed unnaturally quiet, a different world from the paddock I had just left. Moving the torch from side to side, there were only gravestones; cold bleak stones beneath which lay the remains of someone, a person who once lived and worked as I did now.

I moved further on being careful to avoid tripping on any of the grave surrounds or the smaller head stones and began curse my incompetence for not having brought a bucket of meal to rattle about. And while I was thinking this, someone spoke.

'It's a bit cold in here, isn't it?'

I swung my torch round and saw no one. 'Who's there?' I asked.

'Don't you think it's a bit cold?'

This time the voice came from over to my left but when I shone the torch in that direction there was nothing to be seen.

'One day you'll find out just how much cold we have to put up with down here.'

And then I saw something moving, a white circular shape which, as I shone the torch, appeared to float between the gravestones. I felt the hairs lift on the back of my neck and thought it would be a good time to be out of here.

But then every time I went to move towards the style the white shroud seemed to move in front of me, ghosting itself between the stones.

'There's no escape from here,' it said. 'Once you're in here that's it for ever. Don't you think it's cold though?'

That did it for me. Bugger the sheep I was out of there. I put my head down and charged out across the graveyard, dodging the grave stones and trying not to trip over. At one point I stumbled and dropped my torch but I left it where it was. I wasn't stopping for anything and when I arrived back at the style, I was over it in two strides and only then did I pause and look back.

In the gloom of the graveyard I watched as my torch raised itself off the ground, made a large circle in the air and then shone directly into my eyes before darkness descended once more and all was quiet except for the pounding in my ears as my heart thumped away.

I ran down to the house, let myself in. The clock on the kitchen wall showed I had been out for just over half an hour which meant I had an hour and a half before I needed to go out again. I slipped my wellingtons and coat off and headed for the safety of my bed.

All too soon though, my alarm was buzzing again and I

struggled back down into the kitchen, really not looking forward to another session in the dark, looking for sheep in the shadows of gravestones. I pulled on one of my wellingtons and when I put my foot into the other it came up hard against something which shouldn't have been in there. I tipped it upside down and my torch dropped out onto the mat.

'Harry, you bastard,' I fumed, more with relief than anger. 'You scheming old so and so.'

I set off up the yard, torch in hand and called into the barn to collect a bucket which I half-filled with ground barley. But my mind was still fixed on Harry's little prank and as I climbed over the style and lowered myself back into that dark graveyard I found myself wondering if it had been Harry.

Hanging onto the top rail of the style I rattled the bucket just the once and then, with no sheep arriving, I returned to the paddock.

Chapter thirty

Bring out the disc harrows

'How did it go last night, boy?' Harry asked as he filled the teapot with boiling water.

'Oh, there were ten, and all twins, I'm happy to say. And because it was such a mild night, I left them out, rather than bringing them into the pens. Perhaps we can do that this morning.'

'Anything going on with the sheep in the graveyard?'

'Well, to be honest, I couldn't find them. I don't know how you manage it but with all the headstones, it's a job to see them. I even took a bucket out and rattled it but they weren't interested. I'll have a look at them before I start milking.'

Harry disappeared upstairs with Alice's cup of tea and I wandered over to the dairy to get the bucket, thinking that if it had been Harry in the graveyard last night he wasn't exactly scoring on it. Perhaps he was waiting for a bigger audience.

With the cows still to arrive in the collecting yard, I climbed over the style and walked through the graveyard and found the sheep huddled together over by the far wall. No lambs and all well, which was good news – unless they had been frightened witless too.

Anyway, after spending the best part of a night messing around with sheep it was good to be back with my girls, cows which understand how the world works and didn't hide behind gravestones.

Harry waited until breakfast time to spill the beans about his input into the graveyard scene last night, relating the story, I thought, with rather more embellishment than it deserved.

'Oh, you didn't play that stupid trick again did you, Harry?' said Alice. 'Last time he tried that one he ended up stuck in a freshly dug grave with a twisted ankle and we had to pull him out in the morning. I hope he didn't get to you too badly.'

'No, I just thought it was a bit strange hearing someone speaking at that time of the night. It didn't bother me or anything.'

'Oh, come on,' Harry scoffed, wiping the tears from his eyes. 'You were scared out of your wits.'

'Oh well, whatever makes you happy.'

***

By the end of the second week a good two thirds of the flock had lambed and according to Harry, the job was going well. Some of the older lambs were now charging around their field in a big gang and they were a joy to watch even if it did cause their mothers some concern.

'We've been through the worst and it's all downhill from here,' he said. 'And the best of it is the weather has been kind to us for once.'

But the year was moving on and it was time to start working some of the ploughed land down and drilling spring barley. And this meant a return to the forty acres I had spent so many days ploughing at the beginning of the year.

'Take the disc harrows down and make a start,' Harry said. 'If you angle them a bit on the way down you can level out the track.'

The disc harrows were a formidable cultivating tool and comprised two rows of curved steel discs which could be set to run at opposing angles so that the discs cut into the soil and, if the tractor was going fast enough, threw the soil one way and then back again.

With a full tank of fuel on board, I set off down the track and, as Harry had requested I stopped to angle the discs so they would pull soil into the ruts that had formed during the winter. It would take more than one pass to fill them all in but it was a start.

I arrived in Forty Acres and noticed how the soil had weathered since I had ploughed it. Worked on by the frosts, it was now crumbling and completely different to the shiny, raw clay the plough had brought to the surface.

Harry's plan was for me to work across the ploughing at right angles but before I started I should run the discs up and down the plough finishes to try and level them out and make for a smoother ride on the tractor.

Having turned the handle which adjusted the angle of the discs, I set off at full throttle, the tractor bucking over the bumps, soil being thrown all over the place and a great plume of dust following me down the rows.

It was not long before my flock of seagulls were back with me, looking for some fresh worms to eat.

'You ate them all a couple of months ago,' I shouted at them, as I held on to the steering wheel and tried to cushion some of the bumps that three inches of soggy foam did little to absorb.

When I started to cross the ploughing, the ride became even rougher and I had to slow down. Already I could feel the bruising and my whole body was starting to ache as I rode out the sudden dips and violent rises.

But the discs were doing a good job and created a level tilth that looked entirely different from the ploughed land I was having to drive over. When, at about mid-morning Harry appeared he had Ronny with him.

'How's it going?' he asked when I brought the tractor

to a halt beside the Land Rover, the dust slowly drifting past us.

'I think it's doing a good job,' I said, jumping off the tractor.

Harry pushed his boot into the soil and brought it out. 'For spring drilling you want soil to fall of your boot,' he said. 'And we all looked at the front of his boot and watched the soil fall off.'

Ronny then tried to do the same but it didn't seem to work so well with wellingtons but then it might have been the layers of dried slurry on them.

'I think the best thing to do is to let Ronny loose with the discs and finish half the field while we go and sort the drill out,' Harry said.

'Which half do you want me to finish?' Ronny asked.

'Carry on from where John's left off and when you've finished it, do it again in the other direction. And don't forget to do the headlands.'

'Right,' Ronny said, pulling himself up onto the tractor. There was a tremor to his face, like a cat poised to pounce. This was the highlight of his year and I could see that wild look in his eye as he prepared himself. 'I'm going to go like fuck!' he screamed.

'That's right Ron,' Harry said. 'Do your best and keep it going.'

I watched as he started the tractor, put it in gear, opened the throttle and with a wild, heathen cry, released the clutch. The tractor lurched forwards, the front wheels lifted off the ground and the discs began churning the ground, a large cloud of dust billowing out beneath them.

'He's mad,' I said and Harry laughed.

'He spends all year dreaming about using the disc harrows and today's the day. One year he set off like a mad man, went about ten yards and sunk up to his axles in the only wet spot in a thirty acre field and that was another pop-pop recovery job.'

Back at the farm I hooked the Fordson onto a four

wheel trailer, and while Harry went off to look at the sheep, I loaded it with thirty bags of seed barley and the same number of fertiliser bags.

'Don't forget the seed harrows,' Harry said. 'I'll give you a lift up with them so you can lay them along the top of the bags along with the sway bar.'

I then headed back down to the forty acres and parked the trailer on the headland and by the time I had made it back it was lunch time.

'How do you feel about using the seed drill?' Harry asked as he sliced into the boiled bacon.

I wondered what had prompted this question. Every other task else I had been involved in had been largely a case of finding out myself, if we discount the ploughing which was clearly a more intricate operation.

'Alright,' I said.

'Well let me tell you this. It's the most important job on the farm. Get it wrong with missed rows, too deep or too shallow and anything else you can find to do that doesn't put a seed in the place it is intended to be, makes everything we've done before and everything we do afterwards a complete waste of time and money.'

'I can see that. It sounds like a job which calls for a high degree of concentration and care.'

'Exactly. And it goes without saying that the rows also need to be straight. No wandering across the field using your 'doing more work' theory,' he said. 'It's a two-man job so I'll be keeping an eye on you.'

'What's this 'doing more work' theory,' Alice asked. 'I don't think I've heard of that.'

I looked at Harry who was scowling. 'It's just that if you drive in a straight line across a field you cover less ground than if you had some bends to go round, so you're doing more work with each pass,' I explained.

Alice thought about it. 'Yes, I can see that, so why does Harry insist in going in a straight line everywhere?'

'It's a load of nonsense,' he said. 'The quickest way

from to A to B is in a straight line, and that's the end of it,' he slid his tea cup down towards Alice. 'The next thing you'll be telling me is it's the same distance around a five acre field as a ten acre field.'

'Well it can be if the five-acre field is long and thin and the ten-acre is round,' I said.

'Poppy-cock,' Harry replied. 'Come on, boy. We've a field to sow.'

The drill, when I found it at the back of the barn under a dusty tarpaulin, was no spring chicken. Constructed mainly from wood and running on metal spoked wheels it had that faded look about it; the bright red livery it once boasted in the show room had now all but disappeared and the heavy wooden lids covering the seed and fertiliser hoppers were cracked.

'What do you reckon?' Harry asked as we folded up the tarpaulin.

'Well, it looks as if it's done a few acres.'

'It certainly has. My father always said a farmer should be able to make a seed drill last his lifetime.'

There wasn't a lot you could say to that. With the best will in the world, I couldn't see this drill lasting another forty years, either that, or I had seriously over estimated Harry's life expectancy.

We hooked it on the tractor and set off down to the Forty-Acre and I soon learned there was no hurrying with the drill. Shod on little more than wooden cart wheels, every bump was transferred directly to the frame which shook and groaned its discomfort. But eventually drove into the field just in time to see Ronny make the last pass around the headland.

'That was good timing,' Harry told him. 'You'd better make a start on the other half while we sort the drill out.'

'Right oh, Harry,' he said. I looked at him and saw his eyes, still gleaming with the joy of it all, staring back at me through a dusty mask.

We turned our attention to the drill which was little

more than eight feet wide and it dawned on me that we could be in this field for a few days.

'I'll show you the seed metering system first,' he said, removing a wooden cover from the rear of the hopper to reveal a shaft having a number of short arms attached to it which lined up with small exits from the hopper itself.

'At the end of each arm is a shallow cup which, as it rotates, dips into the seed released from the hopper and picks up a couple of grains of seed,' Harry explained. 'When each arm reaches the top of its turn, the seed falls out and drops into the top of the chute, which guides it down to the coulter and into the ground.'

'How do you set the seed rate?'

'The shaft is driven from one of the land wheels by a series of cog wheels and the rate is changed by altering the cogs to provide a different shaft speed. And to knock it out of gear when making headland turns you pull the lever at the end there, which lifts the hopper and its drive clear of the land wheel cog. The same lever also raises the coulters clear of the soil.'

It all seemed a tad basic but then, I had yet to see the fertiliser distribution system.

'If you come round to the front you'll see another hopper and that's where the fertiliser goes.' He lifted the lid. 'You'll probably recognise the metering system because it's similar to the one used by the basic slag spreader you were using – a cog wheel and knocker feed system.'

'Does the fertiliser just drop on the ground?'

'No, it is taken by a pipe to the coulter where it lands in the soil just a bit lower and to one side of the seed so it's ready for the seeds' roots to have a feed on.'

With the tour over we lifted the harrows off the trailer – a group of three – and hooked them onto the sway bar which held them in line at the rear of the drill; the idea being that the short spikes move the soil over the seed to ensure it is buried.

'It's important you don't harrow over your wheel mark

or you won't know where to drive on the return bout,' he said. 'And to do that, the harrows are connected by a chain to a sliding rail so when the drill turns on the headland, the towing chain slips over to an offset position. You'll see how it works when we make a start.'

We filled the hopper with seed from the hundred weight paper bags and then split open four plastic fertiliser bags to fill the front hopper. As ever, there were lumps in it which needed squeezing to break them up.

Harry climbed onto the tractor and I stood on the running board at the back of the drill, realising that if I fell off I would have the harrows running over me, which was not a pleasant thought.

'Everything alright, boy,' he shouted.

I gave him the thumbs up and I hung on as we moved off to the edge of the field.

'OK, boy. Drop her in gear.'

Releasing the lever released the coulters and lowered the hopper and its drive cog onto the land wheel drive. As it meshed, the metering shaft with its arms of spoons began to rotate, dipping into the seed and dropping it down the coulter tube. I looked at each of them to ensure each of the twenty-four coulters was being fed.

If I looked really carefully at the coulters themselves – boat-like objects made from hardened metal which split the soil to create a slot for the seed to fall into – I could see fertiliser granules also being delivered.

'Everything running alright?' Harry shouted.

And before I could answer he screamed, 'Mind your head!'

I instinctively ducked as a low branch sticking out from the hedge, passed over the top of me. And that happened on two or three occasions before we had completed the first circuit of the field. When we drew level with the trailer, we stopped to see if we needed to top up with seed and fertiliser.

'I think we had better,' Harry said. 'Don't want to be

running out on the other side of the field.'

It was when we looked in the fertiliser compartment we noticed that instead of there being a flat level of granules, which would indicate that all the outlets had been fed, there was a pile about a third of the way along it. I dug down with my hands and pulled out the offending lump which had blocked the outlet.

'Bloody artificial,' Harry murmured.

Starting off again, Harry drove in a loop to bring us back into line with where we had already drilled, and I dropped the drill into gear as we approached the point where we had stopped.

In all, we did ten laps of the field before we started to work off the longest side and, apart from a few coulter blockages and a turn which didn't manage to slide the harrow chain over and meant that for about fifty yards the drill's wheel mark was obliterated, all went well.

There was one terrifying moment though, when the sleeve of my jersey caught up on the metering shaft and try as I might to pull it clear, every turn meant the shaft gained a stronger grip on my sleeve. And I was being slowly drawn into the machine. I screamed at Harry to stop but he was concentrating on driving in a straight line and I tried to reach the lever to stop the drive but it was impossible. In the end, just as I thought I was approaching the end, I picked up a handful of seed and threw it at Harry, screaming for him to stop.

Which thankfully he did. 'What's up boy?'

'My sleeve, it's caught up in the metering wheel.'

'Bloody hell, that was a close call,' he said when he took a look. 'Another few yards and I don't know what would have happened.'

'Yes, well if you could cut me free I think I could start feeling my fingers again.'

Harry dug into his trouser pocket and brought out his penknife. 'Never be without a good penknife,' he said. 'Never know when you might need it.'

I don't think I could have used it if I had one,' I replied. 'But if you could hurry up and use yours I'd be very grateful.'

Harry opened the blade and started sawing away at the wool which had become as thick as a rope and about as strong. Progress was slow but eventually he managed to break through and the pressure on my arm released. I flexed my fingers and felt the blood start to flow through them again.

'I hope you're not expecting Alice to darn this for you,' he said holding out the shredded sleeve. 'I think the best you can hope for from now on is a sleeveless jersey but then, another few yards you wouldn't have needed any sleeves; well, only one of them. Still, don't worry, boy. It's all 'armless fun.'

From that point I made sure I kept well away from the rotating arms on the metering shaft, and I wondered how many other operators using this drill had suffered the same nightmare experience I just had.

By half past four it was time for me to go up to the farm and get the milking underway and Harry needed to be with his ewes and have them settled and sorted before night set in. So, with the tarpaulin spread over the drill we hooked off it and headed for the farm.

As we climbed Brier Hill, I looked back and saw Ronny still going like a mad man charging from one end of the field to the other, a great trail of dust following him. I couldn't believe he would have much fuel left and, as I thought it, the tractor came to a halt.

'Looks like Ronny's out of fuel,' I said.

Harry turned round and looked.

'Yes, you're right, it does,' he murmured, and we continued on our way.

Chapter thirty-one

Friday afternoon

It took a couple of weeks but by the end of March we had sown all the spring barley and more importantly, it had chitted and was all growing away.

'Spring barley needs to germinate and continue growing without any hold ups caused by draught, cold weather or waterlogged ground,' Harry said. 'It also doesn't like competing with weeds so before we shut the gate and wait until harvest most crops get a dose of herbicide to take out the charlock, poppies and hopefully anything else that isn't barley – Banlene Plus usually does the trick.'

The farm's sprayer was tractor mounted and had a hundred gallon tank and a twenty foot boom with spray nozzles fixed at intervals along its length. Application rate was usually twenty gallons to the acre and was set as a combination of forward speed and spraying pressure and there was a chart to help work it all out.

Spraying was one of those jobs when you never knew for sure what sort of job it was you were making. It took a few days for weeds to start keeling over and, as a result, any misses with the sprayer only became visible after about a week or so. Which was usually too late to do anything about it.

'I see you've left a nice row of poppies across the middle of Farm Close,' Harry said. 'Very attractive, but tell me, what is it about a twenty foot boom you don't understand? It's not eighteen feet and it's not twenty five feet and why weren't you using the blobber?'

'I was. It's just that the wind blew the foam blobs all over the place. Some of them were a couple of yards away by the time they landed. It was impossible to use it.'

'Ha! A bad workman always blames his tools.'

'Well it proves the herbicide worked where it did land.' I said. 'If I had sprayed every square inch of the field you would never have known that, would you?'

'You mean you didn't leave a strip of poppies so you could pick a bunch for Elizabeth, then?' He was looking behind me and there was a big smile on his face.

'What?'

'Hello John,' Elizabeth said. 'What are you two bickering about now?'

'Oh nothing of any importance. But look, you're here and back for Easter.'

She nodded. 'Yes, we have three weeks before I need to go back. Isn't that just brilliant?'

'You bet,' I said. 'I think we've time to have a look round the sheep and the lambs before milking, if you want to?' I looked questioningly at Harry.

'Go on you two. Go and show Elizabeth the lambs and while you're in Farm Close don't forget to pick her a bunch of your home-grown poppies. If you pick some every day I should think there's enough to last until Christmas. Oh, and if you take your time, you can bring the cows back with you.'

We joined hands and walked up the yard and out into the paddock, the sun low in the sky but still providing some welcome warmth.

'How's the term been?' I asked.

'Not so bad. I'm managing to keep up but I have to work really hard. Sometimes it's past midnight before I can call it a day and then I have to do it all again the next day.'

'It sound's tough but I guess it will be worth it when

you graduate with your honours degree.'

She laughed and I put my arm around her waist and gave her a long kiss.

'How about you?' she asked. 'Have you made any plans to go to agricultural college or anything?'

'It's secret and you must promise to keep it but I have applied to attend several agricultural institutes next year. I have to say though, I have mixed feelings about it.'

'Why should you have? You can't spend the rest of your life working for Harry. There's a big wide world out there and the really good part is that not all of it has even seen a joint of boiled bacon, let alone eaten it.'

'I know, but I'm so happy here. I have the farm, the cows and, best of all, I have you.'

'If you were at a place close to mine we could perhaps share a flat or something,' she said.

I stopped and looked at her. 'Yes, we could,' I said. 'And if I'm honest with you one of the institutes I've applied to is only a few miles away from yours.'

'Not the Yorkshire Institute of Agriculture at Askham Bryan?'

'The very one.'

'But that would be terrific. I'm only just up the road from there.'

We walked on in silence until we reached the gate leading into Badger Close and then, for something to do, we climbed up and perched ourselves on top of the gate.

'That's pretty,' she said, looking out across the field.

'What's that?'

'That splash of red across the middle of the barley. Poppies, aren't they?'

'Oh, don't you start.' I jumped down and put my arms up to help her down but she pushed off too hard and we both ended up rolling about in the dust.

'Oh no,' she said. 'Look at the state of my jeans. What will Alice think when we get back?'

I shrugged my shoulders. 'What do you want her to

think? Come on, let's pick her a bunch of poppies, get the cows milked and then, if you like, we can go out for the evening.'

'Sounds good,' she cried.

***

For the next few weeks I could think of nothing else other than going to an agricultural institute and being closer to Elizabeth but there was a problem. Somewhere along the way I had to tell Harry what I wanted to do and I felt the news would be letting him down.

One breakfast time, after I had come in from taking the milk churns down to the ramp there was a big white envelope on the table and it was addressed to me. I would have liked its contents to have remained private but seeing as the return address printed on the back of the envelope was to the Yorkshire Institute of Agriculture, there was little chance of that.

'Well, aren't you going to open it?' Harry said.

There was no alternative so I picked it up and made a move to tear it open but Alice had a pair of scissors in her hand.

'Use these,' she said.

And I did and then reached in and pulled out what was a sizeable wad of literature. The first sheet was a letter and I quickly scanned it and put it down.

'Good news?' asked Alice.

I looked at her and then at Harry. 'It's to say they are offering me a place,' I said. 'Which, if I accept, will mean I start in September.'

There was then an awkward silence during which Alice flustered about with tea cups and Harry stared up at the ceiling.

'Well done, boy. That's good news,' he said. Alice and I always thought you should go and learn all about the latest methods and all that. We'll be sorry to see you go but we want you to know we think you're doing the right thing.'

I didn't know what to say but I eventually mumbled

something about only being away for a year and I would be back to help out during the holidays.

Harry held up his hand. 'Hey, just hang on a minute. Like I said, Alice and I have been expecting this for some time and we have a suggestion.' He looked across at Alice who was now smiling and nodding her head. 'What we suggest is that you go off to college and make a good job of it and then, if you still want to come back, we could offer you a more...' he hesitated. 'Responsible role.'

'That would be terrific and it's very generous of you,' I said. 'But it's for almost a year and who's going to help you in that time?'

'Oh, we'll get by. The important part is that you get a good education and then come back and tell us how we should all be doing the job – if that is what you want to do.'

***

Everything after that encounter seemed to take on a different slant. No longer was I muddling along from day to day. Now I had an aim and a direction in life, a route which would hopefully take me forward into a world of farming I had always longed for.

When I told Elizabeth she was as thrilled as I was. 'Does that mean we can find a flat or something to share?' she asked.

'I don't see why not. I don't think it will have escaped anyone's notice that I'm attending a college which is only half a mile away from yours.'

'Well no one has said anything.'

'They will,' I said. Anyway, what does it matter?'

Elizabeth went quiet. 'You don't think I'm being too pushy, do you? I mean, you don't have to do all this if you don't want to.'

I put my arm around her shoulders. 'Look, I want to go to college. You were right, I can't stay working for Harry for ever and, more than that, I want to be with you.'

September drew ever closer and I was dreading the day

I would be leaving; the last time I would milk my cows, the last time I would sit on the tractor, the last time I would ever eat boiled bacon.

When the day came, it was a Saturday. I gave each of the girls an extra handful of ground barley and, for Thrifty and Horns there was a special hug. And when milking was over, I took out their buffer feed and spread it about and stood for one last time and looked at them.

'They'll only love you if you love them too,' I said out loud; a sentence which then bounced around in my mind and one I knew I would never forget.

Back at the farm I went to see the first tractor I had ever driven, the David Brown 990, and climbed up and sat down on a wet foam rubber seat. Together we had put some hours in and I recalled the winter ploughing when it was only the heat from exhaust pot which prevented my feet and hands from freezing.

I jumped down and, on the way down to the house called in to the orchard to say good-bye to the pop-pop – the magnificent green Field Marshall whose winch had saved the day when the combine harvester was stuck up to its axles.

And then there was a special good-bye for Pedro; Donkey Derby winner, harvest festival hero and a good friend. I stroked his muzzle while he stared at me with his all-knowing, big brown eyes, and I told him he was the best donkey in the world.

Breakfast conversation was a little stilted. Alice kept asking me if I was sure I had everything I wanted, and Harry filled the time by asking me which way I was going to drive up to York.

But after eating my last slice of boiled bacon, and Harry had finished his second half-cup of tea, I lumped two suit cases out to the pick-up and dropped them in the back. Harry came out with me and pushed an envelope into my jacket pocket. 'That'll keep you going for a bit,' he said and then we shook hands.

'Take care of yourself, boy and keep in touch.'

Alice gave me a big hug and a kiss. 'Yes, take care of yourself, John and give our love to Elizabeth. We're going to miss you and here's a sandwich for you to eat on the way.'

And then I was driving up the yard. In the rear view mirror I could see Harry and Alice, arm in arm, waving at me and at the top I paused briefly and returned their wave.

'I'll be back,' I said.

Please leave a review

I really hope you enjoyed this book and if you can spare a couple of minutes to leave a short review on amazon.co.uk it would be greatly appreciated.

If you loved *Harry me, and boiled bacon,* you will want to know there is a sequel on its way. Find out more by emailing: andycollings@outlook.com

Printed in Great Britain
by Amazon